NUCLEAR WINTER V

DESOLATION

BOBBY AKART

OTHER WORKS BY AMAZON CHARTS TOP 25 AUTHOR BOBBY AKART

Perfect Storm (a standalone disaster thriller)

The Texas Forever trilogy
Black Gold
Black Swan
Black Flags

Nuclear Winter
First Strike
Armageddon
Whiteout
Devil Storm
Desolation

New Madrid Earthquake (a standalone disaster thriller)

Odessa (a Gunner Fox trilogy)
Odessa Reborn
Odessa Rising
Odessa Strikes

THANK YOU

Thank you for reading DESOLATION, book five and the final installment in the Nuclear Winter series by Author Bobby Akart. Join Bobby Akart's mailing list to learn about upcoming releases, deals, contests, and appearances. Follow this link to:

BobbyAkart.com

Or visit his dedicated feature page on Amazon at

Amazon.com/BobbyAkart

PRAISE FOR BOBBY AKART AND THE NUCLEAR WINTER SERIES

"Bobby's uncanny ability to take a topic of 'what could happen' and write an epic story about it is short of preternatural!"

"Characters with depth coupled with an incredibly well researched topic wasn't enough for the golden man of post apocalyptic fiction. Oh no, he went and threw in a murder mystery just to keep everyone guessing as well as what I believe is one of his best crafted cliff hangers."

"I never would have believed that Mr. Akart could outdo himself! Well, he has! *Nuclear Winter First Strike* is quite possibly the best book he has ever written!"

"As with any of the best novels, this book really captures your attention and makes it hard to put down at the end of the day."

"*Nuclear Winter: First Strike* and the Albright family are coming dangerously close to nudging my beloved Armstrong family (Lone Star series) into a tie for first place."

"The suspense, the behind the scenes machinations of governments, the evil unleashed, the world on an uncharted path are all woven into another excellent story."

"I am speechless. By far the most edge of your seat, acrylic nail biting book ever. E V E R.
The characters suck you in on a roller coaster ride of emotions."

NUCLEAR WINTER V
DESOLATION

by
Bobby Akart

Copyright Information

ACKNOWLEDGMENTS

Creating a novel that is both informative and entertaining requires a tremendous team effort. Writing is the easy part.

For their efforts in making the Nuclear Winter series a reality, I would like to thank Hristo Argirov Kovatliev for his incredible artistic talents in creating my cover art. He and my multitalented wife, Dani, collaborate to create the most incredible cover art in the publishing business. A huge hug of appreciation goes out to Pauline Nolet, the *Professor*, for her editorial prowess and patience in correcting this writer's same tics as we approach publishing sixty novels together. Thank you, Drew Avera, a United States Navy veteran, who has brought his talented formatting skills from a writer's perspective to create multiple formats for reading my novels. A round of applause for Kevin Pierce, the beloved voice of the apocalypse, who brought my words to life in audio format.

Now, for the serious stuff. Accurately portraying the aftermath of nuclear war required countless hours of never-ending research and interviews with some of the brightest minds in the world of planetary science.

Once again, as I immersed myself in the science and history, source material and research flooded my inbox from around the globe. Without the assistance of many individuals and organizations, this story could not be told. Please allow me a moment to acknowledge a few of those individuals without whom, and their tireless efforts and patience, the Nuclear Winter series could not have been written.

Many thanks to the preeminent researchers and engineers at the National Center for Atmospheric Research in Boulder, Colorado. Between responses to my inquiries and the volumes of scientific publications provided, I was able to grasp the catastrophic effect a regional nuclear war would have upon the Earth and its atmosphere. They impressed upon me the danger of inundating our air with the results of these massive nuclear detonations. It would result in a climatic event akin to the eruption of the Yellowstone supervolcano.

A shout-out must go to Brian Toon, professor of atmospheric and oceanic sciences at the University of Colorado Boulder. He has been a tireless advocate warning all who'll listen of the consequences of nuclear winter. This quote had a profound effect on me and led to the writing of the Nuclear Winter series—*It could potentially end global civilization as we know it.* In other words, TEOTWAWKI.

At Rutgers University, Distinguished Professor and acclaimed climatologist Alan Robock has been studying the potential threat of nuclear winter with a particular focus on the human impact. The incredibly fast cooling of the planet would trigger a global famine and mass starvation. His models of fires and firestorms in the aftermath of a nuclear war provided me detailed estimates of the extent of wildfires as well as the timeframes associated with the smoke and soot lofted into the atmosphere.

For this final installment in the series, a message of appreciation and admiration to Dr. Alexander Leaf, famed physician and research scientist. His collaboration with Massachusetts General Hospital and Harvard Medical School led to a pioneering study on the impact of nuclear winter on the planet. I share the salient points from his extensive research in my Author's Note at the end of this novel.

Now, to the special friends and acquaintances who helped make my characters realistic. Admittedly, my exposure to teenagers is nonexistent. Yet, from time to time, I have teen characters who speak a different language, sort of. In order to add a sense of realism to their dialogue, I call upon a number of resources to enlighten me on their own unique vocabulary.

Thank you to Pam and Tim Johnson, who reached out to their teenage grandson, Simon Andrews. He's credited with a number of phrases in the Nuclear Winter series, including *Yeet!* Dear reader, this interesting term was explained within *First Strike*, book one.

Thank you to Jessica Devenny, referred to me via Pam Johnson and her bestie, Betsy. Jessica's sons, Jacob and Parker, also helped to fill my *teenspeak* dictionary.

Also, Dani's followers on Instagram were up to the task. Instagram is one of the few social media networks where the vast majority of your interactions are positive compared to Facebook and the downright nasty Twitter platform. When called upon, hundreds of terms and phrases were offered. Thanks to you all!

The cigar selections in *Nuclear Winter: First Strike* were suggested by my friend Brad Levy. Brad has read all of my novels, twice, in most cases. He always looks forward to his day on the lanai, enjoying a fine cigar and a good book. Thank you, my friend!

Finally, as always, a special thank you to my team of loyal friends who've always supported my work and provided me valuable insight from a reader's perspective—Denise Keef, Joe Carey, Shirley Nicholson, Bennita Barnett, Karl Hughey, and Brian Alderman.

For the Nuclear Winter series, several avid readers volunteered to make my writing *more better*: Martin McDonell, Cody McDonell, Diane Ash, Rusty Ballard, Joe Hoyt, Cecilia Kilgore Sutton, Thelma Applegate, Joyce Maurer, Annie Kercher-Bosche, Steven Smith, Leslie Bryant, Tim Coppess, Caryl Lynne Honea, Mike Neubecker, Colt Payne, Pete Steffens, and Kelly Trone.

Thanks, y'all, and Choose Freedom!

ABOUT THE AUTHOR, BOBBY AKART

Author Bobby Akart has been ranked by Amazon as #25 on the Amazon Charts list of most popular, bestselling authors. He has achieved recognition as the #1 bestselling Horror Author, #1 bestselling Science Fiction Author, #5 bestselling Action & Adventure Author, #7 bestselling Historical Fiction Author and #10 on Amazon's bestselling Thriller Author list.

Mr. Akart has delivered up-all-night thrillers to readers in 245 countries and territories worldwide. He has sold over one million books in all formats, which includes over forty international bestsellers, in nearly fifty fiction and nonfiction genres.

His novel *Yellowstone: Hellfire* reached the Top 25 on the Amazon bestsellers list and earned him multiple Kindle All-Star awards for most pages read in a month and most pages read as an author. The Yellowstone series vaulted him to the #25 bestselling author on Amazon Charts, and the #1 bestselling science fiction author.

Since its release in November 2020, his standalone novel *New Madrid Earthquake* has been ranked #1 on Amazon Charts in multiple countries as a natural disaster thriller.

Mr. Akart is a graduate of the University of Tennessee after pursuing a dual major in economics and political science. He went on to obtain his master's degree in business administration and his doctorate degree in law at Tennessee.

A million-copy bestseller, Bobby Akart has provided his readers a diverse range of topics that are both informative and entertaining. His attention to detail and impeccable research have allowed him to capture the imagination of his readers through his fictional works and bring them valuable knowledge through his nonfiction books.

SIGN UP for Bobby Akart's mailing list to learn of special offers, view bonus content, and be the first to receive news about new releases.

Visit www.BobbyAkart.com for details.

DEDICATIONS

With the love and support of my wife, Dani, together with the unconditional love of Bullie and Boom, the princesses of the palace, I'm able to tell you these stories. It would be impossible for me to write without them in my heart.

Freedom and security are precious gifts that we, as Americans, should never take for granted. I would like to thank the men and women, past and present, of the United States Armed Forces for willingly making sacrifices each day to provide us that freedom and security. Also, a note of thanks to their families, who endure countless sleepless nights as their loved ones are deployed around the world.

They are the sheepdogs who live to protect the flock. They bravely and unselfishly confront the wolves who threaten our country, our freedoms, and their brothers in arms from those who would bring destruction to our door.

Choose Freedom!

AUTHOR'S INTRODUCTION

February 2021

Since scientific discoveries in the late 1930s made nuclear weapons a possibility, the world began to realize they posed an enormous threat to humanity. In 1942, with the secretive research effort in the U.S. known as the Manhattan Project, a race toward nuclear supremacy began. Since their very first use in World War II, different leaders and organizations have been trying to prevent proliferation to additional countries. Despite their efforts, more nation-states than ever before have obtained nuclear weapons.

Following pioneering research from scientists in the early 1980s, the world was introduced to the concept of nuclear winter. Researchers had known that a large nuclear war could cause severe global environmental effects, including dramatic cooling of surface temperatures, declines in precipitation, and increased ultraviolet radiation.

The term nuclear winter was coined specifically to refer to atmospheric cooling that resulted in winter-like temperatures occurring year-round. Regardless of whether extreme cold temperatures were reached, there would be severe consequences for humanity. But how severe would those consequences be? And what should the world be doing about it?

To the first question, the short answer is nobody knows with absolute certainty. The total human impacts of nuclear winter are both uncertain and under-studied. The aftereffects of the twin atomic bombs dropped on Japan to end World War II were not analyzed in depth. More research on the impacts would be very helpful, but treaties have limited nuclear weapons testing. Therefore research, other than theoretical conclusions, has been limited.

As to the question of what the world should be doing about it, all nations agree nonproliferation is a start. However, there are still more than sufficient nuclear weapons capable of being launched to bring the world to the brink of Armageddon.

Today, nuclear winter is not a hot topic among the world's leaders. When the Cold War ended, so did attention to the catastrophic threat of nuclear winter. That started to change in 2007 with a new line of nuclear winter research that used advanced climate models developed for the study of global warming.

Relative to the 1980s research, the new research found that the smoke from nuclear firestorms would travel higher into the atmosphere, causing nuclear winter to last longer than previously thought. This research also found dangerous effects from smaller nuclear exchanges, such as an India-Pakistan nuclear war detonating *only* one hundred total nuclear warheads.

Some new research has also examined the human impacts of nuclear winter. Researchers simulated agricultural crop growth in the aftermath of a hundred-weapon India-Pakistan nuclear war. The results were startling. The scenario could cause agriculture productivity to decline by twenty to sixty percent for several years after the exchange.

The studies looked at major staple crops in China and the United States, two of the largest food producers. Other countries and other crops would likely face similar declines. Following such crop declines, severe global famine could ensue. One study estimated the total extent of the famine by comparing crop declines to global malnourishment data. When food becomes scarce, the poor and malnourished are typically hit the hardest. This study estimated two billion people would be at risk of starvation. And this is from the hundred-weapon India-Pakistan nuclear war scenario. A larger nuclear exchange involving the U.S., China, or Russia would have more severe impacts because the payloads are much larger.

This is where the recent research stops. To the best of my knowledge, there have been no current studies examining the secondary effects of famines, such as disease outbreaks and violent conflicts due to societal collapse.

There is also a need to examine the human impacts of ultraviolet radiation. That would include an increased medical burden due to skin cancer and other diseases. It would also include further losses to the agriculture ecosystems because the ultraviolet radiation harms plants and animals. At this time, we can only make educated guesses about what these impacts would be, informed in part by research surrounding enormous volcanic eruptions.

A note on the impact on humanity, we can look to society's reaction to recent political events. Imagine what U.S. cities would look like if the triggering event for protests and riots was based on lack of food. The social unrest would quickly spread into suburban areas, as the have-nots would search for sustenance from those who might have it.

When analyzing the risk of nuclear winter, one question is of paramount importance: Would there be long term or even permanent harm to human civilization? Research shows nuclear winter would last ten years or more. Would the world ever be able to come back from the devastating loss of billions of lives?

Carl Sagan was one of the first people to recognize this point in a commentary he wrote on nuclear winter for *Foreign Affairs* magazine. Sagan believed nuclear winter could cause human extinction, in which case all members of future generations would be lost. He argued that this made nuclear winter vastly more important than the direct effects of nuclear war, which could, in his words, *kill only hundreds of millions of people.*

Sagan was, however, right that human extinction would cause permanent harm to human civilization. It is debatable whether nuclear winter could cause human extinction. Rutgers professor Alan Robock, a respected nuclear winter researcher, believes it is unlikely. He commented, "Especially in Australia and New Zealand, humans would have a better chance to survive."

Why Australia and New Zealand? A nuclear war would presumably occur mainly or entirely in the northern hemisphere. The southern hemisphere would still experience environmental disruption, but it would not be as severe. Australia and New Zealand further benefit from being surrounded by water, which further softens the effect.

This is hardly a cheerful thought, as it leaves open the chance of human extinction, at least for those of us north of the equator. Given all the uncertainty and the limited available research, it is impossible to rule out the possibility of human extinction. In any event, the possibility should not be dismissed.

Even if people survive, there could still be permanent harm to humanity. Small patches of survivors would be extremely vulnerable to subsequent disasters. They certainly could not keep up the massively complex civilization we enjoy today. In addition to the medical impact, the destruction of the power grid, the heartbeat of most nations, would likely occur due to the electromagnetic pulse generated by the nuclear detonations. It would take many years to rebuild the critical infrastructure ruined by the blasts.

It would be a long and uncertain rebuilding process, and survivors might never get civilization back to where it is now. More importantly, they might never get civilization to where we now stand poised to take it in the future. Our potentially bright future could be forever dimmed, permanently.

Nuclear winter is a very large and serious risk. In some ways, it doesn't change nuclear weapons policy all that much. Everyone already knew that nuclear war would be highly catastrophic. The prospect of a prolonged nuclear winter means that nuclear war is even more catastrophic. That only reinforces policies that have long been in place, from deterrence to disarmament. Indeed, military officials have sometimes reacted to nuclear winter by saying that it just makes their nuclear deterrence policies that much more effective. Disarmament advocates similarly cite nuclear winter as justifying their policy goals. But the basic structure of the policy debate is unchanged.

In other ways, nuclear winter changes nuclear weapons policy quite dramatically. Because of nuclear winter, noncombatant states may be severely harmed by nuclear war. Nuclear winter gives every country great incentive to reduce tensions and de-escalate conflicts between nuclear-capable states.

Nation-states that are stockpiling nuclear weapons should also take notice. Indeed, the biggest policy implication of nuclear winter could be that it puts the interests of nuclear-capable nations in greater alignment. Because of nuclear winter, a nuclear war between any two major nuclear weapon states could severely harm each of the others. According to intelligence sources, there are nine total nuclear-armed states with Iran prepared to breakthrough as the tenth. This multiplies the risk of being harmed by nuclear attacks while only marginally increasing the benefits of nuclear deterrence. By shifting the balance of harms versus benefits, nuclear winter can promote nuclear disarmament.

Additional policy implications come from the risk of permanent harm to human civilization. If society takes this risk seriously, then it should go to great lengths to reduce the risk. It could stockpile food to avoid nuclear famine or develop new agricultural paradigms that can function during nuclear winter.

And it could certainly ratchet up its efforts to improve relations between nuclear weapon states. These are things that we can do right now even while we await more detailed research on nuclear winter risk.

Against that backdrop, I hope you'll be entertained and informed by this fictional account of the world thrust into nuclear winter. God help us if it ever comes to pass.

REAL-WORLD NEWS EXCERPTS

CHINA THREATENS NUCLEAR WAR, EXPANDING ARSENAL IN CASE OF "INTENSE SHOWDOWN" WITH UNITED STATES

~ New York Post, June 2, 2021

The Chinese Communist government touted the country's "urgent" goal to expand its arsenal of long-range nuclear missiles in anticipation of an "intense showdown" with the US.

"As the US strategic containment of China has increasingly intensified, I would like to remind again that we have plenty of urgent tasks, but among the most important ones is to rapidly increase the number of commissioned nuclear warheads, and the DF-41s, the strategic missiles that are capable to strike long-range and have high-survivability, in the Chinese arsenal."

RUTGERS STUDY: NUCLEAR WINTER WOULD THREATEN NEARLY EVERYONE ON EARTH

~ The Journal of Geophysical Research, August 2019

If two warring nations waged an all-out nuclear war, much of the land in the Northern Hemisphere would be below freezing in the summertime, with the growing season slashed by nearly 90 percent in some areas, according to a Rutgers-led study.

Such a war could send 150 million tons of black smoke from fires in cities and industrial areas into the lower and upper atmosphere, where it could linger for months to years and block sunlight.

A nuclear winter occurs as soot (black carbon) in the upper atmosphere blocks sunlight and causes global average surface temperatures to plummet by more than 15 degrees Fahrenheit.

Because a major nuclear war could erupt by accident or as a result of hacking, computer failure or an unstable world leader, the only safe action that the world can take is to eliminate nuclear weapons.

THE RISK OF NUCLEAR WAR WITH CHINA IN 1958 SAID TO BE GREATER THAN PUBLICLY KNOWN

~ *New York Times, May 26, 2021*

Newly leaked documents show that US officials in 1958 cavalierly planned a nuclear strike on China over Taiwan.

When Communist Chinese forces began shelling islands controlled by Taiwan in 1958, the United States rushed to back up its ally with military force — including drawing up plans to carry out nuclear strikes on mainland China, according to an apparently still-classified document that sheds new light on how dangerous that crisis was.

American military leaders pushed for a first-use nuclear strike on China, accepting the risk that the Soviet Union would retaliate in kind on behalf of its ally and millions of people would die, dozens of pages from a classified 1966 study of the confrontation show.

Drawing parallels to today's tensions — when China's own conventional military power has grown far beyond its 1958 ability, and when it has its own nuclear weapons — analysts warn of the dangers of the current escalating confrontation over Taiwan.

SCARED STRAIGHT: HOW PROPHETS OF DOOM MIGHT SAVE THE WORLD

~ Bulletin of the Atomic Scientists, May 27, 2021

A team of Australian researchers asked people in the United States, the United Kingdom, Canada, and Australia about how probable a global catastrophe in the near term might be. They found that a majority (54 percent) rated the risk of our way of life ending within the next 100 years at 50 percent or greater, and a quarter rated the risk of humans being wiped out at 50 percent or greater.

The fact is that many scholars who study existential threats agree that the probability of doom is higher today than ever before in humanity's three-hundred-thousand-year history.

From nuclear weapons to killer drones to designer pathogens, humanity is acquiring much more efficient methods of bringing down civilization or causing our extinction than in the past.

Lord Martin Rees, a world-renowned cosmologist at the University of Cambridge, estimates that human civilization has a 50/50 chance of making it through this century intact.

EPIGRAPH

Morn came and went and came and brought no day.
And men forgot their passions in the dread of this, their desolation.
~ Lord Byron, English poet, in *Darkness*

Hawkeye: *War isn't Hell. War is war, and Hell is Hell. And of the two, war is a lot worse.*

Father Mulcahy: *How do you figure, Hawkeye?*

Hawkeye: *Easy, Father. Tell me. Who goes to Hell?*

Father Mulcahy: *Sinners, I believe.*

Hawkeye: *Exactly. There are no innocent bystanders in Hell. War is chock full of them—little kids, cripples, old ladies. In fact, except for some of the brass, almost everybody is an innocent bystander.*

~ Conversation between Hawkeye Pierce and Father Mulcahy on television series *M*A*S*H*

The third big war will begin when the big city is burning.
~ Nostradamus, French seer and philosopher

Out of suffering have emerged the strongest of souls.
The most massive characters are seared with scars.
~ Kahlil Gibran, Lebanese – American writer

Americans learn only from catastrophe and not from experience.
~ President Theodore Roosevelt

Give a man a fish and you feed him for a day.
Teach him how to fish and you feed him for a lifetime.
~ Lao Tzu, Chinese Philosopher, founder of Taoism

The world is a dangerous place, not because of those who do evil,
but because of those who look on and do nothing.
~ Albert Einstein

Great leaders don't set out to be a leader. They set out to make a
difference.
It's never about the role. It's always about the goal.
~ Anonymous

PROLOGUE

One Week Prior
Mount Weather Emergency Operations Center
Northern Virginia

Once upon a time, when you got fired from your job, the boss would simply say, "You're fired!" The words stung, but there was no doubt about their meaning.

When Secretary of Agriculture Erin Bergmann was awakened at six o'clock that morning by Secret Service personnel announcing she'd been summoned to a meeting with the president and his chief of staff, she was certain to hear those dreaded words.

Not that she would've been surprised. President Carter Helton had grown weary of her contrarian's point of view. He was under tremendous pressure throughout the crisis to the point of being confined for a brief time to his presidential suite on advice of the White House physician.

When Erin was called upon in cabinet meetings, she gave her learned opinion on the topics related to the mitigation of the effects of nuclear winter. Oftentimes, her suggestions and recommendations ran contrary to what the president wanted to hear. She was not a polished politician like the other members of the Helton administration. As a result, she hadn't quite learned how to play the game.

However, in Erin's mind, dealing with an existential crisis like the destruction of the planet's atmosphere from the consequences of nuclear war required straight talk. Nevertheless, she deduced as she made the long walk through the corridors of Mount Weather buried deep in the mountains of Northern Virginia, her days as part of the Helton Cabinet were coming to an end.

Erin rolled her eyes as she imagined the upcoming conversation. To ease the mental anguish of an employee's being fired, human resources directors created many alternatives to the dreaded words —*you're fired.*

Personnel realignment. Rationalizing the workforce. Career change opportunity. Workforce imbalance correction. Adjustments in internal efficiencies.

"Mumbo jumbo," Erin muttered aloud, drawing a look from one of her escorts. She noticed the stern look on the Secret Service agent's face, but she didn't return the glance. Instead, she managed a smirk. *Okay, fine. Gobbledygook. Better now?*

Because Erin wasn't a politician, she didn't give a rat's ass about a future in politics, especially in light of the fact that ninety percent of the country would be dead within a year. Therefore, she was determined to go out in a blaze of glory. Her only goal was to negotiate a departure package, more human resources gibberish for *can you at least give me a ride home?*

When the escorts stopped at the double-doored entrance to the presidential sleeping quarters, reality set in for Erin. She was about to be fired and turned out into the cold, literally. Three words came to mind.

Dead man walking.

"The president will see you now, ma'am," said the Secret Service agent, snapping Erin out of her thoughts filled with dread.

"Um, thank you."

She entered the president's quarters, which consisted of an outer office staffed with two armed guards and a desk for the White House secretary, who was not yet on duty. She stood in the entry alone, glancing around at the spartan furnishings. There were several doors leading out of the entry foyer, presumably offices or bedrooms. The space was not intended to be luxurious like the Oval Office in the White House, but it was elevated above the barracks-style quarters afforded others who were living within the protection of Mount Weather.

Another set of double doors was suddenly flung open, and a casually dressed Harrison Chandler appeared in the entry foyer with a smug look on his face. He and Erin had butted heads many times, which didn't help matters. Chandler had the president's ear virtually twenty-four seven. It was the functional equivalent to talking trash to a wife about her husband. The husband had more time to counter your arguments, so it was always a losing proposition.

"Come in, Erin, and take a seat," said President Helton, pointing toward a chair in front of his desk. The Resolute Desk, the nineteenth-century partner's desk used by the president in the Oval Office, was one of the few historic pieces of furniture that had been removed from the White House. During the bug-out process, it had made its way to the underground bunker.

"Good morning, Mr. President," greeted Erin somewhat cheerily. She intended to kill him with kindness before body-slamming him for his feckless policies. "I imagine you're excited for our move above ground to Carlisle." Our *being the operative word, Mr. President. Did you catch that?*

He looked up from the President's Daily Brief, the daily summary generated by the national security team and supplemented by Homeland Security during the crisis. He removed his glasses and leaned back in his chair. His face was expressionless.

President Helton set a dour tone for the meeting. "Erin, the attacks on America and the nuclear winter conditions have changed the dynamic of this administration. Each and every member of my cabinet was hired with a particular role in mind. When I chose you for the Secretary of Agriculture slot, I followed a skill-mix approach that transcended traditional boundaries, specialisms, and levels of engagement."

Erin bit her tongue because she needed to see how this meeting played out. Her thoughts, however, weren't constrained. *Mumbo jumbo, naturally. You gave me the job as political payback and to endear yourself to Floridians with their thirty electoral college votes, the nation's third largest.*

The president continued. "As we transition in the direction of recovery rather than a defensive posture, I will need people around me who are willing to carry out my vision for the future of this great nation."

Erin chuckled somewhat disrespectfully. Her attitude drew a scornful look from Chief of Staff Chandler.

"Yes-men," she interrupted.

"Excuse me?" asked the president.

"You need more yes-men, as if the other fourteen out of fifteen members aren't enough."

"Secretary Bergmann, you're out of line!" shouted Chandler.

She gave him a death stare. "Am I? It's blatantly obvious that my opinions are disregarded because the president doesn't want to hear an opposite point of view."

"I do value your opinions, Erin," countered the president unsuccessfully as he took control of the meeting. Erin wasn't buying it.

Over the weeks since the attacks, Chief of Staff Chandler had wielded more control and power in the Helton administration. The president's stress and anxiety created a power vacuum that Chandler was more than willing to fill. However, with their impending move above ground, as the president liked to call it, Chandler's role was also being diminished. The HR people might call that being *managed down.*

"Well, Mr. President, respectfully, I understand that you may choose not to follow my suggestions or advice. There can only be one decider, to borrow a term from former president Bush.

However, I don't believe it's in your best interests to discard someone who can provide you a different approach."

The president took a deep breath, glanced at Chandler, and exhaled. Erin got the sense he wanted to use the words *you're fired*. However, his chief of staff, who micromanaged the administration's personnel decisions, was always concerned about optics and media perception. As a result, Chandler was careful not to create a situation in which the president was accused of being one of the many labels ending in -ist or -ism.

"For example?" the president asked.

"Let's take Florida, my home state. Sir, your plan to exercise your authority under the martial law declaration to seize property and convert it into America's new breadbasket is a fool's errand. The sandy soil of the Keys won't support agricultural growth. And even if it did, there's not enough land mass to feed the residents of Florida, much less the nation. Plus, with NOAA's hurricane advisory, you should note that anything grown there could be washed away prior to the harvesting season by storm surge."

The president furrowed his brow and studied Erin. She didn't break eye contact with him as he spoke.

"My interest in Florida involves more than growing food for America. We have a situation, as you know, that borders on treason. I cannot allow state and local governments to shut themselves off from the rest of the nation at a time when we need to come together to help one another."

"You're referring to the actions of the Monroe County officials, I presume."

"Of course. The Florida Keys. The Upper Peninsula of Michigan. The barrier islands along the Eastern Seaboard. Hell, the whole state of Texas thinks they can restrict the flow of American citizens and ignore the rule of law. The first order of business is to tamp down this treasonous activity so I can focus on helping people stay alive."

Erin's mind raced as she soaked in his words. He seemed to be acting out of frustration. She also believed Chandler had been chirping in his ear about using the transition to the temporary seat of government at the Army War College in Central Pennsylvania as a logical opportunity to eliminate Erin, who'd been a thorn in the administration's side.

Truth be told, she was tired of playing the political games. She was proud of her accomplishments and verily believed her experience would be an asset to the country. However, this president and his right arm, Chandler, had shown a propensity for making knee-jerk decisions and playing favorites with members of the cabinet. Her contribution would never be acted upon much less appreciated. So she took a chance.

"Maybe I can help you?"

"In what way?" asked Chandler, rudely trying to insert himself in the conversation. Erin responded to his question but remained focused on the president.

"Mr. President, I have considerable ties to Florida's political machinery, as you know," began Erin, who reminded the president why'd he tapped her as Secretary of Agriculture in the first place. Her expertise was in transportation, but the agriculture position gave her the opportunity to help Floridians. "I know the governor well, of course, and I'm also familiar with Mayor Lindsey Free, the county executive of Monroe County. Perhaps I can defuse the situation."

"Secretary Bergmann, the president's decision has been—" began Chandler before the president raised his hand and cut him off.

"Let her finish, Harrison." The unusually stern rebuke drew a slight smile from Erin.

"Sir, I respect your decision to make a change at the Department of Agriculture. Naturally, I would prefer that you not. That said, I serve at the pleasure of the president and will honor your wishes. However, I can serve you in a way that helps solve the problem in the Keys."

"Go on," said the president, who was once again leaning back in his chair and relaxed.

"Sir, I have many contacts there. Send me to the Keys as your emissary, of sorts. With the approval of the governor, I can work behind the scenes to convince Mayor Free to back down from her shenanigans. If not, I can work with other politicos in the Keys to orchestrate a recall or some other similar means to remove her from office. I know the circumstances are unusual, and generally, a change in leadership of any government, even at the local level, is not advisable. However, her actions are almost tyrannical."

"I see you've been paying attention during the security briefings," said the president with a smile. His mood had softened. "Erin, the governor isn't any help to us. While he doesn't have a relationship with this mayor, he doesn't want to appear heavy-handed in dealing with the local county executives. His actions toward one might seem like an affront toward all."

"Makes sense," said Erin. "The federal government has different interests at stake than Tallahassee. For one thing, they've blocked a federal highway. Secondly, from a national security standpoint, the Florida Keys are the closest point to Communist Cuba, a close ally of Russia."

"Very true, Erin. What, exactly, do you propose?"

Erin paused and then laid out her plan. "I have a friend in the Keys whose family has been there since the beginning. He's well liked and highly respected. If you'll arrange travel for me to Driftwood Key, as well as create a direct line of communication to Harrison, I'll keep him abreast of my activities. I'll also consult with him as I work to remove the mayor and anyone loyal to her from office."

The president smiled. "I like it," he said as he turned to his top aide. "Harrison, work with Erin to give her anything she needs."

For the next two days, Erin learned all she could about Lindsey Free and the politicians who ran Monroe County's government. She identified potential allies and met with the Pentagon representatives coordinating the National Guard troop movements.

The day she was supposed to travel by helicopter to Driftwood Key, a devil of a storm swept over the island chain.

PART I

Day twenty-four, Sunday, November 10

CHAPTER ONE

Sunday, November 10
Florida Bay
Florida Keys, USA

Morning came and turned into day, such that it was during nuclear winter. Then another night swept over the Florida Keys, followed by another day of the grayish haze that blanketed the planet. The tumultuous waves and the torrential rains had ceased, bringing an eerie calm over the water. When it was over, Jimmy Free thought he'd died.

It's not uncommon for the living who discover an unconscious body to act with trepidation. They might kick it to see if it stirs. Others might slap the person's face, trying to evoke a reaction. Or, as Sonny Free suggested when Peter's lifeless body was found in a heap on the bridge leading to Driftwood Key, one could simply shoot the poor soul and see if he responded.

It was a surface-feeding fish nibbling at Jimmy's toes that reminded him he was alive. But just barely.

Dehydrated, exhausted, and disoriented, Jimmy had wrapped his arms around a palm tree log. He tried without success to determine his location. From recollection, he thought he was within the confines of Blackwater Sound. He vividly remembered the pounding waves and the hurricane-force winds that had battered him relentlessly for hours.

Once he lost control of his WaveRunner and began to tread water, he was certain Peter would find him. If not immediately, when daylight came. For hours, he was pushed farther and farther west as the storm raged on. One wave after another generated momentum, forcing his body, along with the other flotsam, to move away from Key Largo and toward the western side of Blackwater Sound.

It was a stroke of bad luck that sent Jimmy floating helplessly through the Boggies, a narrow channel that split the mangroves and entered Florida Bay. Thirty feet to either the left or the right would've landed him against the mangrove trees jutting through the water. He would've held on through the hurricane, and when the devilish storm passed, he could've used the mangroves to pull himself back to Key Largo. At worst, he would've been found by Peter or the other boaters during their search the next day.

However, fate brought him into the open waters of Florida Bay, where he drifted with the waves generated by the hurricane. A palm tree's trunk had rammed into him as he floated along. It was his only option to be used as a floatation device. Despite the heavy nature of the waterlogged tree trunk, it kept him afloat and alive throughout the tempest.

When the log crashed into a beach, Jimmy inwardly rejoiced. He was going to live. He convinced himself he was within Blackwater Sound. He was wrong.

Exhausted from the ride through the storm, he lay flat on his back on the sandy shore and passed out. Then he slept for fourteen hours. When he awakened, he unknowingly found himself on Derelict Key, a tiny island disconnected from the mainland, which was approximately four miles from the Boggies.

The storm had passed, allowing him to take in his immediate surroundings, but the hazy nature of nuclear winter had reduced his visibility to only a couple of miles. For as far as his eyes could see, there was only grayish water and the similarly colored skies above.

Other than the salt-filled rainwater he'd lapped up off his skin during the storm, Jimmy hadn't had anything to drink since he had been held at the Infield Care Center at the speedway. It had now been more than forty-eight hours, and his body was feeling the effects of dehydration.

Between the onset of dehydration and the battle he'd fought during the hurricane, Jimmy was extremely fatigued. He was starting to feel dizzy and unable to pee. As he sat on the beach, staring across the water, he cupped his hand and held it to his mouth. His breath was horrible. He started to laugh hysterically as he debated what luxury item he'd enjoy more, a swig of Scope mouthwash or a cherry Popsicle.

It's been said that the grandest of adventures were often imagined on an uncharted island. From visions of pirate's booty to giant apes, the mysterious nature of a tiny speck of land peeking up through a vast ocean has captivated the imagination of children and adults who seek solace from the so-called rat race.

The Florida Keys were able to fulfill some of these visions. Since they were discovered by Ponce de Leon in 1513, legions of ships caught the trade winds along the Florida Straits to explore the Americas. Pirates sailed the waters, stalking the Spanish treasure fleets. British warships tracked the illegal slave ships. Hidden coral reefs held their bony hands near the surface, causing many of the boats to wreck.

Derelict Key was too small for pirate treasure or giant apes. The foot-shaped island was less than a mile from ankle to toe. Jimmy wandered the entire perimeter of the island, assessing his options. He knew there was another island or land mass nearby, as evidenced by the iguanas that inhabited Derelict Key.

The iguanas weren't dangerous or aggressive. Nicknamed the chicken of the trees by the locals, they were considered tasty when cooked as well as a high source of protein. But Jimmy didn't have the strength or the inclination to kill the creatures, nor did he have a means to cook them. Somehow, as desperate as he was, he couldn't bring himself to eat the iguanas raw.

Jimmy made his way to the north end of Derelict Key. The sky had opened slightly, allowing a little more sunlight to shine through. He squinted his eyes and focused on what appeared to be a stand of mangrove trees a thousand feet from the island. Feeling he had nothing to lose, Jimmy decided to swim to the other island.

The decision almost got him killed.

CHAPTER TWO

Sunday, November 10
Driftwood Key

The night before, Hank Albright had introduced Erin Bergmann to Lacey and Peter. Erin also got reacquainted with Mike and Jessica and the Frees. It had been a long day for everyone, as the weary travelers were exhausted, and Mike continued to recover from the attack courtesy of the serial killer Patrick Hollister. It was agreed everyone would get a good night's rest, and they'd take the boats out early Sunday morning to begin an all-day search for Jimmy.

The residents of Driftwood Key, new and old, were desperate to share information with one another. It took a lot of discipline and Hank's putting his foot down to prevent the group from staying up until the wee hours of the morning talking. He offered a sobering reminder that Jimmy was still missing. It was time to bring Sonny and Phoebe's son home.

In the predawn hours, Phoebe began cooking breakfast for the search party. Hank and Erin would take the Hatteras. They'd bring along six five-gallon containers of diesel for the fishing boat that Peter had been forced to abandon in Little Basin at Upper

Matecumbe Key. Once they retrieved the boat, Sonny and Peter would fill up its fuel tank and undertake another search of Blackwater Sound. Jessica and Tucker would join Hank in Florida Bay. The large fuel cells would enable them to cover a much larger search area.

Sunrise produced just enough light to provide the boaters a clear line of sight as they made their way north toward Florida Bay. It took nearly an hour to arrive at Blackwater Sound. Peter and Sonny waved goodbye and peeled off through the Boggies, slowing down considerably to search the mangroves.

Jessica took her Monroe County sheriff's department WET boat northward toward the mainland. She would concentrate her efforts along the barrier islands protecting Long Sound and in the area around Trout Cove. Hank and Erin turned due west with the goal of searching each of the miniscule islands that dotted Florida Bay before they reached the southern tip of the mainland. It was agreed that Jimmy could've floated many miles during the storm. If they exhausted the outer perimeter of the bay, then they'd work their way inward to look at every key no matter how small.

Hank drove the Hatteras from the flybridge while Erin used the marine binoculars to scan both the water and shoreline. Like Jessica, Hank used the boat's external speakers in conjunction with the horn to call out Jimmy's name.

They'd just begun their search by circling the Nest Key, a mostly sandy island in the shape of a three-legged starfish. The two of them were all business as they focused on the task at hand. Hank had a million questions for Erin, and she was anxious to relay the purpose of her trip. However, Jimmy's disappearance had gone on for too long, and everyone agreed to table any other topics until he was found.

Having no luck, they moved to the west. Tiny islands named Lake Key, Tern Key, and Pass Key yielded nothing. Larger islands like Palm Key and Fan Palm Hammock provided no evidence of Jimmy or anything else other than the normal debris that floats ashore. After many hours of searching, Hank's westward route and

Jessica's northern search pattern resulted in the two boats meeting one another at Alligator Bay, the southernmost tip of the Everglades.

"I just spoke to Peter," Hank yelled to Jessica. "He hasn't seen any sign of Jimmy, and he's running low on fuel. He's got just enough to get back to Driftwood Key."

"What's he gonna do?" she asked.

"He doesn't want to quit, but he feels obligated to Captain Jax to bring him the diesel fuel he promised."

"What about the boat?"

Hank shouted across the water to her, "It was a gift, so he can ditch it. I told him we would make good on the diesel later. Can you head over toward the Boggies to pick them up?"

"Yeah," Jessica replied. "We'll start searching the inner islands now, but, Hank, it's getting dark."

Hank sighed and paused as he studied Erin's face. She was detached and unemotional about the search, as she'd only met Jimmy and his family briefly. She was prepared to look for as long as Hank wanted to, but she feared the worst.

"We have to try," she said to Hank, noticing his eyes revealed how he felt.

"Erin, he's like a son to me. His father and I are like brothers."

She smiled and patted Hank on the back. She glanced at the laminated nautical charts that were rolled out on the seat next to her. She'd been learning her way around while searching at the same time. Erin stood and leaned over the rail.

"Okay, Jessica. We'll get started on this upper half of the bay, running an east-west search pattern. You start at the southern end near Whaleback Key. We'll meet in the middle like before."

"Roger!" Jessica shouted and gunned the engine as she swung around and headed toward the Boggies. Hank and Erin could hear her conversation with Peter over the marine radio.

"Thank you," Hank said softly. His shoulders drooped, and the tension was released from his body. It was as if they could speak freely now that they were alone.

"Hey, there's nothing to thank me for," she responded, rubbing the top of his shoulders and his neck. "Why don't you let me drive for a while? I'm no expert, but we're going slow enough that I don't think I can get us into trouble. Maybe a trained set of eyes might be able to scan the water better than I can?"

Hank squeezed her hand and relinquished the helm. He retrieved two bottles of water out of a tote bag and handed one to Erin. Refreshed, Hank took a deep breath and exhaled. He looked all around them and identified a point to their east for Erin to head towards. Once they crossed the bay, they'd make a sweeping U-turn and head back across toward the west. Each of the tiny stands of mangroves atop sand bars would get searched before moving on to the next one. It was a daunting, time-consuming task.

Erin got them started, and Hank began to scan the water, both of them realizing that any hope of finding Jimmy alive was diminishing with each passing hour.

CHAPTER THREE

Sunday, November 10
Stump Pass at Derelict Key
Florida Bay

Under normal circumstances, Jimmy Free could swim several hundred yards in just minutes, whether above water or below the surface. When he dove into Stump Pass, a tiny opening of Florida Bay between Derelict Key and the island just to the north, his mind told him the quick swim would be an easy one.

Halfway across the pass, his body told him otherwise. Jimmy didn't know if it was possible for the body to use up its adrenaline, but it apparently failed to produce enough to carry him the few hundred yards necessary to reach the next key.

He began to tire and suddenly found himself struggling, frantically treading water. Then he floated on his back to catch his breath and regain his strength, but his inability to concentrate resulted in his face frequently falling beneath the surface. The young man who was once capable of holding his breath underwater for more than ten minutes found himself choking for air after a few seconds.

Jimmy furiously began to tread water again, barely ten feet above a sandbar beneath his feet that would appear at low tide hours later. He rolled onto his back and gently kicked his legs to propel himself toward the next island.

Gaining confidence, he kicked a little harder after turning his head and shoulders to gauge his direction. He kept a steady pace over the next two hundred feet. That was when his head was bumped by something floating on top of the water. He quickly turned his body around to see what he'd encountered.

The beady eyes of two water snakes stared at him. In his exhausted, disoriented state, Jimmy panicked. He quickly turned and began swimming in the other direction. Had he been coherent and healthy, he would know that water snakes are nonvenomous in the Keys. The two solid-black salt marsh water snakes were simply foraging for tadpoles in the brackish water. However, his mind refused to allow him to apply logic to the startling confrontation.

Instead of swimming back toward Derelict Key, he took off into the middle of Florida Bay. Within a minute, fear fueled his adrenal glands, and he found the ability to swim again, albeit in the wrong direction. He looked back to see how much distance he'd put between himself and the snakes. He couldn't see them or Derelict Key.

Once again, Jimmy floated on his back to regain his strength. He closed his eyes to force his body and mind to relax.

Focus, Jimmy. Focus.

He began to control his breathing. His mind blocked out the fear and the formidable task of survival. He allowed his mind to float away, imagining being lost at sea with land nowhere in sight. He was similarly situated because of the poor visibility caused by nuclear winter. Although he was near land to his immediate north and west, he couldn't see it and had no way of gaining his bearings.

Jimmy began to tread water in an effort to determine where the sun was in the sky. He had no idea what time of day it was. From morning to night, the gray skies became lighter and then darker. It was impossible to determine if it was eight in the morning or five in the afternoon.

Whether it was exhaustion or the ingestion of saltwater or the dehydration, Jimmy was becoming incoherent. He was having trouble determining where he was and how he'd gotten there. He thought he'd been swimming against the current, back toward Key Largo. However, he became confused. Was he swimming in the direction the hurricane had traveled? Or was he going with the current to the closest stretch of sandbar?

He chose a course and began swimming again. He'd been in the water for what seemed like an hour, but it could've been two hours or twenty minutes. His mind refused to allow him any form of coherent, conscious thought.

He developed a pattern of swimming for ten minutes followed by treading water or simply floating on his back, giving his shoulders and legs a chance to rejuvenate or, at least, to find the stamina to start again.

His mind and body began to recover. He chastised himself for getting spooked by the harmless snakes. He continued swimming toward what he was certain to be east. The sky appeared to be a darker shade of gray than what was behind him. He stopped again, allowing his legs to drop beneath his body as he swung his arms to release the tension. He couldn't see land, but he was certain he knew where it was.

"That way," he muttered as he pointed toward the east. He was partly right. He continued to swim, hoping land would materialize on the horizon. He focused on keeping the lighter shade of sky behind him. His eyes felt scarred from the sea spray the night of the hurricane. He was unable to produce tears to wash them and to help correct the burning sensation.

His legs felt like lead, and his thigh muscles twitched and convulsed. Jimmy was beginning to lose the adrenaline rush, and doubt crept into his mind. The logical part of his brain, the frontal lobe that reasoned, screamed at him to keep going or he'd drown.

Jimmy began to frog-kick and used a breaststroke to propel his body ahead. The change of swimming technique seemed to rejuvenate him. He was making some progress, and then his heart leapt as mangroves appeared in the distance.

He ignored the small, gray-green waves that hit his face each time he thrust his arms outward and pushed the water to swim. He was doing his best to avoid ingesting it, but there was little he could do to keep it out of his eyes.

His muscles screamed in agony, but he continued. Jimmy knew there were many ways to die while stranded in the water. Hypothermia, especially in these atmospheric conditions, was one of them. The reduced temperatures had lowered the water temperature substantially. His core was reaching a temperature that was on the verge of being hypothermic.

Jimmy continued to swim, turning his head as another small wave rolled under his body. His mind began to wander to his parents. Were they worried about him? Were they looking for him? Did Peter make it to safety? If he did, why didn't he bring a search party?

Jimmy had always been attuned to his surroundings, especially on the water. He could recall sounds and smells and tastes regarding the ocean so vividly that they became real even though he might be lying in bed at night. He was using this same application of sensory memory to force his mind to focus on his mother and father. He could smell and taste Phoebe's cooking as if he were sitting alongside her at the kitchen table. He could hear Sonny teaching him about the greenhouse or hydroponics or whatever wisdom a father found necessary to impart upon his son.

He tried not to think about the dire situation he was in. He tried to push out of his mind the requirement to tread water in order to stay alive. He forced himself to remember bright moments in his life with his parents as well as with his extended family, the Albrights.

He started with ordinary activities like fishing or scuba diving, but then he drilled down to the minutiae, every meaningless detail of diving at John Pennekamp Coral Reef State Park. He knew every square inch of those reefs. He recalled the ones he could reach without the aid of scuba gear. He thought about the girls he'd met at the inn, who begged him to take them diving.

This exercise kept him alert and reminded him of how great his life had been. It took his mind off his body and the pain it was enduring to keep him afloat. It took him out of Florida Bay for a moment to a more pleasant place where he wasn't shivering or fearful of losing his life.

The intensity with which Jimmy wanted to see his parents became more than he could handle. Emotion swept over him, and he began to sob. His uncontrolled crying resulted in him taking deeper breaths coupled with more salt water.

Jimmy began to cough up phlegm and the salty fluids. His stomach seized. A massive grip squeezed his insides, forcing bile into his throat. This triggered nausea, and while he was trying to tread water, he began to vomit.

He retched over and over again until the bile once stored in his gallbladder found its way to his throat. Jimmy desperately wanted to crawl onto his hands and knees to let it all out. Empty the contents of his stomach and start over. However, he couldn't.

Jimmy gargled with sea water to clear the nasty taste out of his mouth. He tried to produce saliva and swallowed. He discovered he didn't have enough saliva to soothe his raw throat. He fought the pain and the nausea as he floated on his back. The exertion, salt water and stress were dehydrating him at a rapid rate now. He took a deep breath and slid beneath the surface of the water.

That was when he heard the low rumble of a boat motor in the distance.

CHAPTER FOUR

Sunday, November 10
Florida Bay

Hank focused his attention on the tiny island sitting equidistant between the Boggies and Derelict Key, which he identified on the nautical chart. The key was not identified on the charts, and by Hank's estimation, it barely measured three hundred feet across. It was not the island itself that caught his eye. Something was bobbing in the water, up and down, yet remaining in the same location despite the gently rolling waves that would carry the debris closer to the island.

Hank pointed to the south after tapping Erin on the shoulder. "Slowly make your way toward that island. We can pick up the search again in a moment."

Erin followed his instruction and turned the Hatteras to port. While she did, Hank picked up the handset to the marine radio and reached out to his sister-in-law.

"Jessica, do you copy?"

"Go ahead, Hank."

"We're working our way due west of Buttonwood Sound. Nothing so far."

"Roger," she replied.

Hank slowly pressed the transmit button. "Stand by."

With his other hand, he pulled the binoculars back up to his face and focused on the bobbing debris near the small island of mangrove trees. He leaned forward as if those extra few inches would close the gap and allow him to get a better fix on the object that had grabbed his attention.

Hank's voice became excited. "There, Erin! Do you see it? Just west of the island."

"Okay, barely," she replied as she brought her hand above her eyes to reduce the glare.

Hank fumbled with the charts and tried to get his bearings. He keyed the mic again. "Jessica! Twenty-five degrees, ten minutes, north longitude. Eighty degrees, twenty-nine minutes, west latitude. I've got something. Definitely a body!"

"I see it, Hank! A guy. He's treading water!"

Erin immediately turned in that direction and gave the Hatteras full throttle, forcing the bow upward. From the flybridge, Hank was still able to keep his eyes affixed on the body.

Hank raised Jessica on the radio again. "Almost there. We have somebody in the water alive. West side of the island. Hurry!"

In the distance, the sound of the powerful outboard engines on the back of Jessica's boat coming to life could be heard across the serene waters of Florida Bay. Hank glanced at the depth finder mounted on the helm of the flybridge, carefully monitoring their distance to the sandy bottom as they approached the small island. The draft on his Hatteras was about four feet, making it susceptible to dragging along a sand bar.

"He's waving, Hank! He's waving!"

Hank grabbed his binoculars and focused on the bobbing head. He saw the arm for a moment before it fell below the water's surface along with the man's head. For several seconds, the man's arm from the elbow up was able to wave.

And then it disappeared.

———

Jimmy had slipped below the surface. He'd summoned every fiber of his being to help him stay alive. He'd heard the boat in the distance and tried to tread water to get its attention. He followed it in the distance as it traversed the bay, clearly searching for something.

His eyes betrayed him at first, partly due to the damage caused by the salt water and partly because of his dehydration. Jimmy thought it was a Coast Guard vessel. He suddenly wondered if the National Guard had enlisted the assistance of the Coast Guard to locate their escaped prisoner. Afraid of being captured and beaten again, he considered hiding under water to avoid detection. He glanced toward the small stand of mangroves that seemed to be a good place to hide, as well as hang on to until his body could recover.

Only, he didn't have the strength to get there. Jimmy accepted his fate, assuming that he'd be caught and imprisoned. At least he'd be alive. He made his way closer to the trees until his feet were able to touch bottom. Standing on his toes, his head and upper shoulders protruded above the surface. He tried to shout, but his swollen throat betrayed him. He began waving, but as he did, he lost his balance and slipped underwater.

Jimmy inched closer to the mangroves, hoping to reach higher ground yet still be visible to the passing boat. He was able to get better footing and waved with both arms when he noticed the boat turning toward him. To his rear, he heard another boat approach rapidly from the other direction.

They'd seen him. He was going to be rescued. He began jumping up and down to elevate himself above the surface, waving his arms to grab their attention while suffering the stinging pain of trying to yell.

Up and down, bounding along the sandy surface, unknowingly moving away from the small mangrove-covered sandbar. And then, as is often the case in the ocean, the currents had created a trough along the sandy bottom that dropped off six feet or so. Jimmy lost his footing and immediately slid down the trough until he was more than ten feet underwater.

Jimmy felt something bump his legs. It was large, solid, cold. He frantically twisted his body to avoid the underwater creature. His heart raced, and his face seemed to tingle.

He felt the movement of the current that had created the trough in the sandy floor. It pulled at his legs, tugging him deeper below the water. The sea creature, a large fish of some kind, bumped into him again. Its skin was like rubbery sandpaper as it grazed his feet and ankles.

Jimmy opened his mouth, thinking if he screamed, the monster that circled him would leave him be. He tried and tried, but he had no breath left as he cried for help.

"Where'd he go?" asked Erin. She pulled back on the throttle and allowed the boat's wake to push them slowly toward the island.

Hank scampered off the flybridge and raced onto the bow. He was holding the railing as he walked around the perimeter of the bow, looking into the water.

Jessica was less than a hundred yards away as she raced toward him. Hank turned toward her and raised both hands in the air, urging her to slow down. It had been nearly a minute since they'd seen the man waving his arms high over his head. And then, in the blink of an eye, he was gone.

CHAPTER FIVE

Sunday, November 10
Florida Bay

Jimmy tried to hold his breath and fought death by not panicking underwater. He slowly turned in a circle, waving his arms, just below the sandy bottom before the drop-off, his arms churning the water over his head. He could see the surface and the large boat hovering nearby. It was moving closer to him. His efforts to swim upward weren't working as if his feet were tied to anvils holding him down.

Soon, his body began to tire again. An argument raged in his mind as to what was the best course of action.

You gotta breathe or you'll die!

I can't breathe or I'll die!

He had to make it. He twisted his torso to lay prone underwater. The other way wasn't working. He closed his eyes and allowed his body to go limp. He imagined himself as bait on a hook, awaiting the big fish to carry him away. Or a dead body floating, waiting for the hand of God to snatch him up to Heaven.

Jimmy's mind wandered, wondering how long he'd been underwater. Was he even conscious? Was this what it was like when a person died? He kept waiting for the soothing voice to tell him to go to the light. Instead, a shadow passed over him, covering him in darkness.

Hank jumped off the transom into the water while Jessica dove off the bow of her WET team boat to assist. They both swept their arms in wide arcs and furiously kicked their feet to force their bodies deeper below the surface, fighting the natural buoyancy of their oxygen-filled lungs.

Jessica arrived at Jimmy's body first and immediately waved Hank off. A drowning person may appear docile when first discovered, but she knew from experience that they were prone to panicking when rescued. When a victim begins to flounder, they could easily knock their rescuer unconscious or prevent them from rising back to the surface.

Jimmy was making no effort to kick his way back to the surface. His body appeared lifeless, yet his mouth was closed, a good sign. Jessica was an excellent swimmer and diver as well. She'd saved the life of a drowning victim once before. Underwater rescue training helped, but the real-life experience of dealing with a person on the brink of death proved invaluable as she touched Jimmy.

His reaction was not unexpected. Startled, followed by an intense desire to help his rescuer. Jessica wanted to shout to him— *I've got this, relax!* Instead, she remained calm so she could think clearly and react to his movements.

She moved behind Jimmy's shoulders and reached her arms underneath his arms. Jessica's leg muscles were strong courtesy of good genetics and constant training by running in the sand. She began kicking, and the two of them moved quickly toward the water's surface. Seconds later, they breached the plane, and Jessica quickly took in a deep breath in case Jimmy woke up and pulled them underwater again.

Her mind tried to shut out the cries of joy and shouts of Jimmy's name coming from all directions. There was still work to be done. She moved her hands to brace his head upright. As she did, she felt for his pulse.

There wasn't one. And he wasn't breathing.

Jessica closed her eyes briefly and then rapidly kicked her legs as she dragged him to the back of her boat. As she passed the port side, Peter and Sonny were looking over the rails, shouting words of encouragement to Jimmy.

"Meet me at the back!" she shouted. "Grab the backboard!"

Peter reacted first. Despite his own injuries, he was setting aside the pain he felt in order to help his friend. Sonny was crying, alternating between wiping his tears being shed for his son and gripping the railing of Jessica's boat to get a better look.

"Got it!" shouted Peter from the boat's stern.

"Sonny! I need you to help Peter. You guys need to get on the transom so we can hoist his body onto the backboard."

While she had been in Key West with Mike at the hospital, she'd taken some time to go to the supply depot located at the nearby sheriff's office. She'd restocked the medications and other trauma supplies used on her water emergency team boat. She'd also taken a seventy-eight-inch orange backboard. Made of high-density polyethylene, it was not only buoyant, but the Velcro straps and head immobilizer provided her the ability to secure Jimmy in place while they dragged him on board.

Sonny held his son's face in his hands while Peter and Jessica positioned Jimmy on the backboard. Then the three of them pulled him over the stern and onto the deck of the boat. Jessica didn't waste any time as she rushed to the helm.

Her marine radio remained set to the emergency channel monitored by first responders and hospitals in the Keys. Despite the power outages, some hospitals were still operating using generators, including Mariner's Hospital in Tavernier. She radioed them and advised she was bringing in a drowning victim.

She had to think for a moment as to where the closest marina was located. Normally, they'd bring an accident victim into Tavernier Harbor on the Atlantic Ocean side of Tavernier. On the Gulf side, an ambulance would meet them at the closest marina.

Peter seemed to sense her inability to remember the closest marina. "Jessica, Mangrove Marina in Hurricane Harbor. It's less than a mile up the road."

"Yeah, you're right." She turned her attention back to her conversation with the dispatcher at Mariner's Hospital and then looked over to Hank and Erin. "Go get Phoebe!"

Hank waved and yelled, "Thank you." He and Erin fired up the Hatteras. After Jessica turned her boat around and took off toward Bottle Key to the south, they began their hour-long ride back to Driftwood Key.

Jessica shouted, "Peter, drive! You know where to go."

She knew Jimmy needed immediate medical attention. Even small amounts of water left in the lungs can cause respiratory issues later known as dry drowning. With Peter propelling the boat along the fortunately smooth waters, Jessica began cardiopulmonary resuscitation.

She took a normal breath, gently pinched Jimmy's nose, and covered his mouth with her own, ensuring an airtight seal. She exhaled quickly twice, keeping a watchful eye on his chest to see if it rose. She raised her body and began chest compressions, pressing down about two inches.

"One, two, three, four, five." She counted to force herself to remain consistent and to give Jimmy's chest an opportunity to rise back to normal. "Twenty-eight. Twenty-nine. Thirty. Off."

"Why isn't he breathing?" asked Sonny.

Jessica ignored his question and pointed to the storage compartments underneath the bench seat on the port side of the boat. "Grab me the light blue bag in there. I need to intubate."

Intubation was the process of placing a specially designed plastic tube into an unresponsive patient who was unable to breathe. The flexible tube was carefully inserted into the trachea to create a conduit through which air could be forced using a large squeezable bulb.

"Okay, I'm in. Sonny, I need you to gently squeeze this bulb to force air into Jimmy's chest. Like this."

After Jessica showed him what to do, Sonny recovered emotionally and set his jaw, determined to save his son.

"Okay," she continued, reaching out to Sonny's hand and squeezing it gently. "Let me try compressions again."

She began to pump his chest. She was halfway through the thirty-count when Jimmy's body heaved upward, and he began to cough violently, choking on the intubation tube in the process. Jessica quickly removed it and then turned him over to his side. He immediately spit out some sea water.

"Son, I'm here." Sonny slid across the deck on his knees so Jimmy could see him. His eyes were open, but he was clearly disoriented.

"Jessica! Water!" shouted Peter from the helm. He held up a bottle of water, and Jessica opened her hands to catch it when he tossed it to her.

"I'll need another in a second," she said before turning back to Jimmy. "Let's get you up and clear the gunk out of your throat."

She and Sonny worked together to get him upright. His eyes were darting around wildly, and mucus was dripping out of his nose. Sonny lovingly wiped his face and moved his stringy wet hair out of his eyes. Jessica slowly poured an ounce or two of water into Jimmy's mouth, monitoring his intake so he didn't gulp down too much.

He coughed again, and Jessica gently patted him between the shoulder blades. She spoke in a calm voice. "That's okay, Jimmy. This will take a few times. Slowly, okay?"

She allowed him a little water. This time, he let the soothing moisture trickle down his throat. Jimmy closed his eyes for a moment until a single tear dripped down his cheek. Then he managed a smile and nodded.

All he could manage was a whisper, but his words spoke volumes.

"Love you, Dad."

CHAPTER SIX

Sunday, November 10
Gulf of Mexico

For several minutes after Hank sped away from where Jimmy had been found, he glanced back toward Florida Bay, trying to catch a glimpse of Jessica's WET boat speeding toward Tavernier. He desperately wanted to be with the young man who'd grown up with Peter and practically became a part of the Albright family. Sonny, Phoebe, and Jimmy had lived on Driftwood Key for nearly three decades. They'd experienced loss together and enjoyed the island living the Keys afforded. Jimmy's death would be devastating.

Erin moved next to Hank on the bench seat and began to rub his shoulders. The touch of a woman caused him to break down in tears. Men tried to remain stoic in a crisis. They want to shoulder the burden of solving the problem or being the family rock—strong, solid, and unchanging.

Yet Hank was a considerably empathetic and caring man who tried to put others' emotional needs ahead of his own. That was one of the reasons he was having difficulty accepting the collapse of society that continued to unfold during nuclear winter.

As the proprietor of the Driftwood Key Inn, he enjoyed tending to his guests' needs. It bothered him that he'd had to ask them to leave in anticipation of what was coming. Deep down, he knew it was the right thing to do. His guests needed to get home before conditions worsened.

When Patrick Hollister showed up at their doorstep, figuratively speaking, Hank readily took him in. He wanted to help a fellow *conch* in his time of need. Nowadays, the number of people born in the Keys, known as a conch, were outnumbered by the newcomers. Patrick was an original. He'd also turned out to be a serial killer.

Even that experience didn't tamp down Hank's desire to help others survive. He simply had to change his mindset. For one, he had to ensure he could take care of his own first. That included his immediate family and, of course, the Frees. Secondly, those in need didn't include anyone who tried to steal from him.

As society continued to collapse, the use of violence to survive had increased beyond his wildest imagination. There had been gunfights at Driftwood Key, the kind you see in the movies. Marauders at the gate, so to speak. Hank was certain these encounters would increase as people became more desperate.

He was relieved that his family was together again, albeit without his son-in-law, Owen. He was a good man. A loving father to Tucker and a devoted husband to Lacey. Hank had immediately hit it off with Owen when Lacey brought him home for the first time. The suddenness of Lacey's return coupled with the search for Jimmy hadn't given Hank time to process Owen's death. He wondered if and when life in the apocalypse would allow them the opportunity to talk it through.

Hank took a deep breath and exhaled. This was all weighty stuff, and he desperately wanted to clear his head before he arrived at Driftwood Key. He needed to provide Phoebe hope that her son would survive, without overpromising. When Hank saw her son last, he wasn't breathing.

"Hank, I feel like I know you well enough to feel the heavy burden you're carrying," said Erin, interrupting his thoughts. She stopped rubbing his shoulders and moved around the seat to lean against the helm, where she could study his face. "I spent enough time with you and your family those few days to know that young man is in good hands. He'll pull through."

Hank managed a smile and made eye contact with Erin. He'd been laser focused on the waters ahead of him. There was a substantial amount of debris floating in the Gulf as a result of the hurricane. Because there had been little or no warning to most residents, the normal precautions weren't undertaken to secure their belongings.

Tears began to flow as Hank spoke. "I can't tell Phoebe the truth, but I can't lie either. A mother looks for words of optimism and hope when her child is injured. I can't say he was lying on the deck of a boat, not breathing because he'd drowned."

"I understand. However, I believe Jessica is a very capable, take-charge first responder. In her care, I think Jimmy has a chance. Plus, we don't know for certain; therefore, you can offer her hope."

Hank chuckled and wiped the tears from his face. "My father used to say things like that when he was supporting me as my wife passed away. She had many chances to live and fought hard to do so. In the end the disease defeated her."

"You have to channel your father's words of encouragement, Hank. You've experienced grief, and from what I recall, Phoebe was there to help you through it. Think back to how she helped you when your wife was ill."

"She fed me," said Hank, laughing now as he thought of those days when Phoebe would dote on him like he was her grandchild.

Erin also laughed. "Okay, well, we don't want you to put her in mortal danger, now do we? Perhaps you can find some other way to comfort her without invading her kitchen."

Hank reached out and took Erin's hand in his. She'd gently yanked him out of his melancholy state of mind and turned him back into the rock of the family everyone relied upon.

"Thank you. I was, um, as the kids say, having a moment."

"You can have a moment, Hank. You're entitled." Erin pointed ahead. They were approaching the dock at Driftwood Key. "It appears they heard us coming, so you'd better get your game face on. If you pull into the dock a blubbering mess, Phoebe will most likely freak out."

Tucker led the way, racing through the sand. His momentum caused him to stumble slightly as he hit the dock. After regaining his footing, he got into position to take the line from Erin. His eyes studied his grandfather for a clue as to what they'd discovered, if anything.

His uncle Mike beat him to the punch. "Any news?" he asked as Erin tossed him the bow line. Mike was recovering from his knife wound and healing remarkably well. He was moving slower than normal, as he was consciously aware of his sutures and the pain associated with certain activities.

Phoebe was crying, sobbing and struggling to catch her breath. Erin didn't hesitate. She climbed onto the side of the Hatteras and hoisted herself onto the dock. She immediately hugged Jimmy's mother to console her until Hank could join them.

She forced her tone of voice to be upbeat. "Okay, we have good news. We found Jimmy."

"Oh, thank God," Phoebe said as she continued to cry. She tried to wipe the tears off her face, but they poured out too fast. Her eyes darted between Erin and Hank. It didn't take her long to realize their demeanors were subdued and not celebratory. "Is he …? Is he okay?"

Hank moved closer and lovingly wiped the tears off Phoebe's face. He held her shoulders and looked down into her eyes. "Phoebe, your son is a survivor. However, he's been through a lot. For days, he's managed to fight the hurricane and dehydration to stay afloat in Florida Bay."

"The bay?" Mike asked. "I thought they were in Blackwater Sound?"

"He must've been pushed through the Boggies during the high winds," replied Hank before turning his attention back to Phoebe. "Listen to me. You know Jessica. She's the best there is at helping people outside of a hospital. They're taking Jimmy to Mariner's in Tavernier. Sonny is with them and so is Peter. We need to go, too."

Phoebe nodded her head up and down vigorously. She started to pull away and head toward the beach.

Erin had a suggestion. "Mike, I assume your truck has sirens and lights?"

"Yes, of course, although traffic isn't an issue. It's the stalled vehicles."

She stepped closer and kept constant eye contact with him in an effort to convey the message she needed him to understand. "Your family needs to be together. Can you drive them? You know, as quickly as possible?"

Mike got it. "Yeah. Let's go."

"I can stay here with Erin," offered Tucker.

"I'll be—" she began to argue before Tucker cut her off.

"Seriously, I'll stay. There's been some things happening, and you'll need help."

Erin had a puzzled look on her face, but she acquiesced. Minutes later, Mike, Hank and Phoebe were racing up the highway toward Tavernier.

CHAPTER SEVEN

Sunday, November 10
Mariner's Hospital
Tavernier, Florida

It wasn't an ambulance, but the E-Z go utility cart had a long enough bed to hold the backboard firmly in place atop a one-inch-thick, vinyl-coated pad. Jessica worked with Sonny and Peter to lift Jimmy out of the boat, where they passed him off to a trauma nurse and two orderlies. The trio drove away with the trauma nurse perched in the back to continue checking Jimmy's vitals.

"Guys, let's secure the boat and head to the hospital," said Peter. "It's just over a mile from here."

They wasted no time in tying the boat to the dock at Mangrove Marina. Jessica also locked all of the vessel's compartments. During the process, they'd drawn the attention of several onlookers, and she was concerned her medical gear would be looted.

They began jogging toward the hospital. Just as they approached the end of Hood Avenue where it intersected with U.S. 1, a sheriff's deputy drove toward them. Jessica flagged her down, and the two recognized one another.

The deputy offered them a ride to the hospital, but Jessica declined. She needed a bigger favor. She asked the deputy to watch over her boat. She'd been caught in a conundrum between joining the family at the hospital and protecting her gear. The deputy understood and readily offered to watch it for an hour. She was one of many deputies with the MCSO whom Jessica and Mike had a good relationship with. After working closely together for years, they'd learned whom they could count on and trust in a crisis.

The group ran the last quarter mile to the emergency care entrance to the hospital. The pink and tan stucco buildings surrounded by palm trees epitomized the architectural look of the Keys. The large hospital was far less intrusive on the eye than the retail strip centers and convenience stores found on both sides of the highway.

Jessica led the way into the ER, where they found a large group of people waiting to be seen. Accident victims with injuries ranging from broken limbs to bumps on the head were awaiting treatment. A frenzied triage nurse was doing her level best to assess the injuries in order to categorize them.

Patients had a variety of tags hung around their necks with a clip-on chain. A green tag represented someone with minimal, minor injuries. Scrapes, bruises, and shallow puncture wounds, to name a few. A yellow tag was assigned to those who could have their treatment delayed somewhat because their injuries were non-life-threatening.

Jessica's trained eye scanned the waiting area and the scrum of people huddled around the reception desk. She was relieved that she didn't see any red tags provided to those who needed immediate attention—patients like Jimmy who'd suffered life-threatening injuries. Lastly, she was glad there were no body bags or gurneys with deceased patients marked with a black toe tag.

She shoved her way through some family members milling about in front of the intake desk. Sonny and Peter followed her through the crowd, perturbed that people wouldn't get out of the way once their loved one had been assigned the appropriate tag.

"I'm Jessica Albright with the sheriff's department WET team. I brought a drowning victim in named Jimmy Free. Can you tell me where he is?"

The nurse tucked her hair behind her ears and reached across the desk to take a clipboard from another nurse. She scanned the handwritten notes. "I have a John Doe. Male. Mid-twenties. Brought in by the AmboCart."

"That's him. He's my nephew," she lied in order to be treated as family. "His uncle and father are with me. Where is he?"

"Trauma eight. End of the hallway." She pointed to her right.

The three of them forced their way through the crowd and past a security guard, who made a half-hearted attempt to stop them as they rushed through the double doors leading to the trauma wing. The guard had been preoccupied with a man who was inebriated or high on something.

Jessica led them to the nurses' station in the trauma wing. "What can you tell me about the drowning victim in trauma eight?"

"Are you family?" the nurse asked.

"Yes. All of us are."

The nurse read the notes on his chart. "He was unconscious on arrival. His breathing was light and labored. A team is in there working on him now. Their first steps were to improve his oxygenation and then to stabilize his circulation. We should know something shortly."

"Can I see my son?" Sonny's voice was pleading.

"Sir, he's not conscious, and we really need to let the trauma team do their jobs. It would be best for you to wait in—" She began to point toward the waiting room before Jessica cut her off.

"We'll stand at the end of the hallway by the window. I'm a paramedic with the sheriff's department, and we'd like to be available to provide the doctor his medical history if asked."

The nurse scowled. Before she could order them out, she was called away by a doctor who'd stuck his head out of another trauma room. The loud, steady blare of a patient coding could be heard as the doctor opened the door.

Jessica nodded her head toward the end of the hallway, and the guys immediately picked up on the subterfuge. They moved quietly and quickly away from the nurses' station to the window overlooking the parking lot. Jimmy's room was the closest to them.

Ten minutes later, the door opened, and the emergency room physician exited. She removed her face mask and gloves before wiping the sweat off her brow. The hospital's HVAC system had been adjusted to run for just a few minutes every four hours to conserve fuel in their generators.

Sonny immediately charged toward her. "How's my son?"

The doctor took a deep breath and raised her eyebrows to open her eyes wider. She looked like she hadn't slept in days, or at least since the hurricane swept over the Keys.

"I'm Dr. Golic. And you are?"

"Sonny Free. That's our son, Jimmy. My wife should be here soon."

"Well, Mr. Free, your son is either part fish or has the nine lives of a cat. He's not conscious, but from my examination, I can tell you he's been through a lot."

Peter offered an explanation. "We got caught on the water as the storm hit. He's been missing ever since."

Dr. Golic shook her head in disbelief. "Wow. That explains it. To say this young man is waterlogged is an understatement."

"He'd just dropped below the surface when we found him," said Jessica. "I performed CPR and intubated him to force air into his lungs. He regained consciousness for a brief moment before passing out."

"You intubated him?" the doctor asked.

"Yes, my name is Jessica Albright. I'm a paramedic with the WET team."

A look of recognition came over Dr. Golic's face. "I thought I'd seen you around. You likely saved this young man's life, Jessica."

"Oh, thank God!" exclaimed Sonny as he broke down crying. He looked past the doctor toward the door. "May I go see him?"

"In a moment. The nurses are cleaning up and getting him into a gown. It's a tedious job because he doesn't need to be jostled unnecessarily. Plus, let me explain where we are in his treatment."

Sonny's chin dropped to his chest, but he nodded his understanding.

"Are there complications?" Jessica asked.

"Like I said, your early intubation of the patient made all the difference. The mechanical ventilation was able to keep his arterial saturation at near ninety-two percent. Naturally, because of his time in the water, it was difficult to get accurate readings on the pulse oximeter due to vasoconstriction. However, using the oximeter on his earlobe gave me a reading I was comfortable with.

"His body temperature was a real issue. As we all know, the temperatures in the coastal waters are at least ten to twelve degrees cooler than normal. Even under ideal conditions, remaining in Florida Bay for that length of time in mid-November can bring on hypothermia. We've employed some thermal insulation protocols to bring his temp back to normal."

The doctor paused, and Jessica sensed she was equivocating or perhaps stalling. Sonny was antsy to see his son, and he deserved to know the entire medical prognosis, so she repeated her question.

"Complications?"

The doctor grimaced and nodded. "He was near death when you rescued him. Not surprisingly, he was suffering from dysrhythmia, a medical term for an abnormal heart rhythm. Even advanced cardiac life-support interventions are often ineffective with patients who have low core body temperatures. We tried atropine and lidocaine, administered intravenously. However, I wasn't satisfied with the results. We used defibrillation to steady his heart rate, but we have to continue to monitor it.

"Once he's stable, I've ordered the team to undertake gastric decompression to deal with the amount of water he swallowed. We'll also continue to push fluids to help him recover.

"Lastly, it takes up to six hours for lung injuries to present. We'll continue to monitor him for wet lung sounds, productive cough, and, of course, his irregular heart rate."

"My god, how can I tell his mother?" asked Sonny, who was overwhelmed by the doctor's detailed explanation.

Dr. Golic was about to respond when the team of nurses exited the trauma room. "Doctor, the patient has stabilized as his body temperature increased."

"Great news," said Dr. Golic. She turned to Sonny. "Mr. Free, you're going to be able to tell Jimmy's mother that her son had an intense desire to live under the worst of circumstances. He needs your love and support now. Keep your thoughts positive and pray for him."

Sonny nodded and looked toward the door. He didn't have to ask permission, as Dr. Golic knew he was anxious to go inside. She stepped back and pushed the door open but issued a note of caution as she did.

"Please stay calm. He looks like he's been through hell, and in a way, he has. However, your son is a fighter, and he needs his father to fight alongside him."

Sonny couldn't stop the tears from flowing, and he thanked the doctor before slipping inside. Peter thanked her as well and followed Sonny. Jessica hung back.

"Dr. Golic, have you withheld anything or sugarcoated it for Sonny's benefit?" It was the type of question that some medical professionals would take offense to, but not Dr. Golic.

"That's all of it," she replied with a sigh. "There is, however, one matter that I need to raise that only you can probably answer."

"What's that?" asked Jessica in a concerned tone.

"How did you find him? By that, I mean was he underwater already or on the surface?"

"We were searching and spotted him from a distance, waving his arms over his head. From his body movement, he appeared to be standing in shallow water. Then, suddenly, he slipped below the surface. When I dove underwater to pull him out, he'd apparently lost his footing and fell into a trough created by the current."

"For how long?" asked the doctor.

"Underwater? I can't be certain."

The doctor grimaced, glanced toward Jimmy's room, and then reached for Jessica's arm. She led her several feet away from the door so their conversation couldn't be overheard.

"Increased duration underwater increases the risk of death but also the potential for severe neurologic impairment. If he was below the surface for less than five minutes, the chances are less than ten percent that he'll suffer diminished neurologic function. Over five minutes? The percentages rise to fifty-fifty. More than ten? Then I can almost assure you of some type of neurological damage."

Jessica's eyes grew wide. All of her training had been focused on rescue and resuscitation. She'd never considered the impact on the brain for a drowning victim.

"Okay. By underwater, do you mean unconscious and not breathing?"

"Yes, if you know."

"Again, I can't say for certain, but I'd put it at more than five minutes and less than ten. How much of that time Jimmy was holding his breath, which he's very good at, versus being in an unconscious state is anybody's guess."

Dr. Golic made several notes on Jimmy's chart and then looked down the hallway toward the nurses' desk, where another patient was being assigned a room.

"I'll have a neurologist look in on him once he regains consciousness. He'll assess the young man's mental condition. I just need to emphasize to you that full neurological recovery rarely happens after ten minutes of normothermic submersion. This doesn't need to be shared with his parents yet. Let's keep him alive first."

With those ominous words, Dr. Golic left Jessica standing in the hallway alone. For the first time, she broke down in tears.

CHAPTER EIGHT

Sunday, November 10
Mariner's Hospital
Tavernier, Florida

Jessica checked her watch again. It had been forty-five minutes since she'd left her boat parked at Mangrove Marina in Hurricane Harbor. The deputy had been kind enough to offer her time to watch over it, but she couldn't count on her staying much longer. She needed to relieve the deputy, and besides, Jimmy had not regained consciousness although his vitals had stabilized.

"Guys," she began, "I've gotta get back to the boat. Plus, I'm sure Hank will arrive with Phoebe, and they're only gonna allow so many of us in the room with Jimmy."

"How many?" asked Peter.

Jessica shrugged. "Three, maybe four, but I doubt it. They don't want him to feel overwhelmed when he comes to."

"Maybe I should—?" Before Peter could finish his question, there was a gentle knocking at the door before it slowly opened. Phoebe's worried face appeared.

Sonny immediately rushed to her and pulled her the rest of the way inside. Peter held the door while the parents consoled one another. The tears began to flow again as Sonny relayed to Phoebe what they knew about Jimmy's condition.

Hank and Mike filled the doorway, craning their necks over the distraught parents to catch a glimpse of Jimmy. Mike had spent plenty of time in a hospital bed of his own lately, so he knew what to look for on the monitors near Jimmy's bed. He frowned when he studied the cardiac monitors. Jimmy's body was fighting to live, but his heart appeared to be struggling.

Jessica whispered to the guys, "Let's step outside and give them some time with Jimmy. We don't want the nurses to run us off."

The Albright men exited the room and moseyed over by the window. It was getting dark, and the minimal visibility was getting closer to zero with no ambient light coming from the surrounding buildings.

"How is he?" asked Hank once Jessica arrived by their side.

She went through the list of considerations Dr. Golic had been most concerned with as it pertained to any drowning victim, including one in Jimmy's condition. She avoided any discussion related to neurological matters since it would only lead to speculation and undue worry. She even debated within herself whether she'd tell Mike. She rarely withheld anything from him for his protection. She simply thought there was plenty to worry about regarding Jimmy's recovery without adding possibilities of a less-than-full neurological recovery.

After providing them the update, she explained her concern for the boat. Mike agreed to give Jessica and Peter a ride to the marina while Hank took a few minutes to visit with Jimmy.

He entered trauma eight with trepidation. Hank still felt guilty for offering Jimmy to Lindsey to perform the role of border guard at the two bridges leading onto the Keys. He never suspected that his second son might get caught up in her dubious plan to destroy the bridges.

The three of them stood over Jimmy's bed, watching every part of the young man's body for signs of movement. Sonny told them the doctor deemed Jimmy to be unconscious rather than in a coma. In a comatose person, the brain was so heavily damaged that neither the sensory nor internal networks were functioning correctly. The body rarely moved or reacted to any external stimuli in that state.

Dr. Golic had described Jimmy's condition as unconscious with a hint of exhaustion. His body and mind had been through a traumatic experience. Quite simply, it needed to rest. The doctor doubted it was prepared to expend one iota of energy more than it needed to.

Mike returned from dropping off Jessica and Peter at the boat. They thanked the deputy for taking the time to watch over the vessel and promised her a favor of some kind if she needed one.

"Any change?" Mike asked as he entered the room.

"No, not really," replied Hank. "I've been trying to understand the monitors. They're like the ones you were hooked up to, but I have to admit I was too messed up to learn what they were for."

Mike glanced at the devices and jutted out his chin. "They're slightly better than twenty minutes ago. It might take a while before he wakes up."

"Not really."

The four of them looked at each other. Hank thought he was hearing voices, but when he saw everyone else's reaction, it became clear. Jimmy had awakened.

"Hey, over here," he said in a barely audible whisper. "I'm awake."

Phoebe and Sonny leaned over the railings and gently held their son's hands as they took turns kissing his cheeks. Their tears streamed off their cheeks and noses onto their son. Rather than cry with them, he smiled. He was alive.

"I'll get the nurse," said Mike, who was through the door before anyone could acknowledge him.

Hank was also emotional. "Save your strength, Jimmy. I'm sure the nurses will need to talk to you."

Loud footsteps could be heard in the hallway, coming toward the door. The soles of their sneakers squeaked on the floor as the two nurses pivoted to come inside. All of Jimmy's loved ones immediately stepped back to allow them to check on their patient.

Hank made eye contact with Sonny and motioned for him to come around the bed to join Phoebe. For his part, he stepped out of the way to allow plenty of room for the medical team to work.

Shortly thereafter, Dr. Golic arrived with her stethoscope slung over her neck and shoulders. She nodded to Hank but focused her attention on Jimmy. She pulled out her penlight and studied Jimmy's eyes, speaking to him in soft tones as she explained the purpose of each examination technique she employed.

Afterwards, she issued orders to the two trauma nurses regarding Jimmy's medications and intravenous feeding. She also set new goals for cardiac and respiratory functions. Now that he was awake, it was hoped his recovery would hasten.

"Jimmy, welcome back. You are a remarkable young man. Part fish is the way your family has described you."

Jimmy smiled and rolled his eyes. "I'll never go in the water again."

Dr. Golic laughed as she picked up his wrist and felt his pulse while studying the rate shown on the cardiac monitor.

"Somehow, I doubt that. You are a survivor. Survivors are known to take calculated risks when necessary. You shouldn't fear the water, especially since you've lived through this."

Jimmy smiled and nodded. He turned his gaze upon his parents, who looked like they were staring at a newborn baby, their son. He'd been given a second chance in life and planned on making the most of it.

"When can I go home?" asked Jimmy.

Mike laughed. "Sounds like something I'd say."

Dr. Golic wasn't sure what he meant by that, so she responded to Jimmy. "You've still got some work to do, young man. We need to assess your lungs for the next twenty-four hours or more. Also, there are other specialists on staff who will look in on you as part of our normal protocols."

She avoided getting into the discussion of the neurological

consequences of his near-drowning experience. Not to mention the hospital's psychologist would poke her head into Jimmy's room at some point to assess him for post-traumatic stress disorder.

Jimmy frowned at her response.

"Jimmy, you stay right here," said Sonny. "Your mom and I will stay close. That's okay, right?"

"Absolutely," Dr. Golic replied. She turned to address Hank and Mike. "No more than two. I'm sorry."

Hank nodded. He reached out and squeezed Jimmy's foot. "You rest up, buddy. Lacey and Tucker are home, as is Peter. We'll fix you up a double helping of conch stew. Right, Mom?"

Hank reached out to squeeze Phoebe's hand. The group laughed. Phoebe's home remedy for pretty much anything was a hefty portion of conch in some recipe or another.

The group said their goodbyes as Hank and Mike eased out of the room. A joyous, emotional reunion took place in Jimmy's room moments later.

CHAPTER NINE

Sunday, November 10
Overseas Highway
Florida Keys

The Keys were engulfed in darkness as Mike drove across the Snake Creek drawbridge connecting Islamorada with Windley Key. Finished in 1981, it had been the third bridge to span the two islands since the Overseas Railroad was built in the early twentieth century. It was the only remaining operating drawbridge in the Keys. Or, at least, it was.

After the two brothers commiscrated over Jimmy and his recovery prospects, they rode along for several miles in silence. Then, as the minds of brothers often do, they brought up a subject in near unison.

"We need to talk about Lindsey," said Mike as Hank asked, "Can we talk about Lindsey?"

After laughing and exchanging high fives, the men became more serious.

Mike continued. "She's on your mind, too."

Hank rested his chin in his hand and stared out the passenger's side window. Normally at night, the small shops and restaurants that lined U.S. 1 in Islamorada would be bustling with tourist activity. Now the spaces were darkened, and the streets were abandoned except for the occasional wayward soul searching through trash or a looted business.

"Don't get me wrong, Mike. I bear the responsibility of Jimmy being on that bridge in the first place. I allowed Lindsey to strong-arm me, but I felt it was my only choice since she seemed to say I'd be protected from her plans to put people in our bungalows and seize the food grown in our greenhouses."

"All right, listen up," began Mike in a stern tone of voice. "I can't help how you feel, but I can try to ease your conscience. Lindsey is a straight-up snake. A master manipulator. A true black widow who has a way of getting men to do her bidding before she injects venom into their system. Trust me, I almost fell prey to her years ago, as you know."

Hank nodded. "Mike, I can't decide if she's lost it or if she honestly believes she's doing the right thing for the Keys. Either way, I don't think we're done with her. She couldn't've cared less about her nephew going missing. Sad, really."

"Sad unless you understand how selfish she is, Hank. She's power hungry and will absolutely use these circumstances to advance her agenda. She's been reelected by fooling people. Now she doesn't have to answer to anyone. Hell, look at how she thumbed her nose at Washington, or wherever our capital is now. Blowing up bridges? Are you kidding me?"

Hank turned in his seat to face his brother. The glow emanating from the dashboard showed the concern on his face. "You're more attuned to the happenings in Key West than I am. I avoid the place like the plague. How far do you think she'll go?"

Mike shrugged. "I'd say the sky's the limit if I could see the damn sky. Personally, I've always believed she was power hungry. Now she has unrestrained power, to an extent. I mean, I don't think she can shoot somebody on Duval and get away with it. But, hell, this martial law declaration probably gives her that right."

"I've read it," added Hank. "At least the one issued by the president. She probably does have that power. Keep in mind, she's got her own executive order, too."

"I nosed around the department before I left Key West. Deputies and staff are scrambling in all directions, jumping at the sheriff's orders. I gotta believe he's working closely with her."

"He's an independent, elected official like she's supposed to be," interjected Hank. "I've never known them to act in lockstep on everything."

"Yeah." Mike stretched out the word. "You'd be surprised. They disagree on mundane matters that don't really have an impact on the people who live here. However, on the big stuff, they see eye to eye. There have been policy changes within the department that have us all scratching our heads but afraid to speak out."

"I tried to have a conversation with the sheriff, but it was a waste of time. When I went to Lindsey's office, I felt like the enemy. Not a good feeling."

The men rode on in silence as Mike was forced to concentrate on their surroundings. The bridge stretching from Lower Matecumbe Key to Marathon had been thrust into pitch darkness. There were cars abandoned in all directions, a few of which were being lived in by homeless people or the displaced.

"Before we get home, let me ask you about Erin," said Mike.

"Okay. You know, we're just good friends. Heck, we really barely know each other. We spent some time together while she was here. Then the day she was whisked away, we were having a pretty good time fishing. That's it."

Mike looked over in Hank's direction. His brother stared forward through the windshield. "There must've been something more for her to get a Coast Guard escort to Driftwood Key. I mean, why did she leave Wash—um, you know, wherever the hell they were working from."

"Mike, honestly, we haven't had time to talk about any of that. She arrived, and I was truthfully glad to see her. I've thought about her a lot since she left. Anyway, it had been a long day for everyone, so we all went to bed. Then we put together the search party and took off early."

"She didn't explain her intentions on the boat ride up to Florida Bay?" said Mike inquisitively.

"No. Like me, she wanted to stay focused on finding Jimmy."

"No small talk or anything—"

Hank got annoyed with his brother. "No, Detective Albright, nothing like that."

Mike laughed. "Okay, I deserved that. It's just odd to me that she would show up out of the blue and think that (a) it was safe and (b) it would be okay with us."

"Why wouldn't it be?" asked Hank, who was now on the defensive. "She's a good person, Mike."

"Geez, Hank. I'm sorry. It's just that I'm a little leery of everything right now. I think we have to move forward with the mindset of, um, trust no one."

Hank gently slapped his brother on the shoulder as Mike slowed to enter the street leading onto Driftwood Key. "No problem. We've all been through a lot."

"No doubt. I think we need adult beverages."

"Drinks and cigars," added Hank.

Mike nodded but threw water on the idea. "I'd love to, but the air quality kinda sucks. I don't think we should be hanging around outside."

"Nah, we'll take over the bar."

Mike started laughing. "Phoebe will have your ass if you smoke cigars in the main house."

"It'll clear out by the time they get home, right?"

Mike shook his head from side to side and grinned. "I hope so for your sake."

CHAPTER TEN

Sunday, November 10
Driftwood Key

Jessica and Peter arrived at the dock just as Hank and Mike were exiting the unmarked four-door pickup truck owned by the MCSO. Lacey and Erin greeted them all at the dock. Interestingly, all the adults had the same suggestion to help ease the stress and tensions of the day. Cocktails.

Tucker, who'd slept most of the afternoon, was ready to pull an all-nighter at the gate. Mike had picked up a couple of ThunderPower megaphones during his supply run to the sheriff's department supply depot the other day. Known as the Earthquake Maker, the powerful megaphone was capable of blasting a voice up to two thousand yards, and its shrill warning siren could be heard for a mile or more. Tucker had tested it earlier and found it worked better than the Pyle megaphones they kept on Driftwood Key for marine use.

With Tucker watching the perimeter, the adults raided the kitchen and then made their way into the bar. Illuminated by candlelight, a few windows were cracked slightly so the guys could each have a means to ventilate the smoke from their cigars to the outside, joining the already soot-filled air.

Lacey and Jessica claimed the opposite ends of the leather couch, their legs stretched out so that their feet pressed against each other. While Jessica was older than Lacey, the two enjoyed a sister-like relationship. On the few occasions Lacey had been able to visit Driftwood Key for an extended period of time, she and Jessica had been almost inseparable.

Erin, the inn's only guest, offered to act as the group's bartender. She was comfortable with all the members of the Albright family. After the initial shock of her grand arrival via helicopter, the family had welcomed her with open arms although they were anxious to hear why she'd come there instead of her own home.

Of everyone in attendance, Erin was the only person who'd not suffered following the collapse. She'd been fed and protected within the confines of Mount Weather along with the other top-ranking officials of the Helton administration. She'd confirmed with the help of Homeland Security that her immediate family was safe.

As the evening progressed, she hoped the Albrights' conversations could be somewhat lighthearted. Erin thought they needed a break from reality.

"Okay, everyone. Tonight, you are the guests of the Driftwood Key Inn, and I am your humble bartender. Before you start telling me your troubles, may I propose a toast?"

"Sure!"

"Only if you're humble!" shouted Jessica, drawing a laugh from the group.

Everyone raised their drinks as Erin lifted hers.

"To TEOTWAWKI—the end of the world as we know it!"

Glasses clinked, and drinks were swigged.

Then Erin bowed her head slightly and looked toward Lacey. She raised her glass again. "To those who were loved and lost."

Lacey smiled and raised her glass. She fought back tears and smiled before proposing a toast of her own. "To all of us as we find the strength to move forward as a family."

"Cheers!" several of the group said loudly.

The toasting session managed to empty several glasses, so Erin busily refilled the drinks. Hank, Jessica and Erin enjoyed a scotch. Mike commandeered his own bottle of Jack Daniel's. Peter sipped rum, and Lacey was the sole wine drinker.

Once settled in with a second round, the conversation turned from Jimmy's medical condition to what was happening outside the Keys.

Mike turned to Lacey. "You guys had one helluva road trip. I'm sure you'd like to put most of it out of your mind."

She grimaced and sipped her wine. "You know, it was an odd mix of unfettered violence and people coming together to help. You had some people who'd give you the shirt off their backs, and then there were others who'd take your shirt, after killing you, of course. It's amazing how broad the spectrum was."

"I experienced the same thing," added Peter. "During my trip, I had a lot of time to soak in what was happening around me, and I tried to make sense of it all. I can't tell you how many times I was surprised by people's kindness only to see the dark side of humanity show itself moments later. People became violent because they were frightened and others simply because they were evil opportunists."

Lacey turned to her uncle, whom she adored. "Uncle Mike, other than this serial killer you guys have mentioned in passing, what's it been like in the Keys? Has there been violence and looting?"

Mike glanced at Jessica and then responded, "Fortunately, so far the spikes in crime have related mostly to B & Es. As the crisis started to unfold, the store shelves were emptied by panicked shoppers."

"I have to say, we were part of that," interrupted Hank.

"Yeah, and within the MCSO, some people looked at it as hoarding while others considered it self-preservation. Those of us who reacted quickly to the first signs of trouble are better prepared than others."

"There has been violence, so let's not sugarcoat it, though," interjected Jessica. "In addition to Patrick almost killing my husband and Phoebe, we had gas thieves shooting at us and a well-armed group try to breach our gate. Their bloodstains are still on the bridge."

Mike continued. "These incidents were becoming more frequent, although the hurricane seemed to give us a break from the violent encounters. However, those who had very little to begin with lost everything during the storm. People who relied upon fishing lost their boats. Others who were days away from starvation also lost the roofs over their heads."

"And thanks to Lindsey, anyone who wanted to leave the Keys and stay with relatives are stuck here because the bridges have disappeared," said Hank. He was about to rise out of his chair to get a refill; however, Erin quickly moved across the room to take his glass. The two shared a long, loving look when they were close to one another, something that did not go unnoticed by Mike and Jessica.

After pouring Hank another drink, Erin took her seat on a bar stool and refilled her glass. As she did, Jessica asked, "Erin, what can you tell us about the bigger picture? What's going on elsewhere?"

She took a deep breath before responding, "First, let me commend both Peter and Lacey for what they accomplished. The levels of violence are much higher outside the Keys. The reports out of Miami, like America's other highly populated cities, are shocking. There are armed gangs forming to establish territories. They work in large packs to loot and rob people. Home invasions are too numerous to count."

"Sounds like lawlessness," said Hank.

"It is, in part because there aren't enough law enforcement officers to control it and also because many have quit to protect their own families."

Mike and Jessica glanced at each other. They'd unofficially done the same thing.

"I read the martial law declaration signed by the president," said Hank. "Obviously, he has the military at his disposal to help, right?"

Erin nodded. "The Army has just over eight hundred thousand

active-duty soldiers and National Guardsmen. With the three hundred thousand reservists who have been called up, the Army provides the vast majority of the president's manpower to gain control of the streets.

"As odd as this may seem under the circumstances, America is extremely vulnerable to foreign invasion at this moment. To be sure, all major powers in the northern hemisphere, namely China and Russia, are going through the same thing we are. That said, their populations are used to a different standard of living, or lifestyle, than we are. They're also used to living under an oppressive government. Rather than using their military resources to fight rioters or quell uprisings, they could turn their sights on us while our armed forces are preoccupied."

"Who shot at us to begin with?" asked Lacey.

"North Korea," replied Erin.

Peter, who was very knowledgeable in foreign affairs, returned to the subject of an invasion. "If the nuclear powers wanted to finish us off, they could've easily done so. We most likely exhausted our nuclear defense arsenal against the North Koreans, am I right?"

"Yes," replied Erin. "Both Moscow and Beijing know this. That said, destroying the rest of America wouldn't do them any good. China, especially, needs America with a vibrant economy to survive. If anything, they need us to get back on our feet quickly. That doesn't mean, however, they wouldn't seize the opportunity to acquire key strategic assets while we're defenseless."

"Are you thinking they might seize territories in the Far East?" asked Peter.

"Certainly. Taiwan is a given. They might make a move on American Samoa and Guam. The Northern Mariana Islands are also targets. For Russia, they'd love to invade Alaska. It would be a perfect fit as they expand their presence in the Arctic. Plus, control of the vast petroleum potential in ANWR would change the balance of power in the fossil-fuel industry." The Arctic National Wildlife Refuge was an oil-rich area that was constantly a football in

Washington between those who want to drill for oil and those who don't.

"We had to reroute our trip home because Texas closed its borders," said Lacey. "How can they do that?"

"The same way Lindsey did it, I suppose," said Mike with a hint of snark. "Did they blow up their bridges, too?"

Erin shook her head as she drank. "No, but they certainly blocked them all. Their actions came as a result of the huge number of American refugees fleeing for Mexico. When the Mexican government had had enough of our people infiltrating their country on the way to lower latitudes, they deployed their army coupled with assistance from the drug cartels to close their borders. The Texas governor was facing a humanitarian crisis as millions of people, not knowing that Mexico had shut down access, would be accumulating in his state."

Lacey shared what she and Tucker had observed. "We saw military trucks, even tanks, headed west on Interstate 40 toward the Panhandle. Did they invade Texas?"

Erin sighed. "I wasn't privy to all of the details, but I did hear the whispers in the corridors of Mount Weather. Let's just say it was in the works."

"Were they going to do the same here?" asked Peter before adding, "I saw them staging in Homestead at the Speedway."

"Yes. That was the president's intention. I believe the operation was delayed by the storm and, of course, the decision to blow up the bridges."

"Maybe Lindsey did the right thing after all," Mike said as he poured himself another drink.

Erin's eyes grew wide. So much for lighthearted.

CHAPTER ELEVEN

Sunday, November 10
Driftwood Key

"Come on, Mike," countered Hank in a raised voice. "There were better ways to deal with these problems than blow up bridges." This was the second time Hank and Mike had had a disagreement that day.

"Okay. Okay. Calm down," began Mike. "Just hear me out. Everyone knows how I feel about Lindsey. Trust me, there's no love lost between us. That said, she made two decisions that arguably may have benefited the Keys.

"The first one involved expelling all nonresidents. Think about it, Hank. You did the same thing here, and it was the right thing to do. Those folks needed to go home and take care of themselves. We're going to be facing some difficult times ourselves without trying to feed a dozen extra mouths."

As soon as he made the statement, Erin wanted to shrink within herself. She was one of those extra mouths.

Mike continued. "Imagine all of these tourists wandering around the Keys. Homeless. Hungry. Desperate. Increasingly violent. It would be a bad situation."

"What about the bridges?" asked Hank.

Mike turned to Erin. "So what was the president's plan as he invaded the Florida Keys? Depose the government and become a military occupying force on U.S. soil? Arrest Lindsey and any criminal co-conspirators who set up the roadblocks? They might've taken all of law enforcement into custody until they could decide who was complicit and who wasn't. Think about this. Under the martial law declaration, the president took away all of our rights of due process, speedy trial, trial by jury, etcetera. Jessica and I, and even Jimmy, could be rotting away in a jail cell somewhere."

"I don't think the president would've let it come to that," Erin began to explain before Mike interrupted her.

"Don't get me wrong because I'm not defending Lindsey. All I know is what I hear from people at the MCSO. She honestly believed the National Guard was going to come onto the Keys, by force if necessary, and use all of the powers afforded under the martial law declaration to seize control of the government and anything else it wanted. Including a place like Driftwood Key."

"Lindsey threatened me with the same crap, Mike," said Hank. "She stood right outside this window and all but said fork over Jimmy to stand guard or I'll be back to load up all your food and supplies."

"I'm just saying we're better off with the devil we know rather than the devil we don't," said Mike as he leaned back and folded his arms.

The tensions between them were evident, making the rest of the family uncomfortable. Erin had intended to speak with Hank alone about why she was there, but she decided to address the group before the brothers' relationship worsened.

She took a long swig of liquid courage and stood in front of the Albrights. "There's something I need to say."

Everyone exchanged glances with one another. Lacey turned around on the couch to give Erin her complete attention.

"Go ahead, Erin," encouraged Hank.

She looked at him as she spoke. "I never wanted to leave the boat that day. I can't tell you how wonderful it felt to close out the world and have someone as nice as you come into my life. Being summoned back to Washington like that frightened me because it meant really bad things were on the horizon. Turns out that was the case.

"Hank, not a day went by that I didn't think about you. Well, all of you, really. I worried about your safety and well-being. In fact, I did my level best to keep tabs on what was happening here through my contacts in the intelligence community who worked out of Mount Weather. I was aware of the mayor's actions although I never imagined she'd blow up a federal highway and a state road.

"Anyway, I had become a thorn in the president's side. It was unintentional. In our briefings and cabinet meetings, he'd ask my opinion, and I'd give it. As it turned out, I was too disagreeable for him and was about to be fired. While I was pleading my case to save my job, I seized on an opening he gave me. That's what led me back to you."

"What was that?" asked Hank.

"Everyone, the president went through a period in which the stresses of the crisis overwhelmed him. When he came back, he was angry and wanted to take out his frustrations on anyone, including entire states like Texas, which he perceived to be working against him. The Florida Keys became one of those lightning rods for his ire.

"When he learned of the nonresidents being removed from the Keys, followed by the closing of the two bridges with armed personnel, he blew a fuse. This happened at a time when Texas and other areas of the country were doing the same.

"You see, the president has this utopian vision of everyone coming together to help one another through the collapse. That's possible, but it must be done on a community or more localized basis.

"The president hasn't been on the road like Lacey and Peter. He hasn't had his home fall under attack like you have. He sees everyone coming together to share their resources for the greater good of all Americans."

"Lindsey is the same way," interjected Hank. "In her mind, all the resources in the Keys should be pooled together and distributed according to need. She doesn't care whether a business or family like ours made personal and financial sacrifices to prepare for a catastrophic event like this one. In her mind, it's not fair for some of us to have an advantage over others."

Mike poured himself another shot of Jack, his fourth. "Are you saying you volunteered to return to the Keys to help the president?" His skepticism of Erin's motives came through in his questioning.

"Mike, let me tell you what the president's stated intentions were," replied Erin, who finished her drink, more to quench her dry mouth than to loosen her tongue. "I'm serious when I tell you this. He planned on taking control of Monroe County's government. Then he was going to displace most of its residents by moving them to government-owned housing on the mainland."

Erin took a deep breath before finishing her thought. "He intended to undertake a massive land reclamation project by leveling buildings, trucking in topsoil, and creating large federally operated farms to produce food for the nation."

Mike started laughing. "That's freaking nuts!"

"What would that look like?" asked Jessica. "Big bulldozers mowing everything down and then dump trucks building farmland?"

"It's absurd, you guys, and I told him as much. That's why he wanted to fire me, among other things."

"Is that why you're here?" asked Mike. "To lay the groundwork for this ridiculous idea?"

Erin poured herself another drink and sat back on the barstool. "President Helton is a cunning, conniving politician, not unlike your mayor, except on a much higher level. Here's why he agreed to send me to the Keys. He wants me to recruit Hank to take Lindsey's job through valid elections."

Mike busted out laughing. "Hank? As county mayor?"

"That's right. It was my idea, actually. You see, the president has encircled the Keys with Coast Guard vessels. He has not given up on his plans to take over the Keys although he lied to me about that. I know him, so I made inquiries with friendly military personnel. Gaining control of the situation is the only way to avoid our own military invading the Keys."

"Then why would you go along with him?" asked Jessica.

"Because I know politics and how these things work. Now, correct me if I'm wrong. Your mayor, Lindsey, is a power-hungry opportunist, right?"

"Nailed it," said Mike.

"Okay. She's got some pretty big *cajones* right now because she destroyed the bridges preventing the National Guard from coming onto the Keys. I guess she forgot about the amphibious units, like the Marines, available to the president. She's pissed him off, and he'd come at her with all he's got."

"She'd fold like a cheap tent," said Hank.

"Exactly!" exclaimed Erin. "She'd sell out the residents and businesses throughout the Keys in a heartbeat. He'd let her keep her position while offering her countless opportunities to profit from this. It's the way these kinds of politicians do business."

"I take it he didn't disclose this part to you, am I right?" asked Peter.

"That's right. I didn't give him any inkling that I saw through his façade. Trust me, Peter. You know Washington. We were playing chess, not checkers."

"So what is the plan?" asked Hank. "How do you intend to make me mayor? And then what?"

"By my agreeing to help the president, we can keep any military action at bay. At least for a while. The media will turn on him if they perceive he's being heavy-handed on a bunch of flip-flop-wearing islanders. We have to find a way to work from within to undermine Lindsey's authority. Cause the locals to turn on her and demand a vote, a referendum of sorts, to insert an alternative government."

"Led by Hank?" asked Mike.

"All of you can play a role," replied Erin. "Think about it. Some of the key aspects of any functioning society are government, law enforcement, and the media. All three of these integral parts are sitting in this room. Each of you can contribute."

Hank stood and began pacing the floor. He rubbed his hands through his hair as he contemplated Erin's proposal. "This is a lot to take on, Erin. I mean, we're gonna struggle to survive ourselves."

"If you do nothing, here's what's likely to happen. First, this tyrannical mayor is going to sweep through the Keys like a pack of locusts stripping away anything of value to be redistributed. At some point, the Coast Guard with a contingent of Marines will come ashore to arrest her and anyone connected to her administration. Possibly, like Mike said, law enforcement officers complicit in the destruction of the bridges. Once that has happened, he might go through with his stupid plan to level the Keys and turn it into Iowa."

"Or?" asked Hank.

Erin stood again and walked up to him, grabbing his arms so he'd stop pacing. "Or you can save the Keys."

PART II

Day twenty-five, Monday, November 11

CHAPTER TWELVE

Monday, November 11
Monroe County Administration Offices
Key West

It was early on that Monday morning when Sheriff Jock Daly entered the Monroe County Administration building for his *official* weekly briefing with Mayor Lindsey Free. Old habits never die despite the apocalypse. Each Monday, the sheriff met with the mayor and key members of her staff to discuss law enforcement or safety issues affecting the county. Despite the seven-day workweeks, the tradition continued.

Of course, this early morning gathering was a mere formality. It was primarily designed to be an exercise to lend the appearance of continuity, thus providing the staff a sense of normalcy. The real decision-making between the sheriff and the mayor took place during their unofficial briefings that consisted of drinks, sex, and pillow talk that invariably led to their plans for the county.

"Let's get down to business," began Lindsey as she set her coffee mug down amidst stacks of files. She'd stayed in her office late the night before, perusing tax and deed records of business owners in

Key West. She was ready to begin her confiscation program, and that required a list of targets.

A political animal by nature, Lindsey created a sliding scale of each targeted business based upon a number of factors that included type of product as well as logistical matters such as storage and distribution to the people. Then there were the political considerations. Which of the businesses were deemed political enemies, and which ones, such as heavy donors to her campaign, would be given a pass. The legal pad she'd been working on had been marked through, erased, and pages crumpled until a final working document had been created. She'd turned it over to her secretary the moment she walked in the door.

In attendance was Lindsey's mayor pro tem, Paul Robinson, the oldest county commissioner and also a former political rival for the job of mayor. Lindsey and Robinson were closely aligned and saw eye to eye on almost every issue facing the county. When she'd defeated him in her first primary run, he agreed to take a back seat to the more vivacious Lindsey. He played an important role in keeping the other three county commissioners in line. He provided her an update on the cleanup activities following the storm.

"That hurricane left the middle and upper keys in shambles," he began. Robinson's District 2 included Marathon and, therefore, Driftwood Key. "From Tavernier to Key Largo, I've seen damage that rivals anything that's occurred in the Keys since I've been in office. For the moment, the hospitals are holding their own, but generator fuel will soon become an issue. My biggest concern will be refilling the fuel tanks, which are slated to run out within eighteen to twenty days, in the only operating medical facilities."

"Paul, this briefing will address that issue in a moment," said Lindsey. "What about cleanup?"

"It's an all-volunteer effort," replied Robinson. "County work crews have been redirected to Key West at your request. They have begun the task of removing stalled vehicles from the streets and impounding them in the hotel parking lots as you requested on Saturday. Also, debris is being removed at the same time. The goal is to have Key West cleared by this evening. Tomorrow, we'll move on to Stock Island, Boca Chica, Big Coppitt, and so on. The task will become less daunting as we make our way up U.S. 1."

"When will you be able to tackle Seven Mile Bridge?" asked Lindsey.

"By week's end, barring unforeseen intervening circumstances."

"Good, thank you," said Lindsey with a nod to her most loyal commissioner. She turned to the sheriff. "Jock, are your people ready?"

"We are," he replied. He allowed a sly grin as he spoke. "I got an early start this morning and met with my key personnel. It should go as planned, assuming, of course, no resistance."

Lindsey was well aware what time Jock had gotten started that morning. They had been in bed together.

"As we exercise our authority under the two martial law declarations, the president's and our own, we face several challenges. Clearly, some of these business owners will take exception to our actions, as will the citizens whose property will be affected by this.

"My priorities will focus on water, food, medical supplies, and anything that might generate power for our governmental facilities. That includes everything from batteries for flashlights to generators and the fuel required to run them."

"I brought up the issue of fuel for the hospital generators," interrupted Robinson. "It's my understanding the gas stations have run dry."

The sheriff addressed the logistics of fuel confiscation. "That is correct. As the crisis hit, motorists either filled up to evacuate the Keys or some simply topped off their tanks so they could have more gasoline than the next guy. The first thing we plan on doing is to siphon gas out of any stalled or abandoned vehicles. Next, we'll go door-to-door to extract fuel from the vehicles of those who filled up unnecessarily."

"How do you siphon fuel out of newer vehicles?" asked Robinson.

"I've discussed this with the head of the county's maintenance department," began Jock in reply. "New cars and trucks are equipped with an anti-rollover valve that acts as a siphon-prevention system. I asked him if a workaround would be to drill a hole in the gas tank and allow the fuel to trickle into a pan. He said that would not only be slow, but it could also result in an explosion of the gas tank during the drilling process.

"He said the trick is to use a small-diameter hose that can pass through the ball or butterfly valve, as the case may be, to enter the gas tank. He's experimented with a quarter-inch-diameter rigid line like what's used for the water supply of a refrigerator. With the use of an electric pump, a twenty-gallon tank can be emptied in minutes."

"Do we have these electric pumps?" asked Robinson.

Jock nodded as he sipped his coffee. He was slightly hungover and sleep deprived. Coffee was all the fuel he needed to recover. "All of our emergency trucks assigned to the fire department have as standard equipment a twelve-volt transfer pump that's used for a variety of rescue operations. We have teams trained and ready to empty the tanks of every vehicle in the Keys if necessary to keep our facilities operating until power is restored."

"When might that be?" asked Lindsey's chief of staff.

"Hard to determine," replied Jock. "That's why we're taking these steps to become self-sufficient."

"People aren't gonna be happy," she added, drawing a harsh look from her boss.

"We've been over this," Lindsey snapped at her top aide. "People don't know what's best for them until they see the results of our actions. Then they thank us. In the meantime, we have to make the hard choices necessary to protect them."

Jock continued. "We're well aware there might be resistance. We've assigned a protection unit to each wrecker crew and fuel-siphoning team. Our deputies will be outfitted in full SWAT gear and armed with automatic weapons."

Lindsey interjected some statistics. "Thank goodness we fought back any talk of open-carry laws in the Keys. Less than ten percent of Key West residents have a concealed-carry permit. That's slightly higher in the Middle and Upper Keys."

The sheriff expanded on her thought. "Well, it didn't get any easier for us when the *stand your ground* challenges hit the media years ago. Everyone began to concoct a justifiable reason to sit on their porches with a shotgun in their laps. There's a fine line between defending themselves from a real threat and brandishing their weapons to appear to be a tough guy."

Mayor pro tem Robinson scowled as he raised another issue. "Lindsey, this may be a sensitive issue, but I couldn't help but notice Chief Rainey hasn't attended our last two briefings." Walter Rainey was the Key West chief of police.

Lindsey quickly responded, "Our plans don't involve him, nor do they require his approval. I had a conversation with the chief, and he fully understands his role."

"Which is?" asked Robinson.

"Stay out of my way."

CHAPTER THIRTEEN

Monday, November 11
Driftwood Key

Erin was the first to rise that morning. With Phoebe still at the hospital caring for her son, she felt comfortable making her way downstairs to start the coffee. When she arrived in the kitchen, she noticed the lights had been turned on, and there was evidence someone had enjoyed a bowl of cereal made with powdered milk. She realized Tucker must've completed his guard duty and had been replaced by someone else.

As the coffee brewed, Erin began to wonder if she'd thrust too much on Hank and his family last night. The conversation had seemed to wane after she'd dropped the bombshell, and within minutes, everyone had finished their drinks before going to bed.

She poured a mug of black coffee and gently blew on it to cool it off. She thought about the big picture. Had she used the suggestion as an excuse to get out from under the thumb of a president who was done with her? Was it a ploy to get closer to Hank? Maybe all of the above?

Before they retired for the evening, Hank had asked if she'd ride with him to the hospital this morning to see how Jimmy was doing. She suggested a change of clothes for the Frees as well as Jimmy, assuming he'd be released once he'd sufficiently recovered. Hank seemed to appreciate the thought, and they said their goodnights.

Erin had tossed and turned for an hour before drifting off to sleep. She'd replayed the entire conversation, more than once, in an attempt to discern where everyone stood. Once they were on the road to the hospital, she intended to broach the subject again.

Hank was the next to awaken. "The smell of coffee floating through the inn is far better than a noisy rooster, don't you think?"

He was in a cheery mood, much to the relief of Erin, who was deep in thought, nervously anticipating a contentious conversation that morning.

"Hey," she greeted. "I hope my shuffling around the kitchen didn't wake you."

"Nah, not at all. I have one of those biological alarm clocks that never fails me. You could throw me out of a plane in New Zealand, and I'd still wake up at the same time."

Erin poured a mug for Hank. "Black, right?" she asked as she handed it to him.

"You remembered."

"We both take our coffee the same way."

Hank took a sip and smiled. "How'd you sleep?"

"Great. It was a little different being in the main house compared to the bungalow I had. It was, well, homey."

"Like part of the family?" Hank studied her face.

Erin blushed and nodded. "Yeah, unless you kick me out after last night."

Hank laughed. "Kick you out because the president sent you to displace Lindsey and replace her with me? Nah. That's not a good enough reason. If you snored really loud, then maybe we'd have to talk."

Erin laughed, mostly out of relief that she wasn't in the doghouse with Hank. "Even if I did snore, you wouldn't know it over your brother the freight train."

"Oh yeah, trust me, when Mike's had a few drinks, the snoring is unbearable. Jessica sleeps with earplugs, you know."

"God bless her," said Erin with a chuckle. She took a deep breath and continued. "Listen, about last night. I feel like I should explain where I was—" Erin stopped as Jessica and Lacey entered the back door leading into the kitchen from outside.

"Yes! I told you, Lacey!" exclaimed Jessica, who made a beeline for the coffee pot.

Hank was puzzled. "Jessica, have you been on watch? It's not your turn."

"Mike's snoring was unbearable. Even with my earplugs and constantly telling him to roll over, I couldn't sleep. I caught up with Lacey a couple of hours ago."

Hank and Erin laughed together. "Have some coffee," Hank offered. "We're going to gather a change of clothes for those guys and visit with Jimmy for a while."

Lacey and Jessica filled up two Tervis Tumblers with coffee. They joked about how they never expected to use the insulated drinkware for anything other than something iced and refreshing.

They spoke for another minute and then pulled surgical masks over their faces to return outside. Jessica had picked up a box of a hundred when she was at the hospital the other day. It was the kind of privileges she enjoyed as an MCSO paramedic. The group agreed the masks made sense as the atmosphere thickened with soot.

Hank turned to Erin. "That looked like a good idea. Would you mind fixin' us a couple of roadies while I head over to the Frees' cottage. I'll fill a duffel bag with clothes and toiletries so they can freshen up."

"Are you hungry? I found a box of blueberry Pop-Tarts. It seems Phoebe stocked up on them."

Hank laughed as he pulled his tee shirt over his mouth and nose. "I can't think of a better food to have during the apocalypse. I'll be right back, or you can meet me at the truck."

"Which one? You've added some vehicles since I was here last."

"The Suburban. It was a drug seizure that Mike, um, *requisitioned*. He really took it to load a bunch of stuff for us."

"From the sheriff's department?"

"Yeah, I'll explain on the way to the hospital."

Hank left, and Erin scooted around the kitchen, fixing them coffee for the trip and making a fresh pot for Peter and Mike, who were both still sleeping. She was anxious to spend some time talking with Peter. She knew of him because of his position with the *Washington Times* and the terrorist attack in Abu Dhabi. They'd never crossed paths because he covered a different department than hers. However, she imagined he'd have some insight into what had happened that might assist her in moving forward.

Ten minutes later, Hank wheeled the long Chevy Suburban off Driftwood Key and onto the Overseas Highway. The sky was illuminated by the sun's rays that tried desperately to poke through the haze of nuclear winter. It was bright enough to get a look at the devastation they had been unable to see in the darkness when they'd driven back and forth to the hospital the other day.

"This is devastating, Hank. It's comparable to the damage I've witnessed in the Midwest following a tornado."

"They had no warning," he said with a grim look on his face. He had to focus on the road because of the stalled vehicles and occasional debris. However, he couldn't take his eyes off the results of the furious storm. "Jessica and I were at the hospital with Mike as it started to move onshore. Fortunately, Sonny has a nose for these things. He began to button up Driftwood Key at the first signs of the hurricane. By the time we got there, he and Phoebe were almost finished."

Erin shook her head in disbelief. "They're remarkable people. Unselfish, too. With their son missing, they put aside their personal feelings to protect everything."

"They're a part of our family, Erin. We all grew up together and spend virtually every waking moment with one another. That's why Jimmy is so special to me. He's like a son in all respects."

Hank wiped a tear from his eye and turned away to hide his

emotions. Erin noticed his change in demeanor and rubbed his shoulders. She offered some words of comfort.

"I believe he's going to be okay, Hank. I was very impressed with his doctor and the rest of the medical team. Considering what's going on, they've managed to help people under unprecedented, adverse conditions."

Hank raised his eyebrows and nodded in agreement. "This is part of what bothers me about Lindsey's decision to blow up the bridges. I'm sure the president tried to defuse the situation first. I can't disagree with her decision to send nonresidents off the Keys. And I certainly see why keeping outsiders on the mainland made sense. It just seems like there was a better approach than cutting us off from the world."

"Agreed," Erin interjected before Hank finished his thought.

"How are we gonna resupply our hospitals? There will come a point in time when we'll need to look to the federal government for assistance. One of the functions they perform is to help the country when an unprecedented catastrophic event like this one occurs."

"Hank, that's why I'm here. I took a chance that you could lead the charge to stop this madness. Can you imagine what this mayor is capable of? I mean, she ordered the demolition of two major roads. People died on the Overseas Highway as a result. Jimmy would have if it hadn't been for your son's heroics."

Hank continued to steer with both hands, but he raised his fingers as he shrugged. "She's always had a conniving streak although I've always believed she had her constituents' best interests at heart. She seems to have let this crisis go to her head."

Erin pointed toward a car that had been set on fire since they'd driven by there the night before. It had burned itself out and continued to smolder. Hank slowed to get a long look before leaving Marathon and heading onto Vaca Key.

She turned in her seat to address him. "You've heard the saying *power corrupts but absolute power corrupts absolutely*, right?"

"Yes. As a politician's authority increases, their sense of morality decreases."

"Exactly. All of them are guilty of that. Never let them try to convince you otherwise. Politicians have a strong sense of preservation. They'll use any catastrophe to better their position in the eyes of voters or to thrust themselves onto the national stage. In the case of your mayor, you need to watch for self-dealing. There are no political brass rings for her to grab like state senate or even Congress. Therefore, she can ensure her survival, as well as the survival of her political cronies."

Hank shook his head from side to side. "You nailed it, Erin. That's always been Lindsey in a nutshell. Every decision she makes has an element of subterfuge in it. She will always do what's best for her."

"Can you see how that approach will make any recovery effort in the Keys untenable? It will instantly divide the residents into those close to the mayor and those who are not. Kiss the ring or suffer the consequences. Make no mistake, her actions are not about helping the most people. Sure, they'll get tossed a few crumbs. The real beneficiaries of her overreach will be those within her inner circle and the minions she requires to carry out her directives."

Hank tapped the steering wheel with his fingers as he fell deep into thought. Finally, he asked a rhetorical question. "I wonder if we could secede from the Keys by blowing up the bridge to Driftwood Key."

The two got a hearty laugh out of the idea until they grew silent. Neither imagined this conversation would resume very soon as it applied to Marathon.

CHAPTER FOURTEEN

Monday, November 11
Mariner's Hospital
Tavernier, Florida

"Wow! Look at you!" exclaimed Hank as he entered Jimmy's hospital room. He was still assigned to trauma eight but, apparently, not for long. His expression of surprise was genuine. Jimmy was sitting upright in bed, flanked by his parents on both sides resting comfortably in padded chairs. Jimmy had a plastic cup of water in front of him on a tray as well as a bowl of Jell-O, the preferred cuisine of every hospital chef.

"Hi, Mr. Hank," said Jimmy in a loud whisper. "I lost my voice."

"Peter's the same way," Hank said as he quickly moved to hug Phoebe, who was grinning from ear to ear. "He's getting better every hour, it seems."

"Me too," said Jimmy as he accepted a gentle hug from Hank. He turned his eyes toward Erin. It took him a moment before he recognized her. "You're back."

"I am and so are you, obviously. You're looking good, Jimmy."

He continued to whisper, mouthing some of the words as he spoke. "Feel better, too. I'm ready to leave."

Sonny stood, and Erin presented him with a duffel bag. "Hank picked out a change of clothes for you guys and something to freshen up," she said as she looked from one parent to the other. Then she turned to Jimmy. "And, based upon the way you're recovering, some jeans and a sweatshirt for you."

"I hope they fit," added Phoebe. "The doctor told us Jimmy likely lost a lot of weight. We have to monitor his food intake and keep him hydrated. He should be back to normal eating habits in a week or so."

Hank's face reflected his good mood. "Does this mean he's being released?"

"Actually, we're all watching that clock," replied Sonny, pointing at a basic black-rimmed, white-faced wall clock. The red second hand steadily wound its way around the face. "At noon, the doctor will return to check Jimmy's vitals and, with a little luck, release him with some detailed instructions for us to follow. Having Jessica at Driftwood Key was a major factor in Jimmy's early release. They have a lot of respect for her around here."

"She's earned it, and we're fortunate to have her in our family," said Hank. He then gently squeezed Jimmy's shoulder. "Just like we're very lucky to have you as well."

Jimmy smiled and nodded. Then he asked, "How is Peter?"

"Let me put it this way," began Hank in response. "He's about twenty-four hours better than you are. I'll let him tell you what happened after he discovered you were missing. He's still recovering from dehydration and muscle soreness. His voice is raspy but stronger, as I said. His face wasn't beat up like yours, however."

Jimmy slowly raised his hands to his face to feel the wounds that had opened up due to the constant exposure to salt water. "I had these before I got lost." He immediately regretted whispering the truth in his parents' presence.

"What do you mean, son? Was this from the fall?"

"Um, no. The CIA guy did this. I don't want to talk about it."

Phoebe and Sonny exchanged glances before looking toward Erin. She worked for the federal government, making her the closest available target for their ire.

She made a hollow promise that she hoped she could keep. "Let's get you well. Once you feel better, I want you and Peter to tell me every detail of what happened. It seems there was wrongdoing on both sides of that bridge."

Jimmy nodded, and the Frees let it go, for now. While they took turns in the bathroom, changing clothes and freshening up, the group engaged in small talk. After visiting for twenty minutes, Hank and Erin excused themselves. Hank wanted to look up an acquaintance who worked in hospital administration.

He and Erin took the stairs to the top floor of the hospital and then made their way to the administrative offices. The hospital administrator, who lived in Coral Gables, was assigned to two facilities within the Baptist Health system. He was rarely in the hospital, leaving the majority of the hospital administrative duties to his second in charge, Jeff Freeman. Freeman was the son of another resort owner located in Marathon. He was Mike's age, so Hank didn't know him all that well. However, they were friendly enough for what Hank wanted to discuss.

Hank was told by Freeman's secretary that he was in a conference. Hank explained to her who he was and then introduced Erin as the Secretary of Agriculture. With that information in hand, she gently knocked on her boss's door and slipped inside for a moment to explain Hank's arrival. Seconds later, he and Erin were invited into Freeman's office, where he was meeting with another familiar face.

"Hey, this is a helluva surprise, Hank!" greeted Freeman heartily. He hoisted his heavy frame out of a side chair where he'd been talking with his guest. "I never expected you to set foot off Driftwood Key with all of this going on." He waved his arms as he spoke.

"Hi, Jeff. I have Sonny Free's son, Jimmy, downstairs in your trauma wing. He almost drowned the other day."

"Oh, geez. I had no idea. Is there anything I can do?"

"Nope. He's recovering nicely, thanks to your staff. With fingers crossed, we hope he'll be released this afternoon."

Freeman turned to his other guest, who was now standing. "I think you know Bud Marino. He owns the café and marina in Islamorada."

"Of course, Commissioner."

"Yeah, that too," said Marino with a chuckle. "Lately, Jeff introduces me as the restaurant guy or marina operator. He tries not to tell everyone I'm the district five commissioner. They might jump me or worse."

"I know the feeling," added Erin.

"Guys, this is Erin Bergmann, our—" Hank began to make the introductions when Marino interrupted her.

"No introduction necessary, Hank. Madam Secretary, it's an honor, for the second time, actually."

"Oh?" Erin asked.

"We met at a fundraiser for the governor years ago. I was impressed when the president chose you for Agriculture. I thought for sure Transportation would have been a better fit. You know, don't get me wrong."

"You're correct, the Department of Transportation was where I belonged. I took Agriculture because I saw it as an opportunity to help Florida orange growers and farmers. I was making some real progress with Congress until Iran and Israel started firing nukes at one another."

Freeman's secretary reentered the room with a tray of canned drinks ranging from soda to fruit juices. All were chilled. Each of them grabbed a drink of choice, popped the top, and got comfortable.

Freeman spoke first. "Madam Secretary, I must say—"

"Erin, please. I'm not in the Keys on official business, and the whole Madam Secretary thing made me feel like some television character anyway."

"Okay, Erin," said Freeman. He pointed at Hank. "How do you know this guy? I can safely say he is the most well-known, yet elusive character in all the Keys."

"Well, long story short. I was staying at the inn as the bombs were exchanged in the Middle East." She glanced over at Hank as she recalled the memorable day together on his Hatteras. "He was kind enough to take me fishing when the Secret Service found us. I'd been summoned back to Washington. I barely made it back in time to enter the underground facility at Mount Weather before we were attacked."

Marino asked, "May we assume that the attacks are over since you've been allowed to leave the bunker?"

She nodded before she responded, "The president has reasonable assurance from China and Russia that they will not initiate hostilities against us. I believe that to be true as well."

"What about Iran or North Korea?" asked Freeman.

"Let's just say they are no longer capable of initiating a nuclear attack. They couldn't fire a BB gun at a squirrel at this point."

The two men exchanged glances. Their expressions indicated they got the visual.

"Jeff, I wanted to stop by and see how things are going for you," began Hank. "The realities of the importance of our health care system continuing to function hit home when my brother was attacked by a knife-wielding maniac, and now Jimmy nearly drowned. Are you going to be able to continue your operations?"

Freeman sighed and leaned back in his chair. Interestingly, Marino mimicked his reaction to the question.

"Ironically, we were just discussing that very subject," replied Freeman. He looked over at his other guest. "May I speak freely with Hank and Erin?"

Marino held up his index finger, indicating Freeman should wait just a moment. He turned to Hank. "If I'm not mistaken, Lindsey was married to Sonny's brother, am I right?"

"Yes, divorced," replied Hank before continuing. "And, let me add, not on good terms. I hope this doesn't offend either of you, but Lindsey and I are not on the best of terms either. To be honest, she bullied me into including Jimmy on her faux-deputy detail at the bridge checkpoints. That's how he got hurt."

Marino looked at Freeman and nodded.

Freeman explained, "There's a lot of concern within the Keys that Lindsey is mismanaging this crisis. For one, the concept of transparency has become totally lost on her. She's excluded people who would ordinarily be a voice of reason. She's surrounded herself totally with loyalists who wouldn't dare disagree with her."

Erin thought to herself, *Sounds familiar.*

Marino interjected, "Our regular council meetings have been cancelled until further notice. I still have a few little birdies running around the admin building in Key West who get messages to me by various methods. It appears the mayor pro tem and the sheriff are in. I and the other two commissioners are on the outs."

Hank asked, "What do you mean by that? The decision-making process?"

"Yes, among other things. Here's an example. Supposedly, according to a couple of friendly maintenance personnel, Lindsey has ordered a cleanup of Key West. Now, I can't argue with that. We're doing the same in the Upper Keys. However, she's going one step further. She's starting by moving vehicles into newly created impound lots, and she's ordered the maintenance department to drain their gasoline. After that, she's gonna send maintenance personnel to every house with a parked car to drain their tanks as well."

"People will pitch a fit," said Hank.

"They're going to be accompanied by SWAT," added Marino. "She means business."

Freeman sat up in his chair and leaned forward to the edge. "Here's the thing, Hank. Our hospital will possibly be the beneficiary of these actions. I assume so, anyway. We need gasoline to run our generators. Without a refill, we'll run out in a couple of weeks. Without a bridge to the mainland, we don't have a way to call Tallahassee for help.

"That said, I've got a real problem with her stealing gasoline from people. I know. I know. Harsh words, but it's how I feel."

"As do I and many others like me," said Marino.

Hank thought a moment. These two influential people in the Upper Keys could be an asset. But he needed help in laying the groundwork to execute Erin's plan.

"Bud, where does the county attorney stand in all of this?" he asked.

"True blue friend of the mayor. Hell, he drafted the executive order declaring her to be Queen of the Keys."

Hank grimaced.

Freeman was curious. "Why do you ask?"

"I need someone who knows the county's charter documents together with any recent amendments. I need to see what our options might be in dealing with our not-so-friendly mayor."

"Well, that's an easy one, Hank. Do you remember Cheryl Morton? Her family was one of the original conchs who developed Vaca Key."

"Yes, of course," responded Hank. "She was the county attorney for years. Lives on Morton Street, her family's namesake."

Marino perked up. "Drop in on her. I'll arrange to have my set of all the county's governing documents, including current versions of Lindsey's recent EOs, sent to her home. I see where you're headed with this, and let me say, unofficially, you know, between us, I'm on board."

"Count me in, too," said Freeman.

The group chatted for a moment, and Hank glanced over at the clock on Freeman's desk. It was approaching noon, and he wanted to be in Jimmy's room when the doctor came. Besides, he got more than he'd hoped for in the chance meeting with Freeman and Marino.

He escorted Erin out of the hospital administration suite of offices and into the stairwell. Once the door was closed, she grasped him by the arm and spontaneously kissed him.

"Hank, you're a natural. You're keen. Intuitive. A great listener and very analytical."

He didn't hear a word she said. All he could think about was her kiss.

CHAPTER FIFTEEN

Monday, November 11
U. S. Army War College
Carlisle Barracks
Carlisle, Pennsylvania

The federal government was never known for doing anything efficiently or speedily. However, when President Carter Helton became singularly focused on reestablishing the seat of government in a location above ground, the logistics arms of government moved with lightning-fast speed.

Within a week of making the move to the U.S. Army War College in Carlisle, Pennsylvania, a small town of twenty thousand people located two hours west of Philadelphia, all three branches of government had found new homes.

Ultimately, President Helton's plan was to formally relocate the nation's capital to Philadelphia, where it had been temporarily seated from 1790 to 1800 while Washington, DC, was being built.

Philadelphia was one of eight forgotten capitals of the United States. In 1774, the Continental Congress met inside Carpenter's Hall in Philadelphia. Just two years later, it reconvened in

Independence Hall, where it adopted the Declaration of Independence. Thereafter, as the Revolutionary War raged on and various skirmishes with the British continued, other locations had been adopted on a temporary basis to protect the fledgling government.

Locations included Baltimore near the end of 1776 when the British were closing in on Philadelphia. In 1777, the enemy was once again closing in on Philadelphia, forcing the city to be evacuated. If for only a day, the nation's government operated out of the Lancaster County courthouse in the heart of Amish country.

As the conflict with Great Britain stretched into the end of the century, York, Pennsylvania, Annapolis, Maryland, New York City, and two New Jersey locations, Trenton and Princeton, all claimed the moniker America's capital.

The president, a native Pennsylvanian, relished the opportunity to bring the nation's capital back to Philadelphia. After the crisis passed, he expected there to be calls for a return to Washington. He'd already heard whispers and murmurs within the confines of Mount Weather that DC should be restored and rebuilt. He had other plans.

Because the District of Columbia had been ground zero for a nuclear detonation, he intended to have his Environmental Protection Agency administrator declare it to be too dangerous for full-time residents or office workers. He hoped to rally support for making the former capital a war memorial.

These were just a few of the many ways President Helton hoped to remake America in his vision. He dreamed of leaving multiple lasting legacies so his presidency would be remembered for centuries. One legacy he didn't want associated with his presidency was a perception of weakness because the likes of Texas and the Florida Keys had the audacity to turn their backs on their fellow Americans.

Legacies aside, the president was also presiding over the largest loss of life in the history of mankind. No war. No pandemic. No natural disaster had ever caused this many deaths so quickly.

As the scientists explained it, the onset of nuclear winter was akin to the eruption of one of the world's supervolcanoes. The out-of-control fires polluted the atmosphere in a way carbon emissions from vehicles never could. Just like the models depicting an eruption of the Yellowstone supervolcano, nuclear winter resulted in an unparalleled environmental catastrophe.

That morning, the president had been informed of a new threat as he tried to look forward to spring and a new growing season. The scientists had referred to this threat as *zombie fires*. Due to the rapidly cooling temperatures, snow had already begun to blanket the upper latitudes of the Northern Hemisphere. The wildfires generated by the nuclear attacks had not been extinguished. Beneath the layer of fresh snow, the fires continued to smolder underground, chewing through carbon-rich peat.

The president was advised that in the spring, as the Earth thawed from the throes of what portended to be a brutal winter, these fires would reanimate. Geologists and scientists at the United States Geological Survey used available satellite data and reporting on the ground to develop an algorithm that could detect where the fires were still smoldering under the snow falling atop the ground. A heat map was generated, indicating thirty-eight percent of the land mass surrounding the current blazes would reignite, and there was nothing man could do to stop it.

The president had intended that morning's briefing to be a strategic planning session. He wanted to establish some form of timeline for the recovery. To the best of his ability, he wanted to disseminate to the media and the American people what to expect as they moved forward. By the time the scientists were finished, he'd wanted to bolt out of the room and find a stiff drink, regardless of the early hour.

The briefing was coming to a close when the FEMA director announced their findings on the death toll estimates. It had been twenty-five days since the Iranians had fired the first nuclear missile at Israel. Their actions had triggered the nuclear war that went on for days, culminating with the attacks on the United States on day seven.

By that time, the climatic effect of nuclear winter had already reached America's shores. The detonations on the East and West Coast only accelerated the disaster. However, it was the EMP effect of the nuclear detonations coupled with the subsequent overload of the nation's Eastern and Western Interconnection, the power grid, that exacerbated the catastrophe.

The onset of nuclear winter was a long-term problem that was expected to last a decade. Its impact on sources of water was unseen, but profound. Lakes, rivers, and underground aquifers, fed by rain and melting snow, were the source of the country's water supply. The fallout from the nuclear detonations and the soot generated by the wildfires polluted these natural resources.

With the loss of electricity across most of the country, the nation's critical infrastructure could no longer function. Without power, water treatment plants that employed mechanical processes to filter and purify water so it was safe for human consumption couldn't operate. For existing stored water in large, enclosed reservoirs, the distribution system of pipes and pumps was unable to deliver the clean water to end-users' taps. Neither wastewater nor stormwater could be collected or treated, as sewer systems required electricity to operate.

The human body could only survive three days without water before it began to dehydrate. At first, the effects of dehydration were evident by common symptoms like headache, dizziness, change in urination, and dry mouth. However, after those three days, the complications of untreated dehydration became more profound, and the onset of the problems came rapidly. The body's vital organs simply shut down. Seizures and involuntary muscle contractions overcame the person. As the kidneys shut down, other organs like the heart were profoundly affected as low blood volume caused a rapid drop in blood pressure and oxygen. As the dehydration victim went into hypovolemic shock, death came quickly, and it was brutal.

All around the nation, people suffering from dehydration began to search for anything to rehydrate their bodies. They turned to the natural sources of water that formed the basis for the nation's water supply. However, these lakes, streams, and rivers were polluted by the fallout from nuclear winter. They were beset with dysentery that only hastened the dehydration process.

By day twenty-five, there wasn't a grocery store or a food-storage warehouse in America that hadn't been looted or emptied. Desperate people trying to feed themselves or their loved ones stormed facilities, even those protected by armed guards, in an effort to grab a case of green beans or a container of baby formula.

Neighbor approached neighbor in search of help. If a family had a little extra and they gave it to their neighbor, they'd find themselves answering the door again the next day as the neighbor returned for more. If a family refused the neighbor's pleas, the day after that, he might arrive at the door with a gun. A new father whose wife and newborn child were at home dying of starvation was willing to do anything to help them, including killing his best friend he'd once grilled and shared beers with.

During that morning briefing, the president was given a reality check. He'd been a politician for most of his adult life, insulated from the realities of daily life. His memory of living under the roof of a coal miner who literally dug under the ground to put food on his family's table had waned long ago. He'd lost touch with how quickly the thin veneer of civilization could collapse as people tried to survive. As the FEMA director droned on, portraying a nation that was collapsing all around them, he began to wonder if anyone would be alive to save when it was over.

CHAPTER SIXTEEN

Monday, November 11
Driftwood Key

Jimmy walked gingerly up the sidewalk toward the front porch of the main house with the assistance of his father, who helped carry his weight. He'd been suffering cramps in his legs as a result of his dehydration and his herculean effort to tread water as he battled for survival. The doctors assured him his legs would return to normal functionality.

To assist in his recovery, he had been given several tubes of Hydralyte electrolyte tablets. The effervescent tablets were to be mixed with water and consumed by Jimmy throughout the next several days. They'd even provided him two cases of Essentia purified electrolyte water to ensure he was drinking something that hadn't been contaminated by the fallout.

His limping gait meant nothing to Peter, who fully recovered except for his strained vocal cords. He came bounding down the steps of the front porch and raced toward Jimmy to give his friend a hug. The two young men became emotional as they whispered to one another about their ordeal. Not because they sought privacy, it was all they could muster.

Lacey, who followed close behind Peter, couldn't help herself. "I say we put it to a vote. Raise your hand if you think this mute button on Peter and Jimmy should be a permanent thing?" She quickly raised her hand. To her surprise, Phoebe raised hers as well.

Jimmy mouthed the words, "Mom? Really?"

She simply smiled and kissed him on the cheek. "Children should be seen and not heard, even the ones who've grown up."

The two gave one another a hug and pressed each other's foreheads together for a brief moment. Without a doubt, the Free family, who'd always been close, now had an inseparable bond that could never be broken.

Sonny gave way to allow Peter to take over the job of helping Jimmy inside. Hank and Erin followed behind with the duffel bag and the supplies provided for Jimmy's recovery. Lacey was the first to comment on the surgical masks they were wearing.

"Are you guys contagious with something or what?"

Her father responded, "Let's get inside, and I'll explain what I learned."

Everyone made their way into the foyer until Hank led them into the bar, which had become the family's unofficial living room. The dining area had remained off-limits until Phoebe's return. It was always considered part of her domain within the main house.

After everyone got settled and Jimmy was provided a squeeze bottle bearing the Driftwood Key Inn logo full of electrolyte-infused water, Hank explained what the doctors had told him.

"You know, before all of this happened, I'd watch the news, and the weather guy would go on and on about the air quality index. My eyes would gloss over, and I'd wait to see the forecast. I learned a lot about AQI, the acronym used by the doctor to refer to air quality index. They take into account a lot of things like the ozone levels and particle pollution. She told me the pollution levels from soot particulates is off the charts. And what's scary is you can't really see it. I mean, sure, we all see the hazy skies. However, if you just consider the air in your immediate vicinity, it seems normal. It's not.

"There are all kinds of chemicals that are part of the soot and smoke that we're ingesting. Carcinogens and benzopyrene, the types of substances found in cigarette smoke, can enter our systems through breathing it or by ingesting it through our skin and eyes.

"Let's put it this way, she told me that it doesn't matter how much food and water we have stored; if we don't prevent this crap from entering our lungs and blood system, we'll begin to suffer from respiratory failure, heart issues, and, like smokers, cancer."

Peter rolled his eyes and said in a loud whisper, "Happy, happy. Joy, joy. I've been breathing in smoke since DC got nuked."

"Okay, the masks are a good start," added Lacey. "I guess we can make it a point to cover up when outside. Hats. Long sleeves and pants."

"That's not a problem with how cold it is," said Tucker, who was used to chilly weather hitting the San Francisco Bay Area.

"What else can we do?" asked Lacey.

"Clean," replied Hank. "It was stupid of me to suggest we could smoke cigars and crack the windows last night. We need to vacuum and wipe down everything. Also, we need to find a way to limit the amount of outside air that comes into the house."

"We could come and go through the mudroom," suggested Phoebe. "I'll keep the door to the kitchen closed, and we could spray our clothing off with Lysol."

"I doubt we have enough Lysol to last years, but it's a start," interjected Hank. "Let's all think on it, and we'll come up with a solution. For starters, let's all plan on kicking off our shoes and remove any outerwear to be left in the mudroom. Sonny and I'll create some peg hooks or cubicles to store our outdoor clothing."

Sonny nodded, his weary face reflecting his exhaustion from worry and lack of sleep.

Lacey made a suggestion. "We have lots to talk about, especially as it relates to getting into a daily routine now that everyone is here. Whadya think about letting Sonny and Phoebe get some rest? Jimmy needs to get squared away as well. Tonight, we'll talk about this logistical stuff after dinner. Sound good?"

The group wholeheartedly agreed. Sonny and Phoebe helped Jimmy out of the house through the kitchen.

After they left, Hank turned to the group. "You guys know that I rely upon them a lot for operating the inn." He turned to look in the direction of the Frees' bungalow. "I'm no longer their boss. I'm Sonny's brother. Jimmy is like a brother to Peter. And Phoebe, she's like the glue that holds us all together. I'm saying all of that to say this. We're going to share the responsibilities around here in order to survive. In addition to the obvious concerns, we, as a group, need to be rowing our boats in the same direction. Does that make sense?"

Everyone agreed.

Erin brought up one additional point. "I'm the outsider, and I can't thank you all enough for taking me in. I hope to lend a different perspective based upon what I experienced while I held my position in the administration. Here's how I look at it.

"After the attacks, the nation as a whole went into shock. There wasn't any guidance on what to do or how to react because this whole thing was unprecedented. It was the stuff of scientists' theories or survival thriller novels.

"Once people realized the government wasn't going to take care of them, their primal instincts took over. Survival in a situation like this will take a strong, cohesive group like this family.

"However, there's one more thing to consider. Our world has suddenly become a lot smaller. Sure, we're still part of the United States, and of course you could say we're still Floridians. But what happens in Pennsylvania or Tallahassee or even Miami is of no real consequence to us. We can only control or be a part of what happens here in the Keys or Marathon or on Driftwood Key."

"Forget about the so-called *big picture*?" asked Lacey.

"Sort of," began Erin in response. "There is a big picture, but how it impacts us won't manifest itself for years, I'm afraid. Outside Driftwood Key and Monroe County, people are dying by the tens of millions. I've seen the hypotheticals and projections. And we're only in the beginnings of this catastrophic event. The same will begin to take place from Key West to Key Largo. We need to focus our efforts on controlling what we can."

"That's why you think my dad should get involved in politics?" asked Lacey.

"Yes, and I saw him in action today. He's a natural. You know why? Because he's real. He's a levelheaded problem solver who could bring business leaders and politicians together to stand up to the mayor."

"Shouldn't we focus on getting our own house in order first?" asked Peter.

Hank stepped in to answer that question. "Peter, we learned today that Lindsey has plans to confiscate property and fuel in Key West using the sheriff's department. Many believe it's her goal to move systematically up the Keys with the intention of taking supplies into the government's possession for redistribution."

"Ours?" asked Tucker.

"Yes," his grandfather replied as he placed his arm around Tucker's shoulders.

"How do we stop it?" asked Lacey.

Erin sighed. "We have some ideas, but like any new political campaign, we have to get organized. We need a place or building dedicated to going over strategy that's separate from our living space."

"Bungalow one is the closest," said Hank. "We could remove the bedroom furniture and convert it."

"That means we'd have to go outside a little too often," said Lacey. "What about the game room upstairs? We could move things out and cover the pool table with a board to create a table."

"That would work," said Hank. "I'll get with Sonny. I think he bought some chalkboard paint for a project Phoebe had. Heck, we'll paint a whole wall with it."

"Excellent!" exclaimed Erin, excited about the undertaking. "I say we sanitize the inn first so Phoebe won't be compelled to do it, and then we'll focus on our new war room."

"Grandpa for mayor!" shouted Tucker.

Hank shook his head and playfully snarled at Erin.

CHAPTER SEVENTEEN

Monday, November 11
Driftwood Key

Everyone gathered in the dining room for dinner except for Jimmy, who was still sleeping. All agreed that every moment he could rest, whether asleep or simply relaxing, would help him recover faster. Like Peter, Jimmy was satisfied with a bowl of soup and some crackers. At this point, the guys were more concerned with their sore throats than filling their bellies.

"Phoebe, it's amazing what you can do in the kitchen with our limited options," said Hank as he marveled at the fresh-cut greens and vegetables from their greenhouse garden that accompanied the baked fish. "For the last couple of days, we've all come to realize how difficult it is to manage our food."

Phoebe accepted the compliment and took her seat next to Sonny. "I have to say, having Lacey and Erin around to help made a difference. But, Mr. Hank, we will have to start fishing again soon to keep our seafood levels where they should be."

Sonny added, "And I have to bring all of our sustainable

gardening to its full capability. Remember, we cut back to fool Lindsey into thinking we were just getting by."

Hank nodded as he poured the homemade Italian dressing made by Erin with oil, vinegar, and Italian seasonings Phoebe had stockpiled.

"I remember. It's time to ramp up with a focus on our survival now that we have everyone together, almost," he said. Hank reached over to squeeze Lacey's hand, a gesture designed to remind her that Owen might be gone, but he wasn't forgotten. "We're going to entrust you to portion out our food and related supplies as you see fit. I think Sonny and I are in a position to start fishing again."

"Jimmy will be ready soon," interjected Sonny. "He's already talked about it. I tried to tamp down his enthusiasm, but he's pretty insistent. He responded in typical Jimmy fashion. *Dad, I don't have to talk to fish.*"

The group laughed, but it was Peter who raised a concern. "Listen, I'm okay after what we went through that night. But it was different for him. He almost died."

Phoebe, who worried for her son more than anyone, explained why they shouldn't be concerned. "Actually, I sense the problem is the opposite. He wants to talk about what he went through, and as he recalls a challenge, he explains how he survived it. If anything, he might think he's invincible."

Hank nodded and exchanged a glance with Lacey. Lacey had been pummeled by the hurricane and almost drowned as well had it not been for Tucker's heroics. She'd already told her dad she'd prefer to stay off the water for a while, as in maybe forever.

"Let's play it by ear. No matter what, he doesn't go out without a partner. In fact, that's one of the things we need to talk about tonight. Tucker is on the gate alone right now, but that'll be the last time that happens. We need to establish a buddy system for things like security, fishing, or if absolutely necessary, travels into Marathon or the other Keys."

Mike chimed in, "Hank's absolutely right. Let me bring everyone up to speed. After I left the hospital the other day, I convinced the sheriff to let me create my own MCSO substation for Marathon. I'm basically based out of Driftwood Key, but I was able to get access to the Monroe County Clerk's office. He's assigned four permanent deputies to my command, plus my darling wife."

"Dream on, Commander," said Jessica with a laugh.

"Okay, let's just say the WET team has a Marathon division, and that's Jess."

"Much better." She and Lacey exchanged fist bumps in solidarity.

"Anyway," Mike continued, "I'll oversee law enforcement activities from Knights Key at Seven Mile Bridge up to Lower Matecumbe, at least for now."

"What does that mean?" asked Sonny.

Mike looked at Erin as he responded, "Like cabinet members who serve at the pleasure of the president, right now, everyone is serving at the whim of the sheriff, who seems to be having his chain yanked by Lindsey. I think all of this is subject to change at a moment's notice."

Hank finished eating and rested his elbows on the table as he spoke. "The original plan was for Mike and Jessica to resign from the sheriff's department. However, Mike saw an opening that allowed the two of them to be close to home while remaining tapped into the MCSO resources."

"Resources?" asked Lacey.

"Yeah, to an extent," replied Mike. "I hope to be able to continue to gather supplies, weapons, ammunition, and any other item that might help us get through this. Things are in disarray at the sheriff's depot in Key West. There doesn't appear to be any accountability or watchdog set up. With my new position, I feel like I can continue to siphon a few things for as long as I'm still in place."

"Same for me," added Jessica. "As an MCSO paramedic, I can restock my water ambulance with medical supplies. We're gonna need them, too. Think about it, we're only a few weeks into this damn apocalypse mess and we've lost Owen, had two near drownings, a stabbing, and two gunfights."

Hank took a deep breath. "Let me add, from what Erin and I

learned at the hospital, these medical facilities are in a world of hurt when it comes to filling their needs. They lost access to the mainland just like the rest of us did."

"Hank's right, which means I'll only be able to, quote, *restock*, unquote, until I get cut off." She used her fingers to create air quotes as she spoke. She gathered Mike's plate and stacked it on top of hers.

"All right," said Hank. "I guess the point is our ability to look outside Driftwood Key for supplies or assistance will be coming to an end at some point. Maybe sooner rather than later based upon what Mike is hearing from others within the department."

Mike thanked Jessica for moving his plate. She knew him so well. When having a serious discussion at the dinner table, he tended to get animated and used the table to outline his point as if drawing with his fingers made it more clear for the others.

"The issue of security and the buddy system Hank alluded to is important now more than ever. Admittedly, I've been out of pocket since the stabbing, and prior to that I was still focused on finding our serial killer. I had a meeting with my newly assigned deputies, who told me that the number of break-ins in Marathon has increased.

"They're hitting restaurants first. Porky's, 7 Mile Grill, La Niña, for starters. Last night, they ransacked the Sunset Grille by the bridge. It could be a gang, but not in the sense you might think. Some of the eyewitnesses described it as a bunch of guys with guns. It could be anyone desperate enough to break into a business."

"Are they happening at night?" asked Hank.

"Mostly, until yesterday afternoon. They drove up to Sunset Grille, smashed through the front door with the bumper of a pickup truck, and looted the place. The food was gone or spoiled, so they took all the condiments, the liquor, and the propane tanks for the barbecue grills on the deck."

"Brazen," mumbled Peter.

"Exactly," said Mike. "They aren't afraid of law enforcement intervening or investigating. For one thing, they have us outnumbered. And to make matters worse, my deputies showed no inclination to risk their lives to protect someone's property. I'm lucky they show up for their shift at all. If it weren't for the sheriff's promise of food and the fact they live in our area, they'd probably stay home to protect their own."

The thought of unchecked lawlessness hovered over the dinner table as everyone cleared their plates and exited to the kitchen. The group worked together to wash dishes, allowing Phoebe and her crew of two to relax.

Sonny gathered his clothes and weapon and slipped out of the house to join Tucker at the gate. Phoebe stayed behind in the kitchen at her desk to begin poring over her inventory journals. The rest quietly exited to take the issue up again in their new war room.

CHAPTER EIGHTEEN

Monday, November 11
Driftwood Key

Throughout the day, the guys retrofitted the game room, which was rarely used by guests, to a place where they could gather to discuss their plans to rally other like-minded individuals throughout the Keys with the goal of removing Lindsey from office. The next day, Hank and Erin intended to call on Cheryl Morton, the former county attorney, to discuss their legal options. He wasn't sure what illegal options were available, but he'd discuss them as well.

"Okay, we can modify this as necessary to suit our needs," began Hank as the group climbed the stairs and approached the former game room. "The chalkboard paint hasn't dried yet, but Phoebe hasn't had an opportunity to whip up her concoction to make chalk."

"How is she going to make chalk?" asked Mike.

"Until we can find some chalk, something I hope you can help us with when you go into Marathon, she's going to mix together equal parts of cornstarch and water to go with one of the half-inch paintbrushes from the toolshed. It's primitive, but it can work until we have a better option."

"Sounds messy," said Mike. "Let me work on the chalk tomorrow. I might be able to gain access to Switlik Elementary as part of my rounds. I want to start checking on the county-owned properties in Marathon."

"Okay, I'll let Phoebe know in the morning," said Erin. She looked around the room and thought of a few things that might help. "Mike, if you come across legal pads or any other office supplies. We need to start making some notes as we consider our options."

"Tell us what the process looks like, Erin," said Lacey.

Hank urged everyone to sit down as he turned the floor over to Erin.

"After what Mike told us at dinner, before we worry about Lindsey, we need to make sure these armed, roving gangs don't show up at our doorstep like they have in the past. Mike, what would it take to stop them?"

"More manpower," he replied. "I don't have enough deputies to fight them off."

"Okay, let me think out loud for a moment," continued Erin. "Marathon has residents and business owners who are in the same situation as we are. What if we approached them and laid out the threat? You know, tell them about this gang, or gangs, of armed men who are raiding their key. Do you think they'd band together to stop their looting before they grew larger in number and therefore too strong?"

"I don't like civilian deputies," said Mike bluntly.

"I get it. Vigilante justice isn't always the best way to go, but correct me if I'm wrong. Haven't you guys had to administer that kind of justice at your dock and then later at the bridge?"

"That was self-defense," countered Mike.

"True, but it didn't involve calling law enforcement for assistance. You guys handled it on your own. I'm suggesting you bring the locals together to fight back against this group. Plus, it will have a twofold purpose."

"What is the other reason?" asked Hank.

Erin appreciated Hank's ability to carry the conversation in the direction she needed it to go.

"It will give you an opportunity to show them Lindsey and the sheriff will not come to their aid. It will give them a newfound sense of self-reliance while showing Lindsey's ineptitude. We want them to look to the Albright family for leadership, not the person who is ignoring their needs in order to confiscate property in Key West."

"Makes sense to me," said Hank.

"Follow me for a moment," said Erin as she unfolded a map of the Florida Keys. "From everything we've heard, the mayor, with the aid of the sheriff, is working her way up the Keys. She's started with the largest population areas. Eventually, she'll want to send her minions across Seven Mile Bridge. That's where we need to take a stand and say enough is enough."

Jessica started laughing. "Great, we're gonna blow up another bridge."

Erin appreciated the humor, but she felt compelled to confirm this was not her intention. "Step one is to garner the trust of your neighbors and fellow business owners. Then we need to develop allies in the Middle and Upper Keys who will help us send a clear message to the mayor we're not going to willingly give up our property, including food and supplies, to her administration to redistribute."

Peter, whose voice had improved throughout the day, added, "By the time we have to take a stand, she will have pissed off everyone in the Lower Keys. Taking this drastic an approach would've had a better chance if she had a consensus of opinion on her side. She thinks she can run roughshod over everyone. That may work for those docile people in Key West, but with each day, she'll face more resistance."

Jessica stood and ran her fingers along Seven Mile Bridge. "If we're not gonna blow it up, we can certainly make it near impossible to cross."

"They're not going to stand by and let us do that," said Mike.

"It sounds to me like she's allocated a lot of manpower to her activities in Key West," Jessica responded. "Maybe we can do it quickly to frustrate her plans? By the time she figures out what happened, we'll have a lot of folks on our side."

"Here's my question to you, Mike," began Erin. "How long will it take the sheriff to move toward Marathon?"

"Five or six days, assuming they're thorough," he replied.

Erin stepped backward and sat on a bar stool, one of two sitting next to a rack of pool cues. "We're gonna need to move quickly, and a little luck would be nice."

Hank took the floor. "Okay, for tomorrow. Here's the plan. Erin and I will work the political angle. We'll see Mrs. Morton first, and then we'll reach out to the county commissioner from district three. We know we have district five covered with Bud Marino. District one will be difficult to reach, but by the time her home is raided on Stock Island, she'll be on board.

"Most importantly, I need to touch base with the mayor. Mike indicated he goes into his office every morning. I don't know why, but I need to get him on board with us."

"What about the business owners and this gang?" asked Lacey.

"Let me get a feel for what's going on with these break-ins," replied Mike. "Once I know what I'm dealing with, we can discuss how to stop them with the use of civilians."

For the next hour, the group talked about the likelihood of their success. In the end, they agreed with Hank's statement. It was often repeated and represented the feelings of many freedom-living Americans.

"I'd rather die on my feet than live on my knees."

PART III

Day twenty-six, Tuesday, November 12

CHAPTER NINETEEN

Tuesday, November 12
Driftwood Key

They say it's always darkest before the dawn, and the families who'd finally found their way home to Driftwood Key were prepared to put the pains they'd suffered over the last few weeks behind them. Even with Peter and Jimmy on the mend, Hank hoped to bring everyone together for breakfast that morning to create a routine, some semblance of normalcy, during a catastrophic event that would become increasingly difficult to survive.

He took on the leadership role not unlike the coach of a high school football team would. He had to rally his team to do more than play a game on a crisp, fall Friday night under the lights. He had to convince his charges they could survive the chilly days that had been thrust upon them courtesy of nuclear winter. As they settled in for a breakfast of oatmeal, unusual for the Florida Keys at any time of year, Hank laid out the roles for each member of his team.

"Jimmy, you're healing up nicely," said Hank as he passed a bowl of sugar toward the young man who was the last to be seated. Jimmy said good morning to everyone and smiled at Hank.

"Peter and I were just talkin' about it," he said in a loud whisper as he took his first bite of sugar-coated oatmeal. Phoebe had warned everyone that oatmeal and Cream of Wheat would become a staple of their morning meals. She and Sonny had purchased as much as they could find in those days leading up to the collapse. The two healthy breakfast foods were also easy to prepare when power was scarce.

"He's about a couple of days behind me in terms of recovery," added Peter in order to allow Jimmy to slowly eat his oatmeal. His throat was still sore from the ordeal whereas Peter's had substantially recovered, as had his strength. "Whadya think, Jimmy?"

"Crazy as this sounds, I want to get back into the water to practice holding my breath," he replied. "The doctor couldn't really tell me if I had lung damage. The only way I know how to find out is to test them."

Phoebe rolled her eyes and shook her head. "Let's not, son. Okay? You don't need to do any skin diving right now."

"Mom, I've already been challenging myself while lying in bed. I'm up to six minutes."

His mother playfully swatted him on the shoulder and the back of the head with both hands. "Don't stress me out!"

"Okay! Okay! I was better off swimming with the sharks."

"Sharks?" asked Tucker. "I didn't know …" His voice trailed off.

"I saw one, I think," Jimmy answered. "We have them, but they don't bother anyone. And who knows, I could have imagined it. I was getting kinda loopy out there."

Hank stepped in because he wanted everyone to look forward, not back. "So here's what I was thinking. Mike and Jessica will continue their duties working with the sheriff's department. Officially, they've been assigned Marathon and the surrounding Keys from Seven Mile Bridge to Lower Matecumbe Key. As we all know, their focus will be on our protection and acquiring supplies for us."

Mike interrupted. "The sheriff's office is in disarray, and I'm continuing to receive information about their activities in Key West. It's simply a matter of time before Lindsey and the MCSO SWAT team moves up Seven Mile to knock on the doors of our neighbors."

"And maybe us," added Hank. "Erin and I have a plan, as we've discussed, to rally people opposed to Lindsey's activities. Our efforts will begin today with Mrs. Morton, who can tell us what our options are. Also, we'll be touching base with the mayor, business owners in Marathon, and friends of our family. The goal is to push back against Lindsey. If we can't stop her, then at least we can confine her confiscations to the Lower Keys and Key West."

"What do you want us to do, Dad?" asked Lacey.

"Well, I'd like to divide the rest of you into two groups. Sonny, Phoebe, and Jimmy will do what they've always done for Driftwood Key. Jimmy's fishing duties will wait until we feel he's close to one hundred percent. When he does resume fishing, it will be on the buddy system. Nobody leaves the key alone. No exceptions."

"Okay," Peter confirmed. "Can I assume Lacey, Tucker, and I will handle security and fill in as needed elsewhere. I'm not much for fishing, but I can work with Jimmy when the time comes."

"Just like the old days, right?" said Jimmy with a grin. He offered his fist to Peter, who bumped it in return.

"Yep. I'll drink beer while you reel 'em in."

Jimmy shrugged and grinned. The two friends were reliving their glory days growing up on Driftwood Key.

Hank rolled his eyes and shook his head disapprovingly. He had two teenagers on his hands once again.

Tucker spoke up. "Uncle Mike, would you or Aunt Jess have some time to show me how to use all the weapons? I kinda learned on the fly, if you know what I mean."

Mike glanced at Lacey, who nodded her approval. "Over the last few weeks, he's been forced to grow up. I never thought he'd learn to fire weapons before he got his driver's license, but that's what we have to do. Honestly, I could use a refresher course, too."

"Same," added Peter.

Mike patted Jessica on the arm, who nodded. "Deal. However, dry fire only. We can't risk attracting attention, and we certainly can't afford to burn through our ammo. It's not like we can run out and buy more. That said, I will try to procure more from the MCSO supply depot in Key West if I go that way."

"Aren't you planning to stick around here?" asked Sonny.

"Absolutely, unless the sheriff sends someone to bring me to his office or something," replied Mike. "What I don't want is him coming this way nosing around. I don't know how long Jess and I can keep up this charade."

"Hopefully, long enough for Hank to work his magic on the other residents of Marathon and then Islamorada," interjected Erin. She glanced around the table. Everyone had finished their oatmeal, so she turned to Hank. "We should get going. It'll be a full day."

"I want both of you carrying weapons," said Mike with an authoritative tone. In matters of security, Hank would always defer to his brother. "Handguns with backup magazines are mandatory. Also, at least one long gun. A shotgun would be best."

Sonny spoke up for the first time. "Hank, Jimmy and I can do some fishing today. Close to the shore, of course."

"That would be great if Phoebe agrees," said Hank. "Just keep your eyes open."

Everyone confirmed what their roles were and set out for the day. In Key West, another group was about to take on a job they never imagined doing on American soil.

CHAPTER TWENTY

Tuesday, November 12
Key West

Sergeant Jorge Rivera was an eleven-year veteran of the Monroe County Sheriff's Department. He'd always been loyal to Sheriff Jock and had even petitioned his fellow officers on the force to support Lindsey during her first mayoral campaign. When the sheriff sat down with Lindsey to discuss the mechanics for executing the raids, Rivera was a logical choice to lead the members of the SWAT team. They were perfectly suited to breach the buildings that were to be raided that day.

Their first early morning stop would be a brazen raid upon a local restaurant supply store just a quarter mile away from the U.S. Coast Guard facility on Whiting Avenue. Despite the standoff between the Helton administration and Mayor Lindsey, as the hurricane approached, the USCG facility had been ordered to bug out. A small contingent of base police was left behind to guard the base and would be witness to the activities.

Sergeant Rivera did not expect to run into any meaningful opposition as he conducted his raids. Between the earlier unrest and the hurricane, all of the businesses had shuttered their doors and windows to protect their inventory. Except for a few notable, national companies like Publix, Winn-Dixie, and Walgreens, the businesses were owned by locals.

The omissions on his lengthy list were obvious to Rivera, who was keenly aware of the political affiliations of most business owners in the Lower Keys and Key West, his district. The restaurant supply store's owners had been a vocal opponent of Lindsey's policies, and therefore it came as no surprise they'd be targeted first.

Sergeant Rivera addressed his team leaders, all chosen because of their loyalty to him and Sheriff Jock. Loyalty secured by promises of receiving a greater portion of the seized goods than ordinary citizens.

"We've prepared for this, and it's time to execute. Team A will hit the front entrance and clear the building. Once the all clear is received, team B will position our box trucks at their loading docks while team C takes up perimeter security. Understood?"

"Yes, Sergeant!" the three team leaders replied in unison.

Sergeant Rivera continued. "Team A, once the perimeter is secured, we'll move on to the next location, where two more teams are at the ready. This will be a systematic, efficient sequence of raids designed to catch these people off guard. The idea is to avoid confrontation and an escalation of hostilities."

During the prior two days, the sheriff's office sent out deputies with iPads to photograph the perimeter of each target building and its surroundings. The computer tablet was then given to Sergeant Rivera, who intended to study it as he moved from one raid to another. His breach team would be under his direct command while the teams assigned to emptying out the businesses and perimeter security were left on their own.

Rather than undertaking the raids at night, Sergeant Rivera wanted the benefit of the minimal daylight nuclear winter afforded him. He expected each location would draw curious onlookers, and he wanted his perimeter security teams to be able to make adjustments if something went awry.

The team leaders rejoined their groups, and Sergeant Rivera spoke into the microphone of his encrypted two-way radio. "All teams are confirmed ready. Shock and awe, people. Team A, hit it!"

Years ago, the U.S. government had begun selling off its decommissioned military vehicles. Monroe County had purchased four urban assault vehicles that had never been used except in training exercises. Team A now operated three of them to undertake the initial breaches of the buildings. The fourth remained at the administration building together with a sizable security contingent. Lindsey wanted her castle protected.

The urban assault vehicles raced toward the one-story structure at a fairly high rate of speed. At that hour of the morning, very few people were awake, but the hyped-up drivers were at their highest state of awareness.

After skidding to a stop, three men emptied out of the rear of the vehicles and approached the front entrance. The breach team was made up of SWAT team members and firefighters experienced in extraction methods.

Three SWAT team members with automatic weapons arrived at the plywood-covered plate-glass doors and windows facing the parking lots. The firefighters used cordless saws and their Halligan tools to cut through the plywood. A Halligan was a steel tool used by firefighters and law enforcement when forcible entry was required in an emergency. One of the most important fire rescue tools, it had a two-prong fork used as a claw on one end and a combination spike-duckbill on the other.

With incredible efficiency, the firefighters on team A removed all the sheets of plywood that had been installed to protect the building from the storm and looters. Seconds later, without regard to the damage they were causing, they broke out the panes of glass, allowing the SWAT team members easy access.

Illuminated flashlights sent beams of light dancing throughout the interior of the building. The law enforcement officers called out to anyone stowed away inside, warning them to show themselves or risk getting shot. In less than five minutes, team A had breached the largest restaurant supply store in Key West and gave the all-clear announcement.

Pleased with himself, Sergeant Rivera ordered the other teams to move in, and with the efficiency of a swarm of locusts in a wheat field, they stripped the business of anything left of value.

A large crowd of onlookers gathered at the first target and each location thereafter to beg for a handout or to enter the buildings after the MCSO teams pulled out. They were emaciated and suffering from illness brought on by the lack of nutrition. Their dark, sullen eyes told the story. They were days away from starving to death after running out of their own food supplies.

Sergeant Rivera tried to put the images out of his mind. Their desperation emboldened him to move on to the next target on the list. And the next. And the next. By the time they reached Gordon Food Service on Roosevelt Boulevard, word of the raids had spread throughout Key West. At each stop, the crowds not only became larger, but some also cheered on the SWAT teams.

Thrilled at the success of his raids, Sergeant Rivera and his three armored assault vehicles rolled into Conch Plaza to enter the Gordon Food Service Store. What they encountered was more than resistance. It was a full-frontal assault by the owners and their hired guns.

CHAPTER TWENTY-ONE

Tuesday, November 12
Tarpon Harbour Apartments
Marathon

Don Wallace and his wife had managed the Tarpon Harbour Apartments for more than ten years. Like so many other Keys residents, the Wallaces either came to the island chain in search of a Margaritaville lifestyle, or they were hiding from a past they didn't want exposed. The Florida Keys had many transients in search of a new life, and the Wallaces fell under that category.

Wallace lived in the manager's apartment located on the property on the Atlantic Ocean side of Marathon. They were friendly with all of their tenants and spent a considerable amount of time organizing community events for the one-hundred-and-seven-unit complex.

On this day, the meeting at the complex's clubhouse wasn't set to beach music and free margaritas. It was about survival of the fittest.

Wallace had approached several of the men and women at Tarpon Harbour who'd run out of food. They reached an agreement, one that was born out of instinct. They refused to die and decided to band together to take what they could not buy—fresh water and food.

Several tenants had young children who were suffering. Wellness checks on the tenants in residence began to produce dead bodies daily. Wallace and the tenants began breaking into nearby homes and businesses, taking anything edible and distributing the food products to those in need within the apartment community.

On a few occasions during these home invasions, they were met with a homeowner and a rifle barrel. This prompted the band of burglars to locate weapons of their own. At first, they used aluminum baseball bats and claw hammers to subdue their victims. With each successful nightly set of break-ins, they not only scored food but also guns.

None of the men owned weapons of their own, and very few had ever fired a gun. However, they were prepared to do what it took to continue to feed their families and those in the apartment complex.

Wallace called the group together. What started as a close-knit band of six burglars had now expanded to a dozen. Eight of them were armed with multiple guns. They gathered in the teal-colored clubhouse overlooking the pool, which remained filled with sand and debris following the hurricane. Wallace had only had enough time to cover the windows with plywood and had been unable to put away the lounge chairs that had lined both sides of the pool. The group was talking among themselves as Wallace called them to attention.

"Okay, listen up. We've now confirmed that the sheriff's department has pulled virtually all of their manpower to Key West. From what we've been told by a firefighter who left to join the sheriff's department, the mayor has ordered raids of businesses in Key West and Stock Island. This firefighter friend of mine says the plan is to redistribute the food and supplies to residents."

"How does that help us?" asked one of the men who stood in the back of the open space.

"I don't think it does, for now, anyway," replied Wallace. He ran his fingers through his salt-and-pepper hair. "According to my buddy, they plan on moving up the Keys until they've emptied every place that would have stockpiles of supplies. I think we need to change our tactics before they hit Marathon."

"What do you have in mind?" asked one of the three women who were a part of the group.

"Well, so far we've focused on residences nearby. Mainly, this is because we can hit them and run back to the apartments before we're seen. I think we need to identify the locations in Marathon that would give us the greatest opportunities and get what we can before the mayor beats us to the punch."

Wallace pulled out a tourist map of Marathon and spread it on a banquet table in front of him. The group walked up to the table to get a better look at the markings and Post-it Note flags he'd used to identify certain properties in Marathon.

"We don't have a lot of time if I understand my friend correctly, so we need to hit our most lucrative opportunities first," Wallace began to explain. He tapped his fingers on the map over Marathon High School. "When this whole mess started, the county maintenance people put heavy-duty chains and padlocks on all the exterior doors to prevent entry."

"Do we have bolt cutters strong enough to cut through the chain?" one of the group asked.

"No, but I do have an alternative way into the school," replied Wallace. He stood away from the table and studied the people he would rely upon to break in. "At the food service entrance between the classroom buildings and the community college, there are three roll-up doors that allow delivery trucks to back up to a loading dock."

"We won't be able to open them from the outside," opined one of the men. "I doubt we can even pry them open."

Wallace scowled at the man for interrupting him. "There's another way. You might remember that they were doing some construction work at the school. In the utility yard where the roll-up doors are located, there is a Cat backhoe parked near the roof overhang. We need someone to climb up the backhoe boom, jump onto the roof, and break through the windows into the building. Once inside, you should be able to manually roll up the steel doors from inside."

He studied the faces of the group, hoping for a volunteer. Wallace couldn't do it himself because he had bad knees.

"I've done it before," said a young man as he raised his hand. "I mean, I was a teenager foolin' around, but I did it."

"That makes you an expert in my book," said Wallace with a smile. Then he laid out the rest of the plan. "There's a long concrete wall dividing the loading dock from Sombrero Beach Road. We can hide our trucks behind there while we load up. We can even make several trips if need be."

One of the women spoke up. "I think it's a good idea. As soon as it's dark, let's do it."

Wallace took a deep breath. "I want to do it right now, in the daytime, and here's why. Headlights at night draw attention. Plus, if we are noticed, we can't see anyone sneaking up on us. During the day, with our weapons, we can warn off anyone who tries to interfere. We can't be surprised."

"That's true," said one of the group. "Let them see us. It's not like they can call the cops. Right?"

"Some people have two-way radios," interjected another.

"Man, they're not gonna rat us out. They'll probably just hang around 'til we leave, hoping for a few crumbs."

Wallace liked the fact the group seemed to be in near unanimity with his approach. "Listen, there's no time like the present. Let's get our trucks together and check our fuel levels. I know it's only a couple of miles, but I don't want any hiccups. Also, bring your weapons and flashlights. We'll leave from here in an hour."

CHAPTER TWENTY-TWO

Tuesday, November 12
Morton Street
Grassy Key
Marathon

The Morton family compound jutted into the Gulf from Grassy Key on the eastern side of Marathon. Several properties had been held by the family on Morton Street since Marathon was developed in the early 1900s. The Mediterranean-inspired homes were set in lush, mature tropical vegetation. Each of the three homes had its own jetty projecting out into the water to create a safe space for their boats to dock.

When they arrived, they were surprised to see Commissioner Bud Marino and the other two district commissioners referenced in their conversation at the hospital the other day. They stood on the terrazzo-covered entry leading inside Cheryl Morton's home. The elderly woman stood just inside the doorway and was greeting the commissioners as Hank brought the car to a stop on the driveway.

Marino broke away from the group to hustle to Hank's truck. He opened the door for Erin and spoke to both of them as Hank came around the front bumper.

"I know you're surprised to see me here," he began. He glanced over his shoulder to determine whether they were being observed by their hostess. She'd escorted the other two commissioners inside and left the front door slightly ajar.

"Those two, also," said Hank. "Is this an ambush?"

Marino laughed. "No, of course not. Unless you get caught up in friendly fire. Listen, Hank. This may be presumptuous of me, but I felt compelled to move this thing along a little bit. I have news for you both, if you don't mind waiting until we get inside."

Erin and Hank looked at one another. They shrugged, and Hank said, "Lead the way."

Minutes later, everyone had exchanged pleasantries and got comfortable in Mrs. Morton's spacious living room, which overlooked her private beach. Hank was impressed.

"Let me bring Erin and Hank up to speed," began Marino. "Late yesterday afternoon, Sheriff Daly pulled virtually all of the sheriff's deputies assigned to Islamorada and Key Largo. They, along with several firefighters from our largest fire station, were ordered to report to Key West. The wife of one of the firefighters, who is a paramedic, rode with her husband from Islamorada. She returned just after midnight and pounded on my door, waking me up.

"This morning, Lindsey has Jock sending teams into food warehouses and grocery stores throughout Key West with the intention of emptying them all. Now, as we all know, this was not altogether unexpected. That said, I didn't expect them to act so quickly after the hurricane."

One of the other two commissioners spoke up. "Down our way, we've still got people wandering the streets whose homes were destroyed. I would've thought Lindsey would have more compassion than that."

"She's a vile woman," said Mrs. Morton. "She never should've been put into office in the first place. We're stuck with her, for now."

"I presume you know that's why we're here," said Erin.

"Yes. Before I begin, just so you know, I didn't vote for your boss either."

Erin laughed. "Understood. Half of America didn't. It's a funny thing about elections. Those who are placed into the highest positions of power automatically assume they have some kind of mandate from the people to implement their policies. They lose sight of the fact that half of the voters cast their ballot for the other guy."

"I'll try to bite my tongue when it comes to Carter Helton out of respect," said Mrs. Morton.

Erin studied the matriarch of the Morton family, who'd been a fixture in the Keys for more than a century. She seemed like a take-no-prisoners adversary, which was exactly whom Hank needed in his corner to remove Lindsey from office.

"I'm glad we see eye to eye on this mayor," said Erin. "Is there anything in the county's governing documents that allows for her to be removed from office?"

"Not at the county level, no," replied Mrs. Morton. "Florida laws governing recall must have been elected to a governing body of a municipality or a chartered county. There are twenty chartered counties in Florida; however, Monroe County isn't one of them.

"She is subject to recall under state law if she's served at least a quarter of her term in office, which she has. The next criteria relates to the grounds for the recall. They include, among other things, malfeasance, some permanent disability, conviction of a felony, drunkenness, and the two catchalls—neglect of duty and incompetence."

"I believe we could make a case for two or three of those," added Marino as he made eye contact with each of the attendees.

Hank leaned forward from the sofa he shared with Erin. "Suppose we make this argument to the residents of the Keys, then what?"

Mrs. Morton grimaced. "It's a time-consuming process that

certainly works against what you intend to do. You've got thirty days to gather the requisite signatures. Then the county clerk has a right to confirm them before turning the petition over to the supervisor of elections. Lindsey has the right to issue a statement of defense, followed by a formal recall petition and so on, including a special election. It's meant to require a somewhat lengthy period of time to prevent political lynchings and rash decisions."

Erin took a deep breath and sighed. "Is it possible to obtain a court order to force her to step down due to one of the criteria you listed? Perhaps the mayor pro tem, albeit an ally of the mayor's, would be a little less zealous or heavy-handed."

Mrs. Morton shook her head from side to side as she spoke. "The problem you have is that both the president's declaration of martial law and the mayor's own executive orders have suspended the Bill of Rights, including access to the courts. The streets may be lawless right now, but the halls of justice reek of tyranny."

"There has to be a way," said Hank under his breath.

"The quickest and most expeditious method is to force her resignation," said Mrs. Morton. "I can find nothing under state law or the governing documents of the Monroe County Board of County Commissioners that prevents the BOCC from calling a special meeting for this purpose. Her executive orders don't override the functions of the BOCC, even under these disastrous circumstances."

Marino perked up. "We could call an emergency meeting of the BOCC. The three of us could force her out and select a new mayor."

"We could also select another mayor pro tem," added one of the other commissioners.

"You'd have to show cause, in my humble opinion," interjected Mrs. Morton. "State law may require it, and certainly the will of the people would have to support it. Otherwise, the change might be seen as illegitimate, and you'd face an angry mob on every street corner. In other words, you might make matters worse."

"And we have the issue of Jock Daly," added Marino. "He's

rumored to be more than a loyal servant of the mayor's office. He's much closer to Lindsey than we realize. We'd better have the people on our side, or we'll see what martial law looks like."

"All or nothing, right?" asked Hank.

"That's correct," replied Mrs. Morton.

CHAPTER TWENTY-THREE

Tuesday, November 12
Key West

Sergeant Rivera led the caravan of SWAT vehicles into Conch Plaza's parking lot. A handful of stalled vehicles were scattered about. The Starbucks had been looted, and a tent city had been built in the tree-covered drive-through using tarps and four-by-eight sheets of corrugated steel that had been dislodged during the storm. As the assault vehicles entered the shopping center, out of curiosity the homeless residents followed them toward Gordon Food Service.

All of the other stores in the strip shopping center had been looted, including Bealls Outlet. The windows had been broken out, and the store appeared to have been ravaged. As Rivera's vehicle slowly rolled past, he became puzzled as to how the clothing and home décor store could have been thoroughly looted, yet the adjacent grocery store had not.

Sergeant Rivera, whose mother lived nearby, had visited Gordon's often to purchase groceries for his elderly mother. When the nation began to collapse following the nuclear attacks, he'd insisted his mother move into his home near the sheriff's department. He'd packed her most beloved belongings and food the day of the move. He hadn't returned since.

Gordon's was boarded up, but something bothered him about its appearance. There was no evidence that anyone had tried to loot the business, a rarity in Key West. Virtually every storefront was scarred by some effort to enter it.

The store's steel roll-up doors were one reason it hadn't been breached. The other might have been the vehicles tightly parked together under the canopy covering the portico entrance. A desperate looter might've attempted to gain entry by driving their vehicle into the steel doors, but the cars were arranged in such a way to prevent it.

Sergeant Rivera shrugged and shook off the strange feeling that had overcome him. It had been a safe and successful day thus far. He was certain Sheriff Jock and the mayor would be patting him on the back when he made his report.

All the trucks parked, and their occupants spilled out onto the sidewalk that ran parallel to the portico-covered driveway. Sergeant Rivera began to bark out his instructions to team A as well as B and C, which had rejoined them for this target.

"All right. Firefighters, you're up. Get us through these damn doors!"

The three men approached the easily identifiable roll-up doors. The interlocking galvanized steel slats rode upon heavy-gauge steel channel guides on both the inside and outside of the door frame. To gain access, they used a K-12 Fire Rescue Saw with a twelve-inch saw blade. The men traded turns to cut through the steel using several different angles and techniques. The high-torque engine squealed as it tore through the steel quickly.

After several minutes, an entry point the size of a small door frame had been opened up to allow the SWAT team members inside to clear the building, which was the size of a Trader Joe's grocery store. The six deputies had been inside the building for nearly two minutes when shots rang out.

"Team A, report!" shouted Sergeant Rivera.

The deputies shouted over one another.

"We're taking on fire!"

"They're on the catwalk above the registers!"

"No, at the rear—arrrrggggh!"

Automatic gunfire continued to explode inside the enclosed building. Suddenly, the other two roll-up doors began to slowly open. They were being pulled upward manually by a chain just inside the door. Sergeant Rivera drew his service weapon and ordered the firefighter members of team A to grab rifles out of the assault vehicles.

Rivera shouted into his two-way radio, "Team B! Team C! Report to the front entrance. Now!"

The commotion was beginning to draw a crowd as over two dozen curious bystanders crowded around the assault vehicles to watch. They pushed forward until they were near the canopy and the parked cars. Sergeant Rivera, focused on his team trapped inside, didn't notice the spectators behind him.

Two members of team A emerged from the side entries. As they walked backwards, they were firing wildly inside the dark store in an effort to provide cover for their SWAT team partners to escape.

"Deploying smoke!" a man shouted from inside the store.

"Roger that!" another shouted back.

The sounds of smoke canisters striking the polished concrete floor of Gordon's could be heard. Smoke began to billow through the entrances.

Rivera shouted into his microphone, "Abort! Abort!"

More gunfire, this time sending bullets sailing through the smoke-filled entrance and striking eight people who'd pushed their way toward the front entrance to get a better view.

Rivera continued to call out to his team to abort the mission. He yelled at the bystanders to fall back. He tried to call to the members of teams B and C to stand down, who, in the chaos, began to open fire as well. Soon, bullets were flying in and out of the entrance to the grocery store with neither side capable of seeing their targets due to the smoky conditions.

Several members of Sergeant Rivera's breach teams were wounded or killed. The same was true of more than a dozen civilians who got in the way of the barrage of bullets. Rivera called all of his breach teams to the scene. The rest hid behind their Level III bulletproof shields to move in formation as they reentered the building.

A gun battle raged for an hour or more as the sheriff's deputies fought the owners of the business and their hired guards. When it was over, seven deputies had died and another five were wounded. All of the guards and owners of the business were killed. The civilians who'd exposed themselves to the carnage suffered as well. Eleven died and nine suffered life-threatening wounds.

Sergeant Rivera had secured the food and supplies, but they came with a high cost.

CHAPTER TWENTY-FOUR

Tuesday, November 12
Driftwood Key

After Jessica got called away to help a wounded fisherman, Mike spent some time with Peter, Lacey, and Tucker with the newly acquired weapons he'd retrieved from the supply depot at the sheriff's office. Only a couple were department issue. The rest were confiscations that wouldn't be missed considering the state of confusion the department was operating under.

Tucker was especially attuned to Mike's instructions. Both Lacey and Peter had been weapons trained by their law-enforcement uncle while growing up, but Tucker had never been exposed to guns until the apocalypse. He soaked in the information that Mike imparted on the group and, at times, asked poignant questions that caught the seasoned LEO off guard.

"Do you carry your sidearm with a bullet in the chamber? Couldn't that second it takes to rack a round make all the difference between living or dying?"

Mike glanced at the adults and smiled. In his mind, he was telling them—*"Don't worry about the kid. He gets it."*

"That's a great question, Tucker. For me, I keep a round chambered. Here's the way I look at it. What are the chances that the second it takes to rack it will get you killed or hurt versus the likelihood of an accident because you're carrying a chambered round in the weapon strapped to your hip?

"Here's another way of putting it. If you're in a situation where you don't even have an extra second to move your hand, you're probably in real trouble anyway. Most self-defense scenarios don't play out that way, especially if you have good situational awareness.

"So, to answer your questions, I do keep a round chambered, but I've trained with weapons my entire adult life. For you, I don't think you should carry a weapon that is locked and loaded. What you need to focus on is your situational awareness."

Peter chimed in, "I think I'll follow that advice, too. As for situational awareness, it saved my ass more than once since my experience in Abu Dhabi. I learned constantly being aware of my surroundings was important for my personal security, especially now."

"Peter's right," said Mike. "Since this all went down, I keep reminding myself of a quote from that famous general Jim *Mad Dog* Mattis. He advised his Marines who were in Iraq at the time to be polite, be professional, but have a plan to kill everybody you meet. I've adopted that as my motto for when I have to deal with suspects in my job. I wish I'd applied it to Patrick Hollister. I'd be able to run more than twenty yards without getting winded."

Tucker was about to ask another question when Mike's two-way radio squawked to life.

"Sanchez for Albright. Over." Mike and the deputies assigned to his substation had agreed to dispense with the formalities on their radio calls. He was recognized as their supervisor, but none of them used their ranks when interacting with one another.

"Go ahead, Sanchez."

"A woman came into the substation claiming to have seen several pickup trucks approach the loading docks at the high school. She thought one of them, a teenager, was climbing on top of a backhoe parked near the building."

"Roger that," said Mike. He'd laid down a single law with his deputies when he gathered them together for the first time. The buddy system was always in effect. "I'm 10-53." He was en route to the station.

"Do you think they're breaking in?" asked Peter.

"Probably gonna try. I went by the high school the other day, and the buildings looked secure. But you know kids." Mike laughed as he mussed Tucker's uncharacteristically long hair.

Don Wallace was the group's field general. Everyone looked up to him, and he relished the opportunity to feel important once again. In his prior career, he'd operated a large road-construction business. During its heyday, he'd had multiple contracts with the state of Ohio, building new highways and resurfacing old ones. Then a period of hyperinflation hit America, causing building material prices to skyrocket. At the same time, the labor market became tight, and he was having difficulty keeping employees, much less hiring new ones. After making several large draws that included work that was yet to be completed, Wallace's house of cards collapsed. He allowed the business to close its doors. He liquidated his equipment and kept the advance payments he'd received from the state. Before he could be investigated and prosecuted, he and his wife slipped away and landed in the Florida Keys.

The glass breakage was sure to draw attention, but it was necessary. The young man who had volunteered to climb the boom of the backhoe and jump over to the suspended roof covering the loading dock did so with ease. Seconds after breaking through, he dove in head-first, his legs languishing half in and half out for a brief moment as if he were diving into a swimming pool.

"You two, cover that entrance. I need two more on the other side. If anyone from the neighborhood approaches, make sure they see your rifles. Don't get into conversations with them. The idea is to scare 'em off. Got it?"

With a quick nod, the four took off to man their posts. Wallace had plenty of people with him to locate the food storage within the high school and to load the trucks. What he didn't need was an audience.

"The rest of you, come with me. Let's move quickly through the building and locate what we need. Don't waste time unnecessarily searching through cabinets and desk drawers. This is a high school, not a jewelry store. Understand?"

The men and women agreed. A minute later, they were pacing in front of the roll-up doors, waiting for one of them to open. Wallace was growing frustrated. All the man had to do was come directly to the floor below him. How could he get lost?

"Hey, are you guys out there?" the man shouted from the center door.

Wallace rolled his eyes. *Yes, moron.* "Yeah, what's the problem?"

"The doors are run by a motor. There's no power. I've tried all the switches."

Wallace shook his head in disbelief. He should've sent in a second man with this guy. He nervously looked around. Standing on the platform of the loading dock exposed them to onlookers from the adjacent neighborhood.

"Disengage the locking mechanism," ordered Wallace. "Think of how you manually open your garage door. There won't be a rip cord, but somewhere near the motor or the guides, you'll find a locking bar."

After a minute, Wallace was about to ask the guy if he was doing anything when a series of loud metallic bangs could be heard. The door shook and rattled, startling the group who were waiting to enter. Then a slight gap appeared at the bottom. The man's fingers protruded from underneath.

"Hey, can you guys gimme a hand?"

The twenty-foot-tall steel panel door was heavy and required five men to lift it. Once it created an opening of four feet, a pallet was retrieved from near a dumpster to wedge under the door.

"All right, people. Let's split into two groups. Food service is most likely on the main level. Half of you head to the right, and we'll take the left side. Let's go!"

They broke off from one another, flashlights dancing around the hallways, entering the building as they searched for the storerooms. It took a couple of minutes to find what they were looking for.

"Bingo!" Wallace shouted. He thought he was a winner.

CHAPTER TWENTY-FIVE

Tuesday, November 12
Marathon

Hank and Erin left Mrs. Morton's home encouraged by the support shown by the three county commissioners but wary of whether the group could pull off what amounted to a coup d'état. Lindsey had allies throughout the county, some of whom were likely being compensated through her confiscation program.

The additional complicating factor was Lindsey's relationship to the sheriff. Jock's actions indicated he was in lockstep with her plans, and that didn't bode well. When a state's national guard was preoccupied with societal unrest in major cities like Miami and Tampa-St. Petersburg, a county sheriff's department was tantamount to an army.

"We don't have the luxury of time," began Hank in a defeatist tone. "My guess is Lindsey's been planning something like these confiscations since the president declared martial law. Obviously, Key West was the first likely target. However, it won't be long before Sheriff Jock will have his deputies heading up Seven Mile Bridge."

Erin patted Hank on the leg. "You've made some powerful friends. As I said, you definitely impressed Commissioner Marino at the hospital the other day. So much so, he stuck his neck out and approached the other commissioners."

"What I don't understand is why doesn't Marino carry the torch. He's obviously ready to make a move on Lindsey."

Erin was quick to reply. "He needs a political outsider who's known in the community. The Albright name obviously is respected in the Keys."

"Maybe. I'm just not so sure to what extent our family is that well known on the other keys. We've had very little to do with Key West. Folks in Islamorada know us, but not so much in Key Largo."

"That's where networking and the other commissioners come in," said Erin encouragingly. "You should solidify your support in the areas you know best. Show the other two commissioners this move is viable. Then let the mayor and sheriff hang themselves. Heavy-handed approaches to governing never work regardless of which side you're on. Eventually, the people turn on tyrants. You'll see."

"I hope you're right," said Hank until he suddenly leaned forward in his seat and gripped the steering wheel a little tighter. He pointed through the windshield. "Hey, that looked like Mike's truck with his emergency lights on. He turned by the Winn-Dixie."

"I saw him, too. He was in a hurry, wasn't he?"

"Hold on. Let's see what's going on." Hank accelerated and raced past the International House of Pancakes, which was in the process of being looted. He glanced over at the restaurant and simply shook his head as he focused on finding his brother.

———

"I've got two armed men with weapons at low ready near the utility yard," said Deputy Sanchez, who'd turned in his seat to remove the shotguns from the roof-mounted gun racks. "How do you wanna approach this?"

Mike pointed through the windshield. "They've seen us. What happens next is on them."

Mike raced into the high school parking lot, which was shared with the Florida Keys Community College. The two men retreated behind the wall, but Mike caught a glimpse of another man milling about at the other end. He, too, abruptly disappeared.

The first entrance to the parking lot had been blocked with a stalled car, so Mike drove past it, skidding to a stop on the sand-covered road at the next entry. He sat there for a moment while Sanchez racked rounds into the shotguns.

"That damn wall has our view blocked," Mike complained.

"We have to separate, Mike. Each of us will approach from a different end and converge on them in the middle."

"We need backup!" Mike was still agitated. He was trying to police Marathon with four deputies, one of whom was on Lower Matecumbe Key, and the other two had just gotten off of their shift.

Suddenly, one of the gunmen poked his rifle around the block wall and fired toward the truck. The bullets missed to the right, kicking up sand and asphalt as they skipped past.

"That's it! Idiots!" Mike exited the truck, and Sanchez followed his lead. Each ran in opposite directions to take up positions behind parked vehicles that afforded them a view of the utility yard. Sanchez ran in a low crouch until he reached a green power transformer adjacent to the building. He'd arrived undetected. Mike wasn't as fortunate.

Still easily winded due to his lung injury, he had to slow down as he reached a viburnum hedgerow that separated the utility yard from the school entrance. He was well concealed, but he had little in the way of ballistic protection. Just as he reached the hedges, bullets sailed over his head and ripped through the foliage. The gunmen had no way of knowing precisely where he was located, but they certainly had him pinned down.

Mike dared not shoot back. He remained in a low crouch, hidden from his assailants. He thought for a moment. These shooters weren't disciplined nor were they trained. He keyed the mic on his radio and whispered to Sanchez, "Fire on them. But be ready for them to fire back. I need you to draw their attention."

"Roger," Sanchez responded. Seconds later, the boom of his shotgun filled the air as he broke cover and quickly unloaded on a vehicle parked near the utility yard entrance. The windshield exploded as the pellets struck the truck. Then he shot again, purposefully aiming toward the end of the stucco retaining wall. Hunks of stucco and the underlying foam were torn away from the wall.

"Inside!" shouted one of the men. "Fall back and get inside! Now!"

Mike could hear their hurried footsteps as the shooters found their way to the concrete stairs leading to the loading dock. He peeked through a thin section of the viburnum hedge to get a better look.

Just as he stood to round the hedges and enter the utility yard, he heard a vehicle approaching from the main highway. He raised his shotgun and turned toward the sound, prepared to shoot. He slowly lowered his rifle and exhaled as he recognized the Suburban he'd obtained from the impound vehicle lot. The driver's side window was rolled down, and Hank shot him a concerned look.

Mike began waving his arm at Hank, directing him away from the scene. Shots rang out again as two of the gunmen began firing upon his position from the windows above the loading dock roof. Mike swung around and dropped to a knee. He was approximately two hundred feet away from the shooter, not optimal range for a shotgun, but close enough to cause serious injury.

He fired. The double-aught buckshot reached its target, blasting through the partially broken glass and striking the two men who foolishly failed to take cover. Both screamed in agony as they were knocked backwards. Mike had no way of knowing whether they were killed, but they certainly didn't fire back.

He rushed across the parking lot, glancing up at the building as he went. He noticed Sanchez break cover and run toward the stucco wall to get closer to the loading docks. He reached the Suburban just as Hank and Erin exited, weapons in hand.

"You two need to get back in the truck," Mike said angrily.

"Not gonna happen," Hank shot back. "What can we do to back you up?"

Mike brusquely grabbed his brother by the arm and led him around the truck to get them out of the open. He looked at Erin and then addressed Hank.

"These guys mean business. They fired on us first, Hank. That means they're stupid. Stupid is dangerous. You follow?"

"Yeah, I follow. And I'm not gonna let you take them on alone. I, um, we can handle ourselves."

Mike looked over the hood of the Suburban and confirmed Sanchez was in position. He shook his head but then came to the realization he and Sanchez were greatly outnumbered. He assessed their choice of weapons. Hank had a shotgun, and Erin was holding an AR-15. Both had their handguns tucked into paddle holsters at their waists. Erin even had a backup magazine in her jeans' back pocket.

"Geez, Hank. Are you sure about this?"

Before Hank could answer, another gunman showed up at the upper windows and fired toward Sanchez.

"Yes. Now, what do you want us to do?"

"Okay, Sanchez and I have to flush them out," he began. He turned toward the building and gestured as he spoke. "I need you and Erin to take up positions on each end of that stucco wall. If they come toward you, and they're armed, then you shoot them. Understand? None of this hands-up-or-I'll-shoot nonsense. If they're armed, shoot them."

"No problem," said Erin. Her look of determination gave Mike a comfort level to proceed.

"Agreed," added Hank.

Mike whispered into his radio, "We've got backup. We're moving."

Sanchez readied his rifle and leaned around the corner of the wall, focusing on any movement in the broken window. He responded, "Move!"

CHAPTER TWENTY-SIX

Tuesday, November 12
Marathon High School

Mike and Deputy Sanchez worked together now. With Hank and Erin ensuring nobody else entered the building after they did, the trained law enforcement officers could feel comfortable they wouldn't get trapped. There were four pickup trucks backed up to the loading dock. Mike checked their exhaust pipes to confirm they were still warm from being recently driven. He expected there could be as many as eight armed gunmen inside, plus the two who were likely wounded from his shotgun blast.

He led Sanchez into the spacious receiving room. They both walked in a low crouch, separating once they were inside so as not to present their attackers with a single target. It was oddly quiet. Mike expected to be fired upon as soon as their silhouettes appeared inside the building, but they found themselves alone. There were no whispers or muffled coughs. No footsteps echoing across the concrete floor. The loading docks were devoid of human activity other than Mike and his deputy.

Mike motioned for Sanchez to walk along the perimeter walls of the intake room. He did the same, constantly checking on his partner as they encircled the space that led to a single set of double doors in the center of the back wall.

The fixed door latches had been opened, resulting in the spring-assisted door being left slightly ajar. Mike dropped to a knee and cradled his shotgun with his right arm. Using his left, he slowly pushed the door open, wincing as it creaked on its hinges. He held his breath, assuming a barrage of gunfire would be thrown in their direction.

Nothing.

Great, he thought to himself. Now these guys had found some discipline. Mike knew the dynamics had changed. He put his game face on and made a decision to head toward his left down the corridor. To his right was the community college, and to his recollection, it did not have a full cafeteria like the high school did. Its portion of the storage warehouse was probably dedicated to sanitation supplies and the like.

He whispered across the door opening to his partner. He pointed his hand down the left corridor. "Sanchez, take the lead. I'll cover our back."

Mike pressed the button on the tactical flashlight mounted to the Mossberg 590's Picatinny rail system. He swept the barrel of his shotgun up and down the hallway. Satisfied the corridor was clear, he moved to the right and once again pointed left, indicating Sanchez should get started.

The two men walked in tandem. Sanchez concentrated on the upcoming door openings in the hallway. Mike walked backwards, focusing on their rear while periodically swinging around to check his deputy's progress.

Sanchez had been trained in search techniques by the sheriff's department. In fact, he was one of the better deputies at the MCSO. Mike was lucky the man lived in Marathon, making him a logical addition to the newly formed substation.

They moved quickly along the painted block wall until they reached the first doorway. With their backs flattened near the door opening, they focused their hearing on any sounds indicating movement in the room. They shared a nod, and Sanchez led the way inside, moving to the right while Mike slid along the wall to the left.

While being cautious, they wanted to hit the rooms aggressively with the intention of startling any of the gunmen lying in wait. Tensions were high as their flashlights illuminated the space, searching for a target. Several cubicles were located in the center of the room, providing ample cover for the gunmen. Mike dropped to a knee and swept the flashlight underneath the partitions, which were three inches above the concrete floor.

Satisfied there wasn't anyone hiding in the cubicles, he motioned to Sanchez to move quickly along the outer walls. Just as they'd done in the spacious loading dock area, they kept their backs against the perimeter of the room, their eyes darting around the space in front of them as well as back to the door through which they'd entered.

After clearing the first room, they carefully reentered the hallway to move on to a room down the hall to the right. A large set of double steel doors were closed, unlike the next door in the hallway to the left, which was open.

Mike could've easily assumed this room was unoccupied, but he left nothing to chance. After he and Sanchez were in position, he slowly turned the knob and pushed it open. This open area had windows on the back side, and just enough ambient light was available for him to get a good look at the layout.

The perimeter walls were lined with cubicles, all of which contained a rolling office chair and a desktop computer. In the center, there were half a dozen utility tables with folding chairs around them. The space could've been used as a meeting room or even a break room for the cafeteria and loading dock employees. The sheer amount of clutter and furniture in the room gave him pause.

Mike stepped through the doorway first, attempting to lead by example. Sanchez immediately followed and moved to the right as before. Suddenly, there was a muzzle flash, and several bullets stitched the wall to Mike's left. He dropped to a knee and held his position. He racked a round and fired in the direction of the muzzle flash. The shooter fell in a heap.

Another gunman was in the opposite corner of the room, hiding behind some boxes. He shot in the deputy's direction. However, his bullets were deflected by the metal folding chairs around the tables. Sanchez didn't hesitate to return fire directly into the stack of boxes. Some of the buckshot made it through, injuring the gunman. When he fell into the open, Sanchez pulled his service weapon from his utility belt and shot him again.

Mike and Sanchez quickly approached the two bodies sprawled out on the tiled floor. Blood splatter covered their clothing and the walls behind them. The holes in their chests and throats were all the evidence Mike needed to confirm their deaths.

"They look like soccer dads, not gangbangers," quipped Sanchez.

Mike kept an eye on the door and responded, "Everybody's a banger in the apocalypse."

"Four?" asked Sanchez as he led the way back into the hallway.

Mike whispered his response. "We've still got work to do."

They cleared two more rooms and made their way to the end of the corridor, where two double doors were propped open with cases of bottled water. They had to be extremely careful now, as the gunfire just gave away their approach.

Mike's flashlight illuminated the sizeable storage room that rose two stories to an open-beam ceiling. The interior was filled with steel shelving full of dry goods and pallets of boxes. Above their heads, a catwalk filled with boxes extended around the second level.

This was the high school's storage area and the prize the intruders sought. The numerous obstructions and the potential for gunmen having the high ground would make this a difficult space to clear. Mike took a deep breath and contemplated his best approach. The large size of the warehouse coupled with the amount of shelving in the center made splitting up unwise.

He also wanted to limit the ingress and egress to the room. Mike leaned into Sanchez and whispered his instructions. "Help me with these cases of water. I wanna seal off this exit, or at least make it difficult for them to come in or out."

He and Sanchez worked in near silence as one lifted the water and the other slowly closed the door. This also served to make the room darker, a benefit for the trained law enforcement officers. The two men slid along the wall and dropped into a crouch, using the minimal light to get a feel for the space. Mike's eyes darted around the room in search of light sources. Closing the double doors to the corridor limited their visibility of the lower level, but the catwalk's details had appeared.

"I see a doorway above this one. It's producing the most light, probably from the windows overlooking the loading docks. There has to be an exit into the high school opposite this one. There are a couple of skylights on the back side of the roof, but I'm guessing they're covered in soot because they don't allow much light in."

Sanchez continually scanned the perimeter. "They're here, Mike. I can feel them."

"Me too. Let me take the lead, and you watch our backs. Let's make our way to the staircase leading to the upper level. I'd feel better if we got eyes on the two who were shooting at us from the windows. Plus, I'd rather have the high ground myself."

Sanchez tapped the detective-turned-substation-commander on the shoulder. The two men, separated by a few feet, moved along the wall, keeping their bodies as low to the ground as possible. Just as they reached the staircase, the sound of gunfire outside the building stopped them dead in their tracks.

CHAPTER TWENTY-SEVEN

Tuesday, November 12
Marathon High School

For a split second, it wasn't clear who was more surprised to encounter a man with a gun—Don Wallace as he raced along the viburnum hedge in his attempt to escape, or Hank Albright, who heard the man's footsteps crunching through the dead zoysia grass.

Hank turned the corner and abandoned his cover behind the stucco wall just as Wallace appeared at the end of the hedgerow. Hank's sudden appearance startled the left-handed Wallace, who tried to point his handgun in Hank's direction. His nervous trigger finger fired into the ground beside his feet and then wildly to the right, ricocheting off the school's flagpole with a loud *ping*.

Hank didn't hesitate. He'd already racked a birdshot shell into his marine shotgun and fired at Wallace. The birdshot was designed to wound any would-be attacker before the second shell full of double-aught buckshot finished the job.

However, at a range of just forty feet, the birdshot caused significant harm to the man. Wallace's right shoulder was ripped open, leaving tendons and muscle dangling from where his bicep once was. He spun around and landed on his knees, frozen in that position until he fell onto the sandy soil.

He was not dead. Hank carefully approached the man with his shotgun pointed at his chest. Wallace's chest rose and fell as he gasped for air. Several pellets had torn through his clothing and hit his chest. Yet he still held his weapon in his left hand. He was about to raise it to shoot at Hank when more gunfire emanated from the breezeway connecting the warehouse building to the high school.

Two more men were racing in Hank's direction, carrying handguns. Both were shooting at him, spraying bullets over his head and into the ground on both sides. Hank quickly backpedaled to get cover behind the stucco wall. He frantically searched for Erin, looking behind him toward the other end of the wall, but she was gone.

"Shit!" he whispered loudly to himself.

He was concerned for her safety and had no idea where she went. He intently listened for the approaching gunmen to gauge their location. He dared not look around the wall, as they might shoot him.

Then a single gunshot broke his concentration, followed by an explosion. This was followed by another a few seconds later. Then another coming from the other side of the utility wall. He put two and two together. Erin was shooting out their tires, eliminating their means to escape.

Hank shouldered the shotgun and pulled his handgun. He dropped to a knee and readied his weapon. Mike had always advised him to keep his body low to the ground to create a smaller target and because nervous, untrained shooters had a tendency to fire over the heads of their targets.

Without looking for a target, Hank quickly stretched his hand around the edge of the wall and fired in the direction of the man he'd shot earlier. If Erin was approaching, he wanted to distract the two gunmen.

They fired back at him, embedding several rounds in the top of the stucco wall. They missed their target. Erin did not.

The men's gunshots gave her a point of reference to release several rounds from the AR-15 into the viburnum hedge. Two of the NATO 5.56 rounds found their mark, striking the gunmen in some manner.

Hank holstered his handgun and racked another shell into his shotgun. He didn't hesitate to swing around the wall and immediately shoot toward Wallace's location. The shot hit Wallace and another man who was kneeling on the ground next to him. The man's body was flung backwards as blood and flesh flew across the dying grass.

The third man began running back toward the breezeway, half turning and firing his handgun toward Hank. The bullets missed badly and shredded the hedges. Hank rushed toward the man until he planted his feet and unleashed two rounds out of his shotgun in rapid succession. Both blasts tore through his shoulders and back, killing him instantly.

"Hank!" shouted Erin, who rushed around the hedges with the barrel of her rifle pointed toward the two men left bleeding in the grass.

"I'm good," he replied. He walked back slowly, racking another round in his shotgun while keeping a leery eye on the breezeway. "Are you okay?"

"Fine. Are they ..." Her voice trailed off.

Hank turned to kick their bodies. Neither of the dead men responded. Then, in unison, he and Erin picked up their weapons and tossed them into the shrubs.

"Did you disable their trucks?" he asked.

She glanced toward the loading docks and nodded. "What should we do?"

Hank looked around. A crowd of residents had gathered, remaining safely across Sombrero Beach Road to watch the action. Most were tucked behind the pilings of the colorful homes that faced the man-made canal. Others peered through their upper-level windows, watching the spectacle unfold. Hank focused his attention back on the task at hand.

"Let's do what Mike told us. We gotta trust his abilities on the inside."

———

Mike desperately wanted to leave the building to help his brother, but when the barrage of gunfire rang out, the remaining gunmen panicked. They began to fire their weapons indiscriminately throughout the warehouse. Containers of liquid were punctured. Bags of flour were torn open by the bullets spreading a cloud of white into the air. Canned goods were knocked off shelves, clanking to the floor, making it difficult to differentiate between the sound of their shell cartridges plinking to the concrete and a can of vegetables being knocked off a shelf.

While Mike was ready to dispatch the gunmen, he also wanted to stop the wasteful destruction of food. He used their panicked firing against them by identifying their locations in the near darkness.

One of the shooters was on the catwalk near the single door leading to the upstairs hallway. Mike slapped Sanchez on the leg and took off toward the stairway leading up a level while the panicked shooters continued to fire in all directions without any identifiable target.

Walking silently on the concrete and wood steps, they made their way up to the catwalk. Keeping their bodies close to the shelving attached to the outer walls of the room, they moved rapidly at a low crouch toward the gunman on the upper level, who was now leaning over the rail in search of a target.

All of a sudden, several shots broke the silence. Mike immediately spotted the source through the muzzle flash. The man on the catwalk fell to his knees and began shouting.

"That's me you shot at, dumbass!"

"Sorry. I didn't know."

Mike took advantage of the confusion and moved deftly along the catwalk to get into position. As soon as the gunman on the upper level stood upright, Mike shot him without hesitation. He rushed toward the body and fired another round from his service weapon into the man's chest.

Below, there were panicked shouts coming from the two remaining gunmen. They fired into the ceiling, knocking out one of the skylights. Then their heavy footsteps could be heard running away from Mike's position.

Mike searched for the sliver of daylight coming from the exit door on the opposite side of the building. He had a clear shot at the door. He held his breath, trained his weapon on the exit leading to the breezeway, and waited.

It took just seconds for him to find his target. The men ran side by side and slammed into the doors simultaneously. The moment the panic bars were hit with their hands to open the double doors, Mike fired in rapid succession, sending round after round into their bodies until they crashed through the doors and landed facedown on the concrete sidewalk. Their motionless bodies lay half in and half out of the doorway. Dead.

Any return fire never materialized, so Mike and Sanchez cleared the second floor of the building. When they returned to the catwalk, they could see Hank standing over the two gunmen with his shotgun pointed at their heads. Mike finally exhaled and holstered his sidearm. He cradled his shotgun and turned to Sanchez.

"What's your body count?"

Sanchez thought for a brief moment. "Three up here. Three down there. Those two in the doorway. Plus whatever happened outside. It's possible we missed somebody."

Mike chuckled. "I dare them to stick their heads out of whatever hole they crawled into."

CHAPTER TWENTY-EIGHT

Tuesday, November 12
Marathon High School

Mike and Sanchez joined Hank on the sidewalk, where he continued to stand over the dead men. He cradled the shotgun in his arms and wiped the sweat off his brow. Hank had been through a gunfight before and knew what to expect. He silently said a prayer thanking God for keeping his family safe once again.

He turned his attention to Mike and Sanchez, who squinted to allow their eyes to adjust to the daylight. "You guys good?"

"Yeah," Mike said, mindlessly kicking the legs of the two dead men bleeding on the pavement between them. He half-waved to Erin, who stood over the other three dead men. Her head was on a swivel, looking between the hedges toward the loading dock and across the street toward the crowd of people who'd accumulated in the street. "What's all that?" He pointed toward the onlookers.

"We made plenty of noise, I guess," replied Hank. "Erin shot out their tires, by the way. If there are any stragglers, they're walking home."

"There might be, but I believe they're long gone," said Mike.

"Plus, we have a few dead guys inside. Did they give you any trouble?" His face showed his concern for the onlookers, who were inching closer.

"No, they stayed hidden behind pilings and cars. I doubt they want any piece of this." Hank pointed the barrel of his shotgun toward the two dead men.

Mike took a few steps toward where Erin stood. He studied the crowd, who continued to inch closer. He estimated there were more than a dozen of them. He turned to address his deputy.

"Sanchez, go to my truck and grab a couple of rolls of crime scene tape. I'm not sure it'll keep them out, but we gotta try something."

"Do you think they're gonna rush us?" asked Hank.

"The building. They want what's inside as much as these guys. Only, they aren't willing to die for it." Mike paused and then added as he unconsciously raised the barrel of his shotgun slightly, "I hope."

"Is it full?" asked Hank.

"Pretty much. These morons shot it up, but there are a lot of nonperishables inside."

Sanchez returned with the yellow and black tape containing the lettering CRIME SCENE DO NOT CROSS. Mike instructed him to cordon off both entrances to the utility yard in front of the loading dock and from the hedgerow to the entrance to the high school.

"You know what," began Hank. "Let me go talk to them."

Hank wandered away from Mike and Sanchez to join Erin.

"Is it over?" she asked.

"Yeah. However, we need to make sure these people don't do anything stupid. Wanna help me?"

She nodded and lowered her weapon so as not to appear to be a threat. Erin was aware that the mere appearance of an AR-15 sent some people screaming into the night. They walked side by side toward the crowd, causing some to react by backing up several paces. Hank noticed this first and began to speak as he approached.

His goal was to satisfy the curious and to warn them against interfering.

"Hi, folks! My name is Hank Albright, and this is Erin Bergmann. If you have a moment, let me bring you up to speed on what just happened."

Erin made eye contact and gave him a reassuring smile. Hank nodded his appreciation. What he was about to say would spread around Marathon faster than the *Coconut Telegraph* could be printed.

"Don't you own the inn on Driftwood Key?" asked one woman.

"That's right. And my friend, Erin, is the United States Secretary of Agriculture. She's here to help us through this mess."

"What happened over there?" asked a man in the front of the group.

Hank glanced over his shoulder and then explained. He chose his words carefully in order to send a very clear message. "Those armed gunmen thought they were entitled to something they weren't. Many in our community are suffering. They're sick, hungry, and thirsty. But that doesn't give a few the right to load up in their trucks, arm themselves with guns, and break into a place like the high school to steal. My brother and his loyal deputy took decisive action to protect this food for everyone in Marathon, not just a handful who thought they could take it by force. They paid the ultimate price for their rash decision and brazen attempts to kill two members of our law enforcement."

A shy woman at the rear of the group pushed her way to the front. "There have been people breaking into our homes at night. They carried guns and threatened to kill us if we tried to stop them. They robbed my sister's house across the canal. She was hiding in a closet and overheard them say they were from the Tarpon Harbour apartments."

Erin addressed her. "Thank you for this information, ma'am. We'll provide it to the detective and his deputies. Does anyone else know anything about these break-ins?"

Suddenly, several people in the crowd began to relay what they'd heard and experienced. The home invasions had a chilling effect on everyone in the adjoining neighborhoods, who were just trying to survive. Their plight was made all the more difficult by the brazen robberies.

Hank and Erin listened intently to their stories, mentally taking notes to share with Mike. As the conversation died down, one man was bold enough to ask what was on most of their minds.

"Hey, is there any food in there?" he asked.

"How about fresh water?" chimed in another.

Hank wasn't sure how to answer the questions. He presumed to know why they were asking. "Well, we were a little busy, as you can imagine, to take inventory. After the deputy secures the building, I'm sure some kind of inventory will be taken. Technically, it's the property of the county, so I'm not sure—"

"It sure would help those of us who had our food stolen by those thieves!" a man in the back shouted.

"Can't argue with that!" added another.

Hank began to wonder if the crowd was going to remain friendly. They might not have been armed, but they outnumbered them by six to one. So to pacify them, he lied. He stuck his neck out and made a promise he wasn't sure he could keep.

"I'm going to propose we create a food bank for the residents of Marathon, starting with the food storage held in the high school. We also need to set up some type of barter market or exchange location. You know, someone who might have too much bleach can trade a bottle for someone who has some extra canned goods. It's being done up north and can be done here also."

"That's a great idea, Hank!" shouted a woman who stood off to the side.

"We've all talked about it, but nobody does anything. Thank you, sir!" said a man in the crowd.

Erin chimed in, "We will contact your mayor about a possible location. Maybe we can do it here at the high school or through the churches. It's not such a great idea to be out in this air, you know."

The onlookers were enthusiastically on board with the proposal.

"Let's do it. I have fish to trade in exchange for stuff."

"Same here!"

"When will it start?"

Hank leaned into Erin and whispered in a sarcastic tone, "We're all in now."

CHAPTER TWENTY-NINE

Tuesday, November 12
Administration Building
Key West

Lindsey had just received a briefing from her mayor pro tem and Sheriff Jock. She dismissed her staff and loyalists but asked Jock to remain behind. Once her office suite had been cleared, she pulled a bottle of scotch out of her desk drawer and poured them both drinks in Dixie cups intended for the pitcher of water on her credenza.

"Why do you look so pissy, Jock? I consider this a good start. Not great, but good."

"I lost deputies today." His tone was solemn. He threw back the scotch and poured himself another. He paced the floor as he spoke. "Sure, we had a good run on the most valuable location on our target list, but obviously we were done after the Gordon's debacle."

Lindsey wasn't much for consoling the men in her life. In her mind, emotional men were weak. She used their weakness to lead them to do her bidding. Jock Daly was no different. She'd kept him on a tight leash for years, and she didn't need him to get soft on her now.

She walked around her desk to rub his shoulders. He closed his eyes, and the tension was immediately released from his body. She spoke in soft tones as she tried to lift his spirits.

"Your teams had no way of knowing those guys were locked up in that building. From what your sergeant said in the debrief, they were pros. Ex-LEOs or even military. It could've been much worse."

Jock nodded but still lamented the death of his men. "It's gonna make it difficult to keep our deputies interested in the raids."

Lindsey rolled her eyes behind his back. "Here's what you have to remind them of. A large portion of the food we secure will go to their families. They are being rewarded with the gift of life. Is it risky? Damn straight. Will they die if they don't take the risk? Sooner or later, yes."

"I know. I'll make sure that's drilled into the new teams tomorrow morning before they start again. It's gonna be a bigger challenge, you know. The word spread throughout Key West. Now, you have business owners redoubling their efforts to secure their buildings. Those with guns are marching up and down the sidewalks, threatening to shoot anyone who comes close. There's an angry mob outside demanding to know what happens to the food that's being confiscated."

Lindsey returned to her desk and plopped into her chair with a full cup of scotch. She took a sip while studying her sheriff and occasional lover.

"Jock, you might have to make examples of a few people. Do you follow me?"

"Do you want me to shoot the doughnut shop owner?" he said with a hint of snark.

Lindsey didn't appreciate the retort but admired his spunk. At least he wasn't feeling sorry for himself any longer. "No, not necessarily. Your rules of engagement should remain the same. Return fire when fired upon. If someone tries to shoot one of your people, shoot to kill, and then leave the body for everyone to see. I think that'll tamp down any resistance."

"There were quite a few civilians killed in the gun battle at Gordon's."

Lindsey smirked. "They should've stayed the hell out of the way, then. Listen, Jock. There's gonna be collateral damage in all of this. You understand that, right? It's unavoidable. If word spreads through the town like you said, maybe part of that message will be to avoid getting involved."

"I get it. We'll see how tomorrow goes. However, I get the sense your constituents are rippin' pissed at what happened at Gordon's today."

"They'll get over it when we start handing out rations in a week or so."

The sheriff wandered to the window and looked over the crowd of people who were huddled outside the administration building. They were animated. Agitated. Some were distraught.

"I hope we can make it until then," he mumbled as he finished his second drink.

"We'll be fine. If they make trouble, clamp down. Got it?" Lindsey was ready to move on to the rumors she'd heard from Marathon.

"Are you going to send someone up to Marathon High School to find out what happened today? My staff was told there was a shoot-out between some of your people and armed gunmen who broke into the high school."

Jock didn't have anyone to spare to investigate the shooting. He was going on what he'd heard through the rumor mill. "All we know so far is that a group of men and women, maybe eight to ten in total, broke into the high school warehouse to steal food. Mike Albright, who's in charge of the substation up there, responded with a deputy. They surprised the burglars, and that's when the shooting began. From what I'm told, all of those involved in the break-in were killed."

Lindsey was both perplexed and curious. "By two men?

Detective Albright and a single deputy?" She reached for the bottle of scotch to pour herself another drink and made a mental note to add a state-run ABC liquor store to tomorrow's raid list.

Jock responded as she retrieved the bottle, "Well, no. Actually, they had some help. Apparently, Hank Albright showed up at the scene with a woman. I think her name was Bergmann, or something like that. My source said she claimed to be some kind of Washington bigwig."

The blood flowed out of the mayor's face as it turned ashen white. She slammed the bottle of scotch on her desk and immediately stood up. "Erin Bergmann? Secretary of Agriculture for that scumbag Helton?"

Jock shrugged. He had no idea who the Secretary of Agriculture was and what she'd be doing in the Keys. All he knew was the information genuinely struck a nerve with Lindsey.

"I can find out—" he began to respond before she cut him off.

"Listen to me, Jock. You send someone you trust to Marathon and find out what the hell is going on up there. Confirm whether she's in my county. She could be working with President Helton to come after me."

"Come on, Lindsey. You're just being paranoid."

Her face turned from white with fear to red rage. She slammed the palm of her hand on her desk, causing the Dixie cup half full of scotch to jump slightly.

"I'm not messing around. Find out if this is true and where this woman is staying. Was she with Hank? Why is she here? Who has been in contact with her? Everything!"

PART IV

Day twenty-seven, Wednesday, November 13

CHAPTER THIRTY

Wednesday, November 13
U. S. Army War College
Carlisle Barracks
Carlisle, Pennsylvania

Following the morning briefing, President Helton and Chief of Staff Chandler returned to the presidential office suite to discuss the reports they'd received. In just three weeks, there had been twelve million deaths resulting directly from the nuclear detonations. Another thirty-five million had died indirectly from starvation, lack of clean water, and societal collapse. That number was rising exponentially by the day, with his FEMA administrator estimating that at least two-thirds of the U.S. population would be dead within a year.

"Mr. President, I appreciate FEMA providing us these estimates," said Chandler as he closed the door to the president's office behind them. "However, I think he's overly pessimistic. I believe the American people will come together to help one another."

"I don't know, Harrison. Our power grid is the beating heart of this nation. Our near-total reliance on electricity and what happens when that heart stops beating is beginning to show."

Chandler sighed. "I have to admit the report from Director McClain was dire. As much money as we spend, we couldn't manage to carve out a billion here and a billion there to harden our grid."

Tom McClain was the director of FERC, the Federal Energy Regulatory Commission's Office of Energy Infrastructure Security. During the briefing, he'd accused prior administrations of adopting the proverbial ostrich-head-in-the-sand approach. The consequences of a complete loss of the electrical grid were too terrible to think about; therefore, political leaders didn't. The Helton administration was equally culpable.

President Helton agreed, expanding on his chief of staff's point. "All it would take was to add those neutral current-blocking devices between our major transmission systems. McClain said protecting two hundred of these critical transformers would've prevented the cascading failure we experienced."

"A twenty-million-dollar investment would've prevented this," lamented Chandler.

The two men grew quiet for a moment as they contemplated Chandler's words. Now they faced a monumental task of replacing hundreds of transformers around the country. It wasn't just the cost of replacing them that was daunting. It was the production process. It would take many years for foreign manufacturers to build the transformers to meet America's specifications. Not to mention the single biggest producer of power equipment was China, America's biggest economic and geopolitical rival.

The president was anxious to change the subject, although there wasn't much of anything to lighten the mood. "The Pentagon seems to think they'll have troops and National Guardsmen in a position to take control of the major cities soon."

"That's where the greatest loss of life has occurred," said Chandler with a nod. "The battle for resources, namely food and water, has resulted in anarchy. The problem, however, is that FEMA doesn't have enough supplies stored to last these high-population areas more than a week or so. They may be successful in restoring order, although it won't last as our food and water resources dwindle."

The president spun in his office chair to study a large wall map of the United States. Pushpins and markers identified certain cities as being priorities. Boundaries were drawn around areas that were considered hotspots to be avoided by the military. In other words, hopeless. Examples were the major cities hit by the nuclear bombs and large population areas that were completely lawless.

"Harrison, we have to play god. I can't believe that we're in this situation. But, honestly, the only way to move forward is to decide who to save and leave the rest of the nation to fend for themselves. We simply cannot save everybody."

"I've thought about this as well, Mr. President, but I wouldn't dare bring it up during our briefings. I will say that it's likely on the minds of your closest advisors."

"Has anyone said anything?"

"No, but I've studied them since we began making your cabinet choices. Other than Erin, I've had a pretty good read on them. At some point when you're ready to broach the subject of rebuilding certain parts of the nation first to the detriment of other parts, I believe they'll be receptive."

The president stood to take a closer look at the map. "Do we focus on saving the most? You know, focus on our large regional cities like New York, Chicago, and Philly, of course."

Chandler had given this some thought. "In the short term, seven to ten years, as nuclear winter continues to plague us, I think we should consider midsize cities in the Sunbelt. Their level of societal collapse is less than in the Northeast and the West Coast. Besides, people are already migrating to typically warmer climates."

The president ran his fingers through his thinning hair and sighed. "We've got to resolve this Texas situation. That state could support many refugees in a climate that could still support agriculture. Florida, too."

Chandler brought up Erin. "Bergmann hasn't checked in with me since her arrival in the Keys. I need to touch base with her."

The president turned to his chief of staff. "We have a lot on our platter, but insurrection doesn't need to be one of them. Whether it's small uprisings like what we've experienced in the Mountain West, the UP, and the Keys, or those damn Texans, this has to be dealt with. I don't know who is a bigger threat to our nation. The looters in the major cities or the people who think they can spit on the Constitution."

His chief of staff and longtime friend agreed. "If we don't nip it in the bud, then others will follow their lead."

"What if we make an example of one of these wild-card communities? Obviously, Texas is a whole nother matter. The groups in Idaho are too small and the state is too remote for word to spread of the military successfully tamping down the uprisings. The Upper Peninsula of Michigan is similar."

"The Florida Keys are different," interjected Carter. "Unlike the other regions where armed militia created barricades and warned off federal government personnel, the locals down there destroyed bridges that likely won't be rebuilt until the nation has power. And even then there are other more pressing projects to address."

"So you consider their actions the worst offender?" asked the president.

"Well, Texans are the worst, but to make an example of them would require something akin to a war. The Keys are different. Our Coast Guard vessels with a couple of Marine platoons would bring it to an end."

President Helton tried to imagine the Marines storming the beaches of the Florida Keys. Would they face opposition? How ugly might it be? He took a deep breath and turned to Chandler.

"Reach out to Erin. Tell her the clock's ticking. She's got days, not weeks, to give me what I sent her there to do."

CHAPTER THIRTY-ONE

Wednesday, November 13
Driftwood Key

"Well, that was interesting," said Erin as she reentered the main house. Hank and Mike stood in the foyer, awaiting her return from the unexpected phone call. She'd kept the satellite phone charged intermittently when Sonny ran the generator to maintain the temperature in the refrigerator. During that quick one-hour time period, everyone in the main house scrambled to undertake chores or charge devices, from cell phones to flashlight batteries.

"Was it the president?" asked Mike.

Erin returned the satphone to the charger that sat atop the reception desk along with several other devices, including Mike's police-issued two-way radio. She glanced around the rooms leading into the spacious foyer.

In a whisper, she replied, "Let's talk in the car."

Hank nodded and grabbed his shotgun from behind the door. All of them carried handguns and rifles whenever they left Driftwood Key. For most, a sidearm was strapped to their waist during every waking moment. It had become the new normal.

Mike checked with Sonny and Phoebe in the kitchen before the trio left. Hank took Erin by the arm and led her onto the front porch, where they slipped on their surgical masks. As they did, he leaned into her.

"Problems?"

Erin grimaced. "I'd call it more of an ultimatum. A deadline."

"Or what?" asked Hank, but before she could answer, Mike joined them.

That morning, they'd decided to try a direct approach by appealing to Lindsey in her office. They hoped to stave off an inevitable confrontation with the woman who was once Sonny and Phoebe's sister-in-law. While Hank and Erin tried to meet with her, Mike would spend his time at the sheriff's department to learn what he could about the raids.

After they were secured inside Mike's truck, they removed their masks. The air quality was slowly deteriorating, and the group considered themselves to be fortunate to have a large supply of medical masks from the hospital. After they spoke to Peter and Tucker at the gate, they slowly made their way toward U.S. 1.

Erin explained what she meant by an ultimatum. "Here's what's disconcerting. That was the nicest that Harrison Chandler has been since the day I was sworn in as Secretary of Agriculture. Our relationship has gone south ever since. His sudden change of attitude makes me think he's up to something."

Hank was confused. "But you said he gave you an ultimatum. A deadline. That doesn't sound pleasant to me."

"Oh, make no mistake, Mr. Chandler was all peaches and cream until he whipped out the knives and said we only have days, not weeks, to get Lindsey removed from office."

Mike shook his head in disbelief as he wheeled his truck onto the highway. As he spoke, he maneuvered around a number of stalled cars and entered the Seven Mile Bridge.

"What does he expect us to do? Storm the palace?"

Erin shrugged. "That's the thing. It was an ultimatum, sort of, but he didn't actually tell me what the consequences are. I could read between the lines as to where he's coming from. The president is overwhelmed."

"Not that anyone could blame him," interjected Hank.

Mike disagreed. "Hey, he wasn't drafted for the job. He actually fought tooth and nail to get it."

"According to Chandler, the president is most concerned with the nation not sticking together in the crisis. Sure, there are parts of the country that are on fire, literally and figuratively. Chandler alluded to some tough decisions the president would be making soon, but he didn't elaborate. Anyway, apparently Texas and other parts of the country continue to separate themselves from the rest of the nation. Communities are becoming increasingly territorial. The president feels he needs to put a stop to it before this independent-minded thinking takes hold."

Hank turned in his seat to look at Erin as he spoke. "Is he blaming the Keys for this? I mean, we have no idea what's happening in Texas, and I seriously doubt they know what we're up to."

"I agree with you, Hank," she replied. "This president ain't no Harry Truman. The buck doesn't stop with him. It's always someone else's fault."

"Just like Lindsey," Mike quipped.

"In more than one respect, Mike," added Erin. "Both of them believe they should confiscate property, whether real estate or personal belongings, to be redistributed to those in need. Your mayor is doing it on the localized level, and it's likely the president will institute similar actions on the national level. That's why his martial law declaration was so strongly worded."

Mike had to frequently slow down as they drove along the bridge. The roadway had become clogged with more stalled cars since he'd returned from Key West the other day.

"Where exactly did these people think they were going?" he asked angrily. "The grass isn't greener on our side of the bridge."

"Some of these cars are loaded down with clothing and personal effects," Erin noticed. "Is it possible they're unaware of the bridges being destroyed?"

Hank leaned forward to rest his forearms on the dashboard. "It's possible. Or they thought it was an insane rumor and decided to leave anyway. Regardless, if this continues, Seven Mile may be blocked by the time we return this afternoon."

Mike pointed his thumb toward the rear deck lid covering his pickup's truck bed. "I have empty gas cans to fill up at the depot while I'm down here. Hopefully, if that happens, enough people left their keys in the ignition for us to move them."

"Plus, there's the winch," added Hank. Mike's police truck also had a built-in winch. Capable of pulling ten thousand pounds, he could maneuver stalled vehicles out of the way if necessary. Then Hank had another thought. "I don't wanna get off topic because I hope we're successful in our diplomatic mission, if you wanna call it that. But if Lindsey refuses to cooperate, we have to prepare for her bringing her band of merry men toward Marathon in a day or so. We could use these stalled cars to stop or slow their progress."

"A traffic jam of dead cars," said Mike jokingly.

"Exactly." Hank chuckled and then turned back to Erin. "Based on your phone call, what kind of timetable are we talking about?"

"The man said days not weeks."

"No pressure," interjected Mike.

Hank was dismayed. "Don't they realize this kind of thing takes time? Lindsey's not gonna quit, which means we have to follow the legal route that Mrs. Morton suggested."

Mike slowed once again as the end of the bridge entered Big Pine Key. The road was still washed out due to the hurricane, and he was forced to drive over the sandy shoulder next to the hammocks bordering Spanish Harbor.

"I guess all the road crews quit," he grumbled aloud as he drove around a fallen palm tree.

"Consider this, Mike," began Erin. "What you're seeing here is a microcosm of what's happened around the country. Infrastructure, from electricity to roadways, is unable to be repaired. Seriously, the bridges destroyed by the mayor are likely to remain that way for many years. Electricity will require the same length of time to be reinstated because the government has to rely upon foreign nations to provide us replacement components to the grid. As time passes, the Florida Keys will start to revert to the way it looked when your family first settled here."

"That sounds drastic," Mike said.

"Yes, but that's also very possible. What happens in the next few days will dictate whether we can help your neighbors survive or they will face the type of mayhem taking place in large population centers around the country."

Hank took a deep breath. "Lindsey thinks she can prevent that from happening by making sure everyone gets an equal share of what's available."

"It never works that way with dictatorial governments, Hank. They will keep the largest portion of any assets they confiscate and distribute it among their cronies. The rest will suffer that much quicker."

"Days?" asked Mike.

"That's what Chandler said, but he didn't provide an *or else*."

Hank sighed. "I'm starting to feel squeezed. How about you guys?"

Neither Erin nor Mike answered as they both fell deep in thought.

CHAPTER THIRTY-TWO

Wednesday, November 13
Key West

Mike dropped Hank and Erin off a couple of blocks away from the administration building. Hank thought it was best to keep some semblance of separation between him and Mike, especially when his brother was on official business. As they walked along Whitehead Street, they discussed their approach to dealing with Lindsey. Hank reminded Erin that they most likely wouldn't be welcomed after the harsh words he and Lindsey had exchanged following the hurricane.

"It seems Lindsey takes issue with her constituents showing up unannounced," he opined. "It's not like I can pick up the phone and schedule an appointment."

"Are you sure bringing me into her office is a good idea?" asked Erin.

"Can I answer that after we see her?"

"No, you coward," Erin replied before giving Hank a playful shove.

"Well, okay, but you might not like the answer."

"Try me."

"I think Lindsey would probably blow me off like she tried to do after the storm. However, the fact you're with me will pique her curiosity."

Erin shoved him again. "I see how it is. I'm not arm candy. I'm more like a ticket to get in the door."

"Right! Makes sense, doesn't it? Lindsey is a selfish person, and unless I can be of use to her, she'll ignore me. However, we both know she's had a run-in with the president, or at least his staff. The fact a member of his cabinet is at her office door will make her intrigued or worried. Either way, she'll let us in."

Erin grabbed his arm and stopped them just short of the entrance. "Oh, about that. I'm no longer Secretary of Agriculture. I've been removed from the cabinet. However, I am still a special assistant to the president."

Hank thought for a moment. "You and Lindsey have met, right?"

"Yes, years ago at a fundraiser for the governor. I'm not sure she'll remember me."

Hank placed his hand on Erin's back and urged her ahead of him as they approached the entry. "She'll remember. I won't lie and say you're still the Ag Secretary."

Erin interrupted him. "Just say I'm in the Helton administration. It's the truth."

Hank nodded. "Got it. Here we go."

He opened the heavy entrance door, and the two of them entered the stuffy building. They removed their surgical masks and shoved them into their pockets. Like before, the building was bustling with activity, but the first thing Hank noticed was the increased police presence. With the power outage, the metal detectors were not operable. However, they were still being used to funnel people into the building. Hank and Erin had both left their guns in Mike's truck, as they anticipated Lindsey might confiscate them.

The two of them made their way to Lindsey's office suite without difficulty. A few people recognized Hank, and he took the time to speak with them at length. Visiting Lindsey was only one of their goals in coming to Key West. Hank wanted to get a feel for how her government operations were holding up and to touch base with as many acquaintances as he could. He might need a friend in the building at some point.

Hank knew Lindsey's secretary, and the two made small talk. As discussed, he introduced Erin as being with President Helton's administration. Hank and Erin had barely settled into the seats in Lindsey's outer office when her doors flew open. The secretary exited, leaving Lindsey standing alone in front of her desk to greet her visitors. Like Chandler's uncharacteristic friendly attitude during his conversation with Erin on the satellite phone, Lindsey acted genuinely appreciative of Hank stopping by with his friend to meet her.

"Come on in, Hank. I won't bite, I promise."

Hank gestured for Erin to enter first, and Lindsey stepped forward with a toothy grin to shake hands. "Well, Madam Secretary, this is quite an honor."

"It's a pleasure to meet you, Mayor. But, please, call me Erin."

"Lindsey for me." She backed away without shaking Hank's hand and motioned for the two of them to take a seat in front of her desk. Lindsey resumed her customary position of power, separating those beneath her by sitting behind the mayoral desk. Her desk acted like a shield against anyone who would do her harm. It gave her a sense of comfort when dealing with adversaries, and she was certain Hank and Erin were. "What in the world would bring you to the Florida Keys during such a period of turmoil?"

"You may not be aware of this, but the administration has established a temporary seat of government at the U.S. Army War College in Carlisle, Pennsylvania. That's in fairly close proximity to Philadelphia, where the government will reestablish itself until a decision can be made about DC."

"Surely, the president plans on rebuilding Washington, right?" asked Lindsey.

Erin knew the small-talk game. It was a way to both size up and disarm an adversary. She was not much of a politician, but she was certainly capable of mental chess.

"There's a lot of work to be done around the country in order to save lives first and restore our critical infrastructure second. This process will take many years. One thing is certain. The president is laser focused on doing whatever is necessary to make that happen."

Lindsey feigned an itch to her nose so she could mentally wipe the smile off her face. She knew this wasn't a social call. "That's good to hear. Like him, I'm interested in the health, safety and welfare of the citizens of Monroe County. He may not believe that, but it's true."

Hank sat back and watched the two women joust with one another. He wondered if Erin was going to continue to dance with Lindsey or bring out the big guns. He didn't have to wait long to get his answer.

"I know you're aware of how he felt about the roadblocks," began Erin. "The decision to destroy the bridges, one of which happened to be a federal highway, was probably not a good one. The roadblocks might've been the functional equivalent of a gnat in the president's ear. Blowing up the bridges was more like murder hornets coming for the jugular."

Lindsey stood firm. "I did what I thought was best for the Keys. As it turned out, I was right. He sent the National Guard, from out of state I might add, to Homestead. If it weren't for the hurricane that his administration failed to warn us about, they would've taken over the Keys for lord knows what. Was my decision rash? Yes. Do I stand by it? Absolutely!"

If Hank didn't dislike Lindsey so much, he would've been impressed by her strong will in the face of a purported representative of the president.

Erin continued with the full-court press. "Are you aware that the Coast Guard has been sent to cordon off any boat traffic in and out of the Keys?"

"I've heard about that."

"And you do know that the next logical step is to send in a

couple of Marine battalions to finish what the National Guard was authorized to do, right?"

Lindsey leaned back in her chair and clasped her fingers together in front of her. "I suppose he could do that, but the world wouldn't stand for it. He'd generate a political firestorm and an unparalleled boondoggle in modern American history."

Erin glanced at Hank, who remained stoic. He was aware of the time constraints placed upon Erin to act on behalf of the president. Accordingly, she had to play hardball.

"Do you think he's bluffing? I would not underestimate him. He sees your actions as fostering discontent in other parts of the country. He might just make an example of you."

Lindsey laughed. If she was threatened by Erin's straight talk, she didn't show it. She abruptly stood, catching Hank and Erin off guard. "Well, I've got a county to run, and this conversation isn't very productive for me to continue. I get the sense the president is taking my actions to protect Monroe County's citizens a little too personally. When you speak to him, may I suggest he focus on his own shit?"

And with that, the conversation was over, and the two of them were summarily dismissed.

CHAPTER THIRTY-THREE

Wednesday, November 13
Key West

They had barely left the administration building when Erin issued her opinion of Mayor Lindsey Free. "She certainly chose the right career. That woman is a vulture who belongs in the halls of Congress."

Hank let out a nervous laugh. He was not a confrontational person by nature, so the toe-to-toe exchange between the two politicians had made him somewhat uneasy.

"She's always been stubborn and righteous, too. There's no way she'll leave office willingly. We've got a helluva fight on our hands."

"Sadly, you're right. If anything, she'll set her sights on us as soon as she can."

Hank glanced at his watch. He hadn't worn it in the nearly four weeks since the nuclear missiles began flying. There were no appointments to be kept or places to be. Today, however, Mike had given them a precise time when he planned to return to the administration building to pick them up. It was more than two and a half hours from now, which gave them plenty of time to start walking along Truman Avenue toward the sheriff's department.

"Are you up for a walk?" asked Hank.

"Yeah. I'd like to see more of Key West."

Hank broached the subject carefully without doing anything to offend Erin for the approach she'd taken with Lindsey. There was no good way to talk to the mayor, so he couldn't fault Erin for trying to make her points.

"Is there a chance the president is bluffing? I mean, would he really send in the Marines?"

She raised her eyebrows and shrugged. After rolling her head around her neck to relieve some tension, she replied, "I could answer that question better if I'd been in the room with the president when he issued his instructions to Chandler. I don't trust Chandler, and the subtle threat may have been his own doing. That said, the president can be flighty. Oftentimes making decisions ruled by his emotional state at the time. Even if he didn't say it, Chandler spoke for him, so I have to assume it to be his directive."

"Would we have better luck by staying out of everybody's way and allowing the military the opportunity to take care of Lindsey?" he asked.

"If it goes that far, the president will want to install one of his political cronies. Most likely someone who'd receive the blessing of the governor. Better the devil you know than the devil you don't. Especially when you consider the law enforcement duties could be taken over by the U.S. military instead of your sheriff and those serving beneath him."

Hank grimaced. Lindsey had put them all in an untenable situation, and now they had to move quickly before the president lost patience or confidence in Erin's ability to deliver a peaceful resolution.

As they walked up Truman Avenue to the point where it became Roosevelt Avenue, they both pointed out the looted buildings and the number of people who were sleeping in makeshift tents. Several businesses had been burned out, and most had their windows broken. The town looked like a war zone, and it was just a matter of time before every business was stripped of anything of value.

Even the car dealerships across from the marina weren't spared. People desperate for gasoline had attempted to siphon what little fuel the dealership's vehicles had in them. A row of three Jeep Rubicons had caught on fire, likely because someone had attempted to drill a hole in the underside of a gas tank, creating sparks that ignited the fuel.

Up the street, the scooter rental store was being pillaged as they walked by. Hank quickly pulled Erin with him to cross the street so they didn't come into contact with the looters. The scooters weren't the target of the thieves. They wanted the bicycles that had been shackled together in front of the store. One man tried to hold a bike on his back as he pedaled away on another one he'd stolen. He could barely control the handlebars as he pedaled.

"It will go on like this, Hank, until somebody steps in and stops it," said Erin. "Every retail store followed by residences of all types will be looted."

They walked another ten minutes, pointing out damage to property and the occasional dead body that had been covered with palm fronds. It was a disturbing and depressing scene that started to weigh heavily on Hank.

Then they came upon the Gordon's Food Service location. The aftermath of the sheriff's office raid and the ensuing gun battle shocked them both. Bloodstains filled the parking lot. Torn sheets and bedding were used to cover the dead, held in place by small coquina boulders. People were still filing in and out of the building, desperate to find any morsel of food to sustain them for another day. While Hank and Erin paused to take in the scene, a man approached them.

"Say, do you have anything to eat that you can spare?"

"No, sir, we don't," replied Hank. "I'm sorry. Can you tell me what happened here?"

"Sheriff's department came in like stormtroopers. The store had been boarded up, and all of us who live around here knew it was being guarded. That's why we never messed with 'em."

"Who?" asked Erin.

"Hired guns," he replied. "Some were ex-military. Others were just tough guys who were good with a weapon. Anyway, the SWAT team showed up in their military trucks and began to peel off the plywood. That's when the bullets started flyin'."

Hank pointed at the dead bodies and the pools of blood that had soaked into the asphalt. "The SWAT team was all the way out here?"

"No, sir. That's what I'm sayin'. The bullets were flyin'. Most of these dead people are my neighbors. They were in the wrong place at the wrong time. You know what I mean?"

Hank closed his eyes and shook his head. Erin reached over and squeezed his hand.

She looked to the old man. "Did you hear the sheriff's deputies say anything about what they were doing?"

"I didn't, but my buddy over there did," he replied and pointed toward the shaded areas in front of Centennial Bank, where several newly homeless people gathered around. "He said the mayor ordered these raids to feed everyone. When we asked for food, they said we had to wait for the distributions in a week or so."

"I'm sorry this happened to your friends," she said sincerely.

"Yep, me too. It didn't stop the sheriff, though. They're just up the street at Publix and Winn-Dixie doing the same thing. You can keep walking that way, but I'd keep my distance if I were you."

The man wandered off, and Erin grasped Hank's hand to draw his attention from the carnage. "Listen, there's nothing we can do about this. I do want to see their tactics. How far is it to these two grocery stores?"

"Winn-Dixie is right around the corner, and Publix is up the street from there."

"Come on," said Erin, who tugged at Hank's hand and began to walk briskly up North Roosevelt Boulevard. The shopping district that was once filled with tourists and locals alike loading up on staples was in shambles. It had only been a few weeks since the attacks. Erin began to wonder what their surroundings would look like a few weeks from now.

CHAPTER THIRTY-FOUR

Wednesday, November 13
Key West

A deputy sheriff was yelling through a bullhorn at the crowd gathered in the parking lot in front of the Winn-Dixie grocery store on North Roosevelt Boulevard. Just an hour before, they'd hit the Publix around the corner with a force twice as large as they'd used to raid the Gordon's location the day before.

Sergeant Jorge Rivera had met with the sheriff after the boondoggle that resulted in the deaths of several members of his team. He and the sheriff agreed that a repeat of the event would turn the locals against the sheriff's department more than they already were.

Since the start of the collapse, the mayor had made several difficult decisions that she considered to be in the best interest of her constituents while consolidating power within her inner circle.

Evicting nonresidents was considered harsh but necessary by those who were permanent residents. Even closing the bridges was praised as a way to prevent outsiders with no place to stay or no means to sustain themselves from invading the Keys. The sheriff's plan to keep the checkpoint open for returning residents was applauded, and although it was chaotic at times, the border worked.

It was Lindsey's paranoia over the National Guard staging in Homestead that had forced the decision to destroy the only two bridges leading onto the Keys. Her approval rating, if one had been polled, sank precipitously thereafter. Locals who prayed for their traveling family members to return to them were distraught. Those who had properties in other parts of the country, where they believed they had a better chance of survival, considered themselves prisoners with no means of leaving the Keys.

The confiscation effort, something Lindsey thought would be appreciated by starving or homeless residents, was off to a rocky start. They didn't need another black eye, so the sheriff and Sergeant Rivera agreed to slow down the pace of their raids. Instead of trying to cover many locations quickly, they brought a larger force to overpower any resistance and to maintain crowd control.

Nearly a hundred people had gathered in front of Winn-Dixie after word of the Publix raid spread through the adjoining neighborhoods. Some came for the spectacle while others hoped a crumb would be left behind.

Dressed in full riot gear, Sergeant Rivera's deputies formed a line to block the residents from interfering. Unlike Gordon's, which was a locally owned and operated business, Winn-Dixie was a national concern. There weren't any armed guards holed up inside the store, awaiting looters.

It had been a smooth operation for Sergeant Rivera's teams thus far. Both grocery stores yielded several truckloads of household supplies and sundries, but very little food, as the corporate giants had remained open for as long as there communication between them and the mainland. Once the power was lost and the bulk of the food products sold, the managers closed the stores and shuttered the glass storefronts to prevent looting.

Hank and Erin were about to step into the parking lot when they noticed Mike's pickup truck approaching. It was pure chance that they were able to flag him down. He was an hour ahead of schedule, and had he passed thirty seconds later, they would've missed each other.

Erin moseyed into the parking lot past the Ross Dress for Less store while Hank waved Mike over. She was mesmerized by the scene, taken in by the police presence and the disheveled appearance of the onlookers. Granted, the deputies were dressed in uniforms and riot gear that obscured their features. Overall, they appeared healthy, clean shaven, and well fed.

By contrast, the locals who'd gathered to watch the raid were thin, gaunt, and unkempt. Their hair was long. Their bodies were thin. And their clothes hung on them like they were several sizes too large.

Her mind instantly went to some of the television programs she watched from time to time that were set in medieval times or even fantasy pieces like *Game of Thrones*. The elite and powerful stood out among their subjects. The contrast was noticeable in those fictional depictions portraying the haves and have-nots. Erin wasn't watching a movie today. She was observing the natural consequences of economic and societal collapse in which those in power thrived while the rest of society fought over crumbs.

Mike and Hank pulled up next to Erin, who continued to walk toward the police line that formed a semicircle around the trucks being loaded by MCSO personnel. The bullhorn had fallen silent as the crowd around the deputies grew larger.

"Erin, we need to go!" Hank shouted through the window as Mike eased forward through a couple of stalled cars.

Erin ignored him as she approached a woman who was standing alone sobbing in the middle of the parking lot. Tears had soaked her face and two layers of tee shirts. She'd wrapped her arms tightly around her withering body as she stared at the deputies.

"Ma'am, are you okay?" Erin asked. Despite her soft tone of voice, the woman was startled by Erin's sudden appearance behind her.

She turned to respond. She was emaciated. Her once tanned skin had turned wrinkly and crepey. Erin had thought the woman was in her seventies, yet her features indicated she was much younger.

"I've lost everything," she said as she continued to bawl. She pointed her arm over her shoulder and waved toward the Winn-Dixie.

Erin, who thought she was referring to the grocery store raid, was genuinely confused. "Um, did you work at Winn-Dixie?"

It was difficult to make out her words as she blubbered uncontrollably. "No. They broke into my deli. It was all I had left after our house burned and my husband ..."

Erin slowly approached her and held out her arms. The poor woman needed a hug; however, Erin didn't want to frighten her unnecessarily. The two made eye contact, and the woman stepped forward to allow Erin to embrace her. Both women were crying now as they held each other for a long moment without speaking.

Hank exited the pickup while Mike turned off the engine. The men kept their distance but were vigilant as they surveilled their surroundings. The crowd continued to build, and they wanted to keep their distance from the center of activity.

Erin pulled away, extended the sleeve of her sweatshirt over her hand, and gently wiped away the tears mixed with mucus that covered the woman's face.

"Honey, do you wanna tell me what happened?" she asked the woman, who'd calmed down somewhat following their hug.

She began to slowly shake her head from side to side as she relayed what had happened to her in the last week. "My husband and I lived a few blocks away on Seidenberg. He was a boat captain, and I ran the deli down the street. We were so happy."

She began crying again and buried her face in her hands. Crying was personal, exposing someone's inner emotions at a time when they were most vulnerable. Covering her face gave her a sense of privacy and a chance to maintain her dignity as the emotional pain tore through her body.

Erin had suffered loss and understood. She gently rubbed the woman's hands and whispered to her, "You don't have to talk about it if you—"

"No, I need to. I don't have anyone or, um, anything, now."

"Okay. I'm listening." Erin continued to speak softly, but the crowd was beginning to get stirred up. The line of deputies started to move toward the crowd with their ballistic shields to force them away from the trucks being loaded. The man with the bullhorn began yelling again.

The woman, distracted by the noise, turned for a second. The activity seemed to shake her out of her devastated frame of mind. She took a deep breath and poured out her heart.

She and her husband had been planning how they could survive the collapse. He had calculated the amount of fuel he had in his truck. They had friends who lived in Central Florida near Lake Okeechobee. He thought he could load up everything of value that would enable them to fish and hunt. If they showed up at their friends' remote home, they wanted to be useful.

After word of the bridges being destroyed reached their neighborhood, they became angry but began to focus on another option. His fishing boat was fully fueled, so he began to calculate the distance if they left Key West to Lake Okeechobee via the waterway connecting the lake to the Gulf. They could just make it and were set to leave the following day.

That night, a fire broke out in the adjacent home. The property had been broken into by transients, and in an effort to stay warm, they built a fire in the fireplace. The transients passed out drunk and left the fire unattended. A spark ignited a blanket, and soon the place was engulfed in flames.

Her husband had grabbed a fire extinguisher and raced over to the neighbor's property to douse the flames. He was overwhelmed with smoke and was forced to crawl back outside. In the meantime, the fire jumped to their own home. The woman was outside trying to help her husband when he suddenly recovered and raced inside to retrieve the boat keys as well as the family's photo albums. He never came out.

With all of her belongings destroyed and no way to access their boat, her only option was to move into her nearby deli a couple of doors down from the Winn-Dixie in the shopping center. She and her husband had already secured the plate-glass windows at the front. She was able to come and go through the rear door using a push-button, manual door lock. She was safe and had access to food while she grieved the loss of her husband.

"Earlier, while they were busy raiding Publix, a group of men took advantage of them being preoccupied. I could hear them trying to break into Winn-Dixie. When they couldn't get inside, they moved on. They looted GNC and the AutoZone. Then …"

Her voice trailed off once again. She began to cry, and Erin did what she could to calm her down. The woman simply shook her head and steeled her nerves to continue relaying what had happened to her.

"They broke into my deli. It was all I had left in the world. They knocked me down and kicked me." She raised her shirt to show Erin her bruised ribs before continuing. "I ran out of the store, looking for someone to help me. The police were driving into the parking lot to set up in front of Winn-Dixie. I ran toward their trucks and tried to get their help. Instead, they almost ran over me. When I finally got one of them out of the truck, he shoved me to the side and told me I was interfering with sheriff's department business."

Hank had inched toward Erin's side now and was listening intently to the woman's heartbreaking story. He was about to introduce himself when several gunshots echoed off the stucco façade of the grocery store.

CHAPTER THIRTY-FIVE

Wednesday, November 13
Key West

Hank had never seen an actual powder keg explode, but he certainly was witnessing what the saying was intended to describe. Afterwards, none of them were able to identify where the initial shots came from. Regardless, as the crowd built and began to push forward against the line of deputies, shoving and vulgarities began to create a tense situation. A fuse was burning, and the single gunshot reverberating off the stucco walls of the shopping center resulted in mayhem.

Still on edge following the gun battle the day before at Gordon's, Sergeant Rivera was determined to protect his deputies and the firefighters who helped break into the grocery store. He grabbed the bullhorn from the deputy's hands and started screaming.

"Back off! Now! We will shoot to kill!"

It was those last three words that were misconstrued by one newly deputized recruit who'd been used by Sheriff Jock and Lindsey to bolster their ranks at the bridge checkpoints. He was on the front line, face-to-face with the angry mob. He gripped his shield in his left hand and spontaneously pulled his service weapon from its holster with his right. Afraid for his life, he fired wildly into the crowd.

Three shots. Three bodies dropped to the asphalt.

Rather than retreat, the crowd turned on the deputies and rushed them despite the line of ballistic shields they faced. Within seconds, the deputies were overrun, and the crowd was beating them while attempting to take their weapons. Others ran past the scrum and raced toward the entrance of Winn-Dixie.

More shots rang out, this time from automatic weapons issued to team A under Sergeant Rivera's command. The civilians at the front of the crazed mob were torn to ribbons. Blood flew into the air, and screams of agony permeated the shopping center.

Hank and Erin stood frozen for a moment as they witnessed the carnage. The woman they'd been talking to ran away, disappearing with the rest of the crowd, who fled toward Kennedy Drive.

Mike jumped out of the truck and yelled, "Come on, Hank! We gotta go!"

"Hey! He's a cop!" screamed a young man from fifty feet away.

Another one turned his attention to Mike. He shouted his question. "What kinda shit is this, asshole?"

"Yeah!"

"Let's teach this one a lesson!"

Hank and Erin began running back toward the truck. Mike took a shooter's stance and drew his sidearm. He flipped on his red-dot laser sight and lit up the chest of the man in the front of the pack that approached him.

Mike angrily warned them. "Stay back! Stop where you are!"

"You can't shoot us all!"

The mob slowed their pace, but they continued marching toward him.

Hank drew his weapon, and Erin did as well. Hank quickly moved between Mike's truck and the threatening mob.

"Yes, we can and will if you don't stand down! Stop!"

Erin moved alongside Hank and pointed her weapon at several

of the people standing just behind the most vocal members of the mob.

The group slowed as the men leading the charge began to reassess. Their eyes darted from Mike to Hank and Erin until they eventually stopped. They mouthed off again, but they'd lost their will to fight. When another burst of automatic gunfire was heard from the storefront, they turned and disappeared into the fleeing crowd.

Mike didn't have to ask his partners again. Hank and Erin rushed toward the truck and were sliding into their seats just as Mike started the truck. He threw the gearshift into reverse and spun the tires on the thin layer of sand that had accumulated on the asphalt parking lot. He was almost on the road when Erin shouted for him to stop.

She flung the door open and jumped out of the back seat. She began running toward the mayhem. However, instead of drawing her weapon, she pulled another weapon equally as effective—her iPhone.

Cell phones were no longer capable of making calls or sending texts. However, they still functioned. She started filming the battle between the civilians and police. She switched to her photo function and began to take pictures in rapid succession. She wouldn't know how devastating they appeared until later that evening when she sat down to view them. Somehow, she knew they'd become a powerful weapon in their fight against Lindsey and the sheriff.

Mike sped forward to pull alongside her as Hank rolled down the window, imploring Erin to get back in the truck. Seconds later, Mike was once again spinning the truck's tires as he backed out of the parking lot. He almost ran over three women racing up North Roosevelt on bicycles stolen from the scooter store earlier. Mike jammed on the brakes, cursed the women, and then spun the tires again as he headed up the highway to leave Key West.

Hank was still agitated over the entire ordeal. He misguidedly focused his ire in his brother's direction. "What the hell, Mike? Is this some kind of gestapo operation your boss is running?"

"Hold on, Hank. I don't condone any of this shit, and besides, he's not my boss. I threw my badge on his desk a little while ago."

Erin tried to calm the brothers down, who appeared to direct their anger and frustrations at one another. "Guys, come on. Let's catch our breath and talk about what just happened."

Both guys were still cross when Mike drove onto the divided highway just past the Marriott resort. He sped up, and the mere act of driving onto the bridge from Stock Island to Boca Chica seemed to relieve tensions in the cab of the truck.

Erin looked around the back seat and found stacks of handguns in their hard cases together with military ammo cans that must've weighed fifty pounds each. She also noticed for the first time that Mike's truck bed lid was propped up several inches and tied down with ratchet straps.

She'd learned in her brief time around the Albrights that Mike was the more emotional of the two men and oftentimes expressed his emotions through anger. Hank tended to suppress his emotions and rarely got agitated. As a result, Mike was made out to be the bad guy when in reality, he simply let it out whereas Hank boxed it in. Erin wasn't sure which was worse.

She tried to change the subject by asking what had happened to Mike. "I gather you resigned."

He managed a slight laugh. "Let's call it a mutually acceptable separation. He was peppering me with questions about you and what you were doing in *his islands*." Mike emphasized the words *his islands* as he spoke.

"Lindsey must've contacted him after we met with her," interjected Hank.

"Maybe," said Mike. "Although our conversation got pretty heated, and he never mentioned it. He was already in a foul mood after what happened at Gordon's yesterday."

"We heard," said Erin. "I think what we just witnessed was worse."

"Well, all I know is that there were deputies lost in the gunfight yesterday, including a guy I know. He had a family, you know, with young kids."

"Tragic," said Hank. "So he was still upset over that, yet he quizzed you about Erin?"

"Yeah. I don't know how he knew Erin was with us. Maybe Lindsey did contact him. All of this went down about thirty to forty minutes ago."

"Timing would be about right," Erin added.

"In any event, we got into it, and things were said. Maybe I should've bit my tongue, but I called him a sellout for raiding these businesses. I said he needed to focus on protecting our residents and not doing Lindsey's bidding."

Hank laughed. "Dang, brother. I thought Erin was tough on Lindsey. You shoved it right up Jock's—"

"You got into it with Lindsey?" asked Mike, cutting off Hank's sentence. He glanced into his rearview mirror to study her face.

"Pretty much. Let's just say she doesn't take kindly to threats, nor does she seem to worry about them."

Mike nodded and glanced at Erin again. "That's because she's got big *cajones*. She uses Jock as a shield and a protector. She'd never do this unless he was in bed with—"

"Wait!" shouted Hank. "What if that's it? What if …? They're sleeping together!"

Erin wasn't so sure. "C'mon, Hank. That's a little soap-operaish, don't you think?"

Mike sighed. "You have to know her history, Erin. Lindsey chews men up and spits them out if the taste isn't good anymore. If there was a better option than Jock, she'd jump on it."

"Literally," said Hank, causing the group to break out laughing.

With the tensions eased between the brothers, they settled down and talked about what they'd observed at Winn-Dixie. Erin couldn't get the conversation she'd had with the distraught woman out of her mind. She desperately wanted to hug her and bring her back to

Driftwood Key. Unfortunately, a single crazed serial killer had ruined that for everyone.

She sat in silence as Mike and Hank spoke back and forth about the additional supplies he'd taken from the sheriff's office before quitting. She tried to process all of the relationships between the people she'd come in contact with on the Keys. She came to the realization that the usual method of attacking a snake by cutting off its head might not apply here. Perhaps they should attack the body, one rattle at a time.

PART V

Day twenty-eight, Thursday, November 14

CHAPTER THIRTY-SIX

Thursday, November 14
Driftwood Key

The group stayed up into the night as everyone relayed their experiences that day. Lacey, Tucker and Peter encountered a dozen separate instances of people wandering across the private bridge leading onto Driftwood Key. Most of the stragglers appeared harmless and quickly turned when they were subtly threatened by the guards' rifles. Between the sunglasses to block glare, the surgical masks to protect them from the soot-filled air, and the guns, most interlopers immediately left. However, everyone agreed this was a sign of things to come.

Sonny and Jimmy went fishing together. They had quite a haul. That afternoon, the Frees worked diligently to clean and then smoke the fish. Phoebe was an expert at preparing the brine mixture so that once the smoked fish was prepared, it could be preserved for up to three weeks. It was an excellent source of protein and served as a great snack for when some of them were off the key or patrolling the perimeter of their island.

Jimmy provided everyone an honest assessment of his recovery, and Sonny confirmed it. Peter was now declared to be a hundred percent, and Jimmy felt he'd be there in a day or so. To avoid complications requiring a return trip to the hospital, he agreed to take it easy until Jessica signed off.

Everyone started their day. Mike was concerned for Jessica because he'd left the sheriff's department on what might be described as bad terms. His resignation hadn't exactly been under amicable conditions. Jessica had been on a roving duty status, which meant she would be on call from Marathon northward toward Islamorada. If she received a call on her marine radio for any reason that required her to travel toward Key West, she'd ignore it.

Hank, Erin, and Mike convened in the war room on the second floor of the main house. Following the shoot-out at the high school, Mike had had the presence of mind to grab several boxes of chalk off a utility rack in the warehouse. This was helpful as the three plotted out their day.

While they spoke, Erin transferred edited video snippets and photographs from her iPhone to Hank's and Mike's using her Lightning cable. As they made their rounds, they'd show the videos and pictures to prove Lindsey's intentions.

"Mike, how many sheriff's deputies are located in the Middle and Upper Keys?" asked Hank, who went on to qualify his question, "And by deputies, I mean the real ones not the recruits like Jimmy."

"It's not that many," he replied with a grimace. "Four here and another four in Islamorada. Key Largo has the most, as they were too far away for Jock to summon to Key West."

"Are your people loyal to you or the sheriff?" Erin asked.

"Before yesterday, I would say definitely me. Now that I'm out, the dynamic has shifted. It's the first order of business when I leave here this morning."

"Okay," began Hank. "Even if they're wary of their relationship with you, in light of these pictures, can you get them to stand up to the sheriff?"

Mike shook his head. "TBD. I'll try to be convincing. It's a big ask, Hank, because they're gonna be promised the moon. You know, in terms of feeding their families."

"We have to try to do the same," interjected Erin. "I have an idea in that regard."

"What is it?" asked Mike.

"Well, do you have access to the county-owned buildings in your, um, former district?"

"Yeah, unless my deputies were told to lock me out," he replied. "I'm hoping Jock got distracted after what happened at Winn-Dixie. That's why I want to get to my people before he remembers he's mad at me."

Erin explained her reason for asking. "If you're successful, I think we need to raid their buildings before they make an effort to raid ours. We also need a means of storage and dissemination. It has to be a place we feel is secure and overseen by those we trust."

"Churches," said Hank.

Erin smiled and winked at Hank. "Exactly! First off, churches have been there to help their communities throughout history. In a crisis, denominations and beliefs don't usually come into play. It's not like politics. At least not in the Keys, I hope."

"This is a great idea," said Mike. "You know, I've known the rector, Reverend Canon Debbie Messina, at St. Columba for a while now. She is a great person and will certainly be open to helping out. Plus, they have a recreation center that can hold food and supplies. They're not on the main highway like some of the other churches, so it could fly under the radar of Jock's people."

"It's also near the high school, so transferring the food and supplies down the street will be quick and easy," added Hank.

"Will you see her?" asked Erin.

Mike nodded. "First thing after I determine where I stand with the deputies. I'll approach a couple more churches, one on each end of Marathon."

Hank added a thought. "I believe this will make it easier to bring other business owners on board if they know that a nongovernmental entity like a church will be involved with distribution to those in need. It'll be a tough sell if we have to take on a role not that dissimilar from what Lindsey and Jock are doing."

"Fellas, I have one more concern," began Erin. "I'm not saying that Mike made our task more difficult. The separation was inevitable. However, we no longer have an insider at the sheriff's department. We need to establish some means of surveillance and warning. And, like we discussed in the trip down to Key West yesterday morning, we need to consider blocking the Seven Mile Bridge to thwart their efforts."

Mike agreed. "I've thought about both of those things. I know several guys who have powerful winches on the front of their trucks. I wanna get them on board, but once I do, my idea is to drag the vehicles until they're parked sideways. Maybe even flatten their tires so they can't easily be moved."

"Are we okay with closing off access to Key West?" asked Hank.

"It wouldn't be completely closed off. Pedestrian and bicycle traffic would still go back and forth. Just not Jock's SWAT vehicles. Besides, there's always the option to travel by water."

Erin unplugged her phone from Mike's and handed it to him. He thumbed through his apps and opened the photos to look at the images.

She addressed the surveillance issue, drawing on her newfound knowledge of the Keys' geography. "We need some people to camp out at Big Pine Key and let us know when there's activity there."

Hank stood and shoved his phone in his pocket. He was anxious to get started. "Let's make that part of our conversations today with everyone. First, we have to convince them this is necessary by letting them know what's happening in Key West and that soon it'll be at our doorstep. Once that's done, we'll recruit manpower to help."

"Do you think they'll be on board?" asked Erin.

Mike laughed and wrapped his arm around his brother's shoulders. "Oh, yeah. Fear is a great motivator."

CHAPTER THIRTY-SEVEN

Thursday, November 14
Marathon

Prior to the collapse, there were eight thousand full-time residents located in Marathon and the adjacent keys. Four weeks after the nuclear wars broke out, the population had been cut to less than half. Many had traveled north to be with family. Many had died.

Mayor Juan Ramirez, who owned the local electrical supply store, had been a fixture in the community for a generation. His family of carpenters and electricians had helped build the homes at Key Colony Beach, an upscale community on the Atlantic Ocean side of the Keys. As his family aged, they turned to construction-related retailing. They owned an Ace Hardware franchise as well as the electrical supply business. His sister operated a gardening center specializing in hydroponic gardening and container gardening.

Hank had relied heavily upon Lisa Ramirez when he constructed the greenhouses and hydroponic system for Driftwood Key. She helped him assimilate the key's sandy soil with bags of dirt they imported from the mainland to create a soil mixture that would produce vegetables, herbs, and fruit for years.

She'd also taught him the importance of the seeds he chose. They recommended non-GMO, microgreen seeds in addition to heirloom seeds. The term *non-GMO* meant the seeds were not created with the use of genetic engineering. Some GMO crops were modified to make them resistant to certain antibiotics. This resistance was then directly passed on to humans either through eating the vegetable or indirectly by eating a meat product that fed on GMO feed. There was a growing concern globally that humans were becoming increasingly resistant to antibiotics and therefore susceptible to a wide range of bacterial or viral infections.

Microgreens could easily be grown from seed to salad in just a week. Full of intense flavor coupled with high nutritional value, a small portion of the flavorful stems and leaves provided a powerful punch of nutrition.

Heirloom seeds enabled the grower to save seeds from harvested fruits and vegetables to be used in the next growing season. Just as important, during a catastrophic event like nuclear winter, heirloom seeds were not genetically modified to ripen all at once like hybrid or GMO seeds. In a world in which refrigeration and lines of distribution were virtually nonexistent, the heirloom seeds enabled growers to sustain themselves year-round if they had a means to grow the plants.

Hank and Erin had arrived at the mayor's office early that morning. While they waited, Hank provided some background.

"Juan has been the mayor for years, and he's the closest thing I've ever seen to someone being apolitical. I mean, I'm not even sure he identifies with one party or the other. If you talk to him, he might lean a little bit to the left side of the spectrum on social issues, but then he's always preaching fiscal responsibility when he chairs the city council meetings. The bottom line, I guess, is that Juan always tries to do the right thing for the people who live here."

"How many would that be?" she asked.

"Eight thousand, maybe? I'd say ninety percent of those are white, not that it matters. It's a funny thing about the Keys. We're all kinda color-blind down here."

"What's his relationship to Lindsey?"

"Neutral, at least in Juan's eyes. He didn't back anyone in Lindsey's races."

Erin stared across the highway at the Marathon airport. A few fixed-wing aircraft remained parked on the tarmac. It appeared most who had the ability to fly left. She found that ironic, as Lindsey's biggest fear was the Keys being inundated by outsiders, yet those who had the ability to bypass her roadblocks through the air chose not to.

"Here's the thing about politicians, Hank. They are constantly feeling out fellow politicians to determine where they stand. The phrase *you're either with us or against us* very much applies to their interaction with others of their ilk. Your friend may not admit it to us, but there's a reason he didn't throw his support behind Lindsey. I hope we can use that to our advantage."

"Here he comes," said Hank, interrupting Erin. He pointed toward the windshield. "It looks like Lisa is with him. We can cover a lot of ground this morning."

Hank and Erin exited the truck. They casually stood by while the mayor and his wife parked. It had been more than a month since the two men had spoken, but their warm greeting spoke volumes.

Hank introduced Erin, who struck up a conversation with Lisa about their common interest—agribusiness. While they talked, Juan led them into the recently renovated, one-story building.

"Bear with me until we get to my office," Juan began as he waited for the women to enter before locking the door. "It's a little dark in the hallway, and I apologize for the musty smell. It's amazing how quickly the humidity invades a building when there isn't any air circulation or filtration."

As he led them through the hallway, Hank glanced inside the offices of the staff. The desks were neat and tidy. Files had been put away and chairs straightened. It was if the entire City of Marathon government had been sent on vacation and told to keep their workspaces presentable until they returned.

Juan noticed Hank glancing into each door. "This catastrophe is tragic on so many levels, Hank. I come in to work every day although I don't know why. I guess it's out of a sense of obligation to the people I serve. I mean, look around this building. These offices were occupied by civil servants who helped our town grow. They provided fire protection. They ensured businesses properly engaged with their customers. They collected taxes and paid the city's bills. All daily activities that have ceased to function."

He paused as he stood aside, gesturing for the group to enter his corner office near the main entrance facing Overseas Highway and the airport. While they waited, he moved to each corner of the room and turned on several battery-operated Coleman lanterns that provided a soft, warm glow to their surroundings.

The local mayor continued. "Anyway, what brings you to city hall? I don't get many visitors."

Hank exchanged glances with Erin, and then he took a deep breath. He was going to ask Juan to pick a side, something out of character for the independent-minded mayor.

"Juan, Lisa, there's trouble coming."

Lisa chuckled. "It can't be worse than the hurricane."

Erin, who'd established a rapport during her brief conversation with the mayor's wife because of their common interest in agricultural issues, addressed her comment. "Yes, unfortunately, it is. Mayor Lindsey Free is on a rampage in Key West, and she intends to bring it to Marathon within days."

"Are you talking about the raids?" asked Juan.

"We've heard rumors," interjected Lisa.

Erin looked at Hank for approval as she retrieved her iPhone from her pocket. He provided her an imperceptible nod and returned his attention to Juan and Lisa.

"We witnessed her actions firsthand yesterday. I caught it on video. Please understand something. This is raw and unedited. And, um, disturbing."

Erin navigated to the video she'd taken. She made sure her phone's volume was up, and she pressed the play button. She leaned forward and turned the phone so they could watch.

Their reactions were not unexpected. Juan's face grew red with anger, although once he closed his eyes for a long moment in an effort to unsee what he'd seen. Lisa's mouth fell open, and she unconsciously covered it. Her eyes began to well up in tears as the visuals of people being beaten and shot by sheriff's deputies filled the phone's screen. When the video was finished, Erin offered to show them the photographs she'd taken, but both said they'd seen enough.

Juan was the first to speak. "This happened yesterday?"

"Yes, at the Winn-Dixie," Hank answered. "The day before that, something similar happened at Gordon's Food Service down the street. Juan, Lindsey has instructed Jock to take whatever steps are necessary to strip businesses of their assets. Food, water and gasoline are high on their priority lists, but we've been told they are taking everything of value."

"For what purpose?" Juan asked.

"Using Lindsey's words," Hank began to reply, "the greater good."

Juan began shaking his head before leaning back in his chair to stare at the ceiling. He was genuinely angry. "This doesn't surprise me about Lindsey. She's always been someone who felt she could tell you how to run your life or business because she thought she knew better. However, Jock …" His voice trailed off.

Erin spoke up. "I'm an outsider, so my opinion should not carry the same weight as the three of you. It seems that the sheriff has been placed in an untenable position. Perhaps he agrees with Lindsey's plans and therefore devised a mechanism to carry them out. I think he underestimated the desperation of the people. Business owners are not going to stand idly by while their businesses are raided."

Lisa bowed up in her chair. "This one certainly isn't."

"Our philosophies have always differed from Lindsey's," added Juan. "She believes in giving a man a fish. I believe in teaching him to fish." He was referring to the quote from Chinese philosopher Lao Tzu, which translated as give a man a fish and you feed him for a day. Teach him how to fish and you feed him for a lifetime.

"We agree one hundred percent," said Hank. "And we have an idea that you can help us implement. But first, we have to protect ourselves, Juan. Lindsey and Jock's people are coming for us. By us, I mean your business and my business, and everyone else in Marathon who has anything she might want."

"What are you suggesting?" asked Juan.

Hank took a deep breath and exhaled. "We need to circle the wagons and then rally the community to help one another."

CHAPTER THIRTY-EIGHT

Thursday, November 14
Marathon

As predicted, the deputies under Mike's command in Marathon knew nothing of his resignation. They also had no idea how violent some of the confiscation raids had become. When he met with them that morning at the offices they'd assumed in the county clerk's annex, he considered delaying the revelation that he was no longer their boss. Instead, he chose to be completely transparent and forthcoming. It was a decision that earned him even more respect from the small detail assigned to protect Marathon and Lower Matecumbe Key. Now he had to convince them of the larger role he needed them to play.

"I am not going to ask you to violate the oath you took when you became a deputy. Nor am I going to ask you to break any laws, although which laws are enforceable and which aren't at this point is hard to determine. I might ask, however, for you to remain focused on Marathon, where you and your families live.

"You all grew up here. This is where your kids went to school. You have to understand, for the foreseeable future, this is our world.

These Keys, strung together, are going to have to sustain us for many years. In order for that to happen, the people who survive have to know they can count on you to protect them and, most importantly, do the right thing by them. That means opposing Lindsey's plans for Monroe County. Unfortunately, that also means standing up to our boss. Or, in my case, former boss. You guys need to pick a side."

"What do you need us to do?" asked Deputy Sanchez, who'd gained tremendous respect for Mike during the high school break-in.

"Protect and serve."

"That's a given," said Sanchez. "I mean, how can we protect our people?"

"Initially two things. Please give me the courtesy of a heads-up if you hear something from the sheriff or if you no longer think I'm doing the right thing for our neighbors and families."

"Agreed," said two of the deputies in unison.

"Second, I'm not asking you to participate in what I'm going to do this afternoon."

"What is it?" asked Sanchez.

Mike took a deep breath. If he was going to alienate the deputies, it would happen at this point. He chose to remind him of the video and images he'd shown him at the start of their meeting. He showed them the screen again where the video had paused. One of the deputies in riot gear was beating a man cowered on the ground.

"I refuse to allow what happened in Key West in the last few days to occur in Marathon. I'm going to stop them from coming across Seven Mile Bridge."

"How?"

"Create the traffic jam from hell."

Mike went from referencing hell to visiting a woman who led lost souls to Heaven. He arrived at St. Columba Episcopal Church and was surprised at the number of people who were amassed outside its doors. Despite the fact that he was no longer a deputy, Mike pulled on the lightweight jacket bearing the sheriff's department logo. The jacket, combined with his appearance as somebody associated with the authorities, enabled him to gently push his way through the crowd to enter the church. He was amazed at what he'd discovered.

Once inside the narthex, he found tables lined up with church elders handing out bagged meals and bottled water. He searched out Reverend Messina, who was affectionately known as Reverend Deb in the community. She wasn't among the church elders, so he moved through the narthex.

The sanctuary had been turned into a massive refuge for those who'd lost everything. Every pew was full of blankets, pillows, and a person's belongings. Some people slept while others read books, including the Bible. Many were deep in thought and prayer. Mike shook his head in disbelief at the number of people who'd been packed into the church. They were in generally good spirits, but the look of despair on their faces wasn't lost on him.

He set his jaw and stood a little taller, resolved to continue his family's efforts to help as many people as they could. He spotted Reverend Messina leaning with one arm on the pulpit. She was casually dressed in jeans together with a light blue shirt and her white collar.

"Reverend Deb, I don't know if you—" began Mike before she recognized him and politely interrupted.

"Of course I do, Detective. It's so good to see that you're well. I hope your family is, too."

Mike nodded, and then his mind wandered to Owen. He genuinely liked Lacey's husband and really hadn't had the time to process what his death meant to the Albright family. He wondered if the passage of time might prevent them from properly mourning his loss.

"My niece, Lacey, lost her husband as she and Tucker traveled home. It was tragic, but they're doing okay."

"I'm so sorry, Mike. Please convey my heartfelt condolences. His name was Owen, am I correct?"

Mike was surprised that Reverend Messina remembered. He wasn't even sure they had met. "Yes, it is, um, was."

She reached out and patted Mike on the shoulder. "Please, let's talk for a moment. I could use a respite." She directed Mike's attention to the carpeted steps leading behind the pulpit. She sat first.

"Thanks for taking the time for me when you have so much going on," said Mike as he joined her.

"God's work, Mike," she said as she tugged at her clerical collar. She noticed Mike watching her, so she explained. "Habit, of course. You know, there's an old joke among us clergy types that a curate wears a collar at all times, even a shower. Most, like me, wear them at all times, although not in the shower. Even during this devilish disaster, I find it to be a comfort to my parishioners and, honestly, to myself. God has placed us in quite a test, don't you think?"

Mike nodded and glanced throughout the church. There were at least a hundred people residing in the small sanctuary.

"I do, and that's why I'm here," he replied. "Reverend Deb, the other day a group of men broke into the food-storage warehouse at the high school. We were successful in stopping them. However, they breached the building in such a way that the supplies could easily be stolen."

"I heard the shooting. One of the residents is a church elder. I didn't know that involved you since, you know, you're a detective."

Mike gulped. He hadn't lied to his deputies, so he'd darn well better not lie to Reverend Messina. He explained the circumstances regarding his resignation and offered to show her the pictures from Key West. She respectfully declined and assured him she would trust his judgment.

They spoke for a moment about the logistics of what he wanted to accomplish. The reverend promised to help by sending out her two most trusted aides to recruit other churches in Marathon to assist in the humanitarian project. With his approval and the deputies' supervision, they'd handle the removal of the supplies from the high school.

In the past, Reverend Messina had helped many people in crisis, especially during hurricanes. She'd established a program known as the Five-Dollar Bag Sale. Members of her congregation would donate clothes, toys, tools and other household items to be included in simple, brown grocery bags. For a five-dollar donation to the Hammock House, a local charity, purchasers could receive a wide variety of useful things for their homes.

"We are a close-knit group of clergy across all denominations," she explained. "Our parish strives to be a strong partner in the community, which is why I've been involved in so many charitable endeavors. Other churches in Marathon also offer consistent and tangible ways to help people in need. I have no doubt everyone will pitch in."

Mike smiled and thanked her for her assistance. In addition to making an important partner to help people survive nuclear winter, his day was now freed up to systematically create the mother of all bottlenecks on Seven Mile Bridge.

CHAPTER THIRTY-NINE

Thursday, November 14
Near Big Pine Key

Lacey and Tucker volunteered to conduct surveillance along the Lower Keys to monitor the sheriff's department confiscation teams. There was too much ground to cover between Big Pine Key and Key West, so they opted to use the boat given to Peter by Captain Jax in order to search for Jimmy.

The nondescript center-console fishing boat was like thousands of others found through the Keys. It was stripped down and devoid of the modern accoutrements found on most boats capable of fishing on the ocean and gulf waters. Nonetheless, it served their purpose.

Peter had left it adrift in Little Basin near Islamorada when it ran out of fuel that day. He'd tried in vain to locate Jimmy and simply ran the vessel for as long as he could. They'd retrieved it on the way back from Florida Bay after Jimmy had been found and taken to the hospital aboard Jessica's boat.

The fishing boat was one of several new acquisitions that had been added to the Driftwood Key fleet. Because there were too many to tie off to the dock, the fishing boat was moored just off the beach. Of all the boats in their possession, this particular boat was considered a throwaway. In other words, if it was lost, damaged or stolen, there was no great loss.

Lacey's memory of the waters surrounding the Keys had returned. Like her brother and Jimmy, she enjoyed the turquoise blue waters. She'd frequently traveled to visit friends in the Lower Keys by water, avoiding the often-congested traffic on A1A.

At Jessica's suggestion, she crossed into the Atlantic through Knight Key at the start of the Seven Mile Bridge. This would enable them to closely monitor the highway from a safe distance as it hopscotched from key to key between Key West and Marathon.

Sonny and Phoebe packed up food and water for the two of them to stay away several days if necessary. They would try to stay in communication via their marine radios and the two-way radios Mike had taken from the MCSO supply depot. If they observed a potential threat headed their way, they could quickly make their way back to Driftwood Key by water.

Before they left, the group had gathered in the war room in the main house to brief Lacey and Tucker on where to focus their attention. Based upon the first few days of the sheriff's raids, it appeared grocery stores and wholesale food warehouses were the primary targets.

They discussed each of the keys in between Stock Island near the sheriff's department and Marathon. Most of the islands were small and primarily residential. The three most likely to garner Sheriff Jock's attention would be Big Coppitt, the closest to Key West, followed by Cudjoe Key and then Big Pine Key, where Seven Mile Bridge terminated in the Lower Keys.

"This is Shark Channel," said Lacey as she slowed down in the shallow waters just off Big Coppitt Key. "Uncle Mike thinks the sheriff may bypass Big Coppitt altogether. Let's hang out here for a while and see if anything develops."

Tucker had grabbed the high-powered binoculars off Hank's Hatteras before they left. He handed them to his mom so she could focus on the stretch of highway running through the center of the Key. Tucker would scan the highway that crossed the channel and watch for any boats that might approach them.

After an hour or so during which time they made small talk, Tucker brought up Owen. "I think about Dad every day. I really feel guilty because, um, it's like I can't really remember everything. There's no reminders of him anywhere, you know?"

Lacey, who was wearing dark, polarized sunglasses, nodded. The sunglasses helped her hide the tears welling up in her eyes. "That's understandable, son. I miss your Dad more than anyone can imagine. It's just, well, since he died, you and I have been forced to survive alone for most of the time. After we survived the hurricane, my thoughts were focused on our safety. There will come a time when we can sit down and reminisce about your dad. We'll be able to laugh as we recall our good times together. The memories may have faded for now, but they're not forgotten or abandoned."

Tucker fell silent as he absorbed her words. He turned his attention away from the highway and studied the activity, or lack thereof, at Naval Air Station Key West. He couldn't see any military aircraft. There was a single Coast Guard helicopter near an administration building, but it had been covered to protect it from the hurricane. It was as if the military airport had been abandoned by the government, along with the rest of the Keys.

"I've got something, Mom," announced Tucker suddenly. "Use your binoculars to look across the runways toward the highway. Doesn't that look like a convoy of trucks. I mean, those first four are like those MRAPs they used in Oakland to deal with the riots." MRAP was a military term for mine-resistant ambush protected tactical vehicle. They were similar in style to the SWAT vehicles deployed by the sheriff's department for their tactical raids.

"I see them!" she said excitedly. "There are several patrol cars behind them, followed by at least six box trucks. You know, like U-Hauls and Budget trucks."

"Are they slowing down?" asked Tucker.

Lacey didn't immediately respond as she followed the convoy until they disappeared from sight for a moment.

Then Tucker answered his own question. "Here they come! They're crossing the bridge to ..." His voice trailed off, as he didn't know the name of the small island that was next in the chain.

Lacey quickly lowered her glasses. "They're headed for Sugarloaf. Hold on!"

She handed Tucker the binoculars and quickly slid behind the center console. She fired up the engines and took off toward the ocean, winding their way past Pelican Key at full throttle. As soon as she cleared the shallow reefs, she veered to the left and gripped the wheel. The fishing boat refused to plane out, so their ride was bumpy as she sped along the desolate beaches of Saddlebunch Keys. She was finally able to suppress her adrenaline and trimmed the engine so the boat was riding over the water to encounter less wave resistance.

"Where are we going?" asked Tucker, who continued to grip the handles of the center console.

"I'm gonna take us deep into Cudjoe Bay so we can get a good look at them as they go by. Uncle Mike wanted us to get vehicle and personnel counts. We'll want to be settled in as they go past our position. I don't wanna draw any attention."

"Gotcha," said Tucker, who pulled out several sheets of copy paper that had been stapled together. It was a list of grocery stores and markets located on each of the major keys they were tasked with surveilling.

"Mom, there really aren't any places for them to raid on Cudjoe Key, according to this list. There's a little seafood store and a couple of restaurants. The next store is on Summerland Key called Murray's Market. I can't imagine it's big enough for all those guys to bother with."

Lacey slowed her pace as she turned the boat toward Cudjoe Bay. She glanced toward the list, so Tucker folded the pages to make them easier for her to read while she navigated closer to U.S. 1. As she entered the center of the small bay, she throttled back and studied the list.

Darkness was approaching, although the perpetually hazy skies didn't give them much warning of the lateness of the day.

"You're right. I wonder ..." Lacey paused, her voice trailing off as she kept her thought to herself.

"What is it, Mom?"

She pointed toward the binoculars that Tucker had set into a pouch on the port side of the boat. He retrieved them, and she got her bearings straight.

"Do you have the Sharpie?"

Tucker retrieved it from his pocket and waved it in front of him. "Yep."

"Okay. I'm gonna call out what I see, and you make notes. Then we're gonna haul our cookies to Big Pine Key to see if they make it that far. In the meantime, I need to call Uncle Mike and let him know what's going on. I hope he's ready."

CHAPTER FORTY

Thursday, November 14
Seven Mile Bridge

Mike threw his two-way radio into the front seat of his truck and wandered around the concrete pavement, running his fingers through his sweaty hair. This was happening way too fast. He thought he'd have days, if not a week or more, to prepare the bridge and get Marathon ready. He'd miscalculated, and now he'd have to ask the impossible of his tired volunteers.

After he left his meeting with Reverend Deb, Mike drove through Marathon, touching base with his acquaintances who owned trucks with winches. He was appreciative of Reverend Deb's offer to recruit the other churches for him. It took an inordinate amount of time to explain why he needed the men's help, and once they were convinced, he had to get fuel for their trucks. It was already early afternoon when they'd gathered at the start of Seven Mile Bridge. After a lengthy back-and-forth on the best way to approach the problem, they began.

Unfortunately for Mike's schedule, it was agreed they had to clear the road in order to clog it up again. The stalled and abandoned vehicles were in the way of the far end of Seven Mile Bridge closest to Big Pine Key. They had to clear one lane to get there. It was determined that the group of six trucks be split into two teams of three. One would focus on clearing a lane for the other. They leapfrogged down the two-lane highway for most of the afternoon. They were midway through the process of doing so when Lacey reached Mike on the radio.

"Okay," began Mike after he gathered himself. He waved down the men, who shut off their trucks and joined him. He passed out bottled water and allowed them to catch their breath before he explained. "They're approaching Big Pine Key. It hasn't been their normal MO to conduct these raids at night, so I wanna believe they're staging for tomorrow."

"What if they're coming now?" asked one of the men. "We just made it really damn easy for 'em."

Mike didn't need to be reminded of that fact. He had two options. "Well, we could work under the assumption they're gonna stop for the afternoon and pick it up again tomorrow morning."

"That's possible, Mike," began one of the men. "But here's the thing. If they keep on coming, we're busted. I don't wanna go head-to-head with Jock's people after the video you showed me."

"I'm with him," said another volunteer. "Maybe we oughta just cut bait and hope for the best?"

"That would be a helluva mistake," said Mike. "I get that you guys don't want to gamble taking this all the way to Big Pine Key. I can't really disagree with that."

One of the men interrupted Mike. "Big Pine is barely a mile wide. If they're gonna make camp, or whatever, they'll be able to see and hear us in the dark. They'll be all over us, Mike."

Mike knew they were right. The risk was too great. They were halfway down the bridge. Three miles of gridlock was better than none.

"Let's do this," he began. "We'll start our road blockage right here at the halfway point. We can start towing cars from down the highway, leaving enough room for our trucks to get through. Then, one by one, we'll pull 'em sideways and flatten the tires. It'll take them forever to clear the mess."

"Then what?" asked one of the men who was the most argumentative.

Mike screamed the answer in his head. *I don't know! That's my brother's job!*

He took a deep breath before he verbally responded, "We'll cross that bridge when we get to it." He instantly cringed at the corny pun. However, it served to ease the tension between him and his volunteers, who found the use of the expression incredibly funny under the circumstances.

So after a good laugh and a few slaps on the back, morale was high, and the men got to work again.

CHAPTER FORTY-ONE

Thursday, November 14
Big Pine Key

After the caravan had passed and entered Big Pine Key, Lacey was off again. She had to rush to get to the other side of the island, as it was only a mile or so across. She had to travel well south through the aquatic preserve and then back around to the highway where it crossed the Spanish Harbor Channel.

Because the tide was low, they were able to ease the fishing boat through the half-moon bridge supports that held the bridge up between the two keys. This enabled them to get a direct point of view down the highway where the business district was located. Even as the tide rose, blocking their access back across the highway, Lacey was in position to race back to Driftwood Key from there.

"There they are, Mom," said Tucker, who was using the high-powered binoculars. He had to look down a short stretch of street in a residential area that was lined with vegetation. The gray skies of nuclear winter had taken the lives of the trees, enabling Tucker to have a fairly unobstructed view. "They're parked sideways across the highway. We're too far away for me to see what they're doing exactly."

Lacey took the binoculars from Tucker and tried to get a better look. From memory, she thought they were a mile away or slightly more. She set the binoculars down and studied the house on pilings in front of them. Its hurricane shutters had all been closed, and there were no vehicles parked underneath. Furthermore, the dock jutting out into Harbor Channel was empty.

"Let's get a closer look. Whadya think?"

"Will our stuff be okay?" asked Tucker.

Lacey looked at the camping gear she'd brought in case they needed to make their way onto one of the keys for the night. She took the other pair of binoculars and studied the home again. There was a fence together with a locked gate protecting it. The road ended at the water's edge, and there were no signs of life.

"Yeah, let's dock the boat."

Fifteen minutes later, the two of them had tied off to the dock, and they were walking briskly up Avenue A toward US 1. By the time they reached the activity, another raid was in full swing.

An angry crowd of people had gathered at the intersection that led to Winn-Dixie. According to one onlooker Lacey spoke with, they had been informed by a deputy that the food was being confiscated to be sent to Key West.

Lacey considered warning them about the violence that had occurred in Key West but opted to stay out of the way. Her job was to conduct surveillance, not engage an angry mob.

"Mom, here come the trucks. The cops are walking them down the road with their guns."

"They're not messing around, Tucker. Let's get back toward the boat."

The people started to push toward the row of sheriff's vehicles and the armed deputies lined up behind them. They began shouting at one another as the crowd became increasingly hostile. Most demanded that the trucks stop to share the food with the people who shopped there regularly.

Suddenly, the tactical vehicles appeared from behind the box trucks and began roaring toward the crowd. This startled the onlookers, who turned and fled in all directions. To force the issue, warning shots were fired by some of the deputies high over the head of the angry mob. They began pushing and shoving one another as they couldn't get away fast enough.

Lacey and Tucker joined a group racing east on A1A. She turned slightly as she ran and saw the box trucks turning toward Key West. She counted six vehicles leaving along with two of the tactical vehicles. The rest of the convoy she and Tucker had counted earlier remained behind.

She grabbed Tucker by the arm and told him to stop. She pointed toward the canopy of a Tom Thumb convenience market, where the two of them settled in behind the gas pumps to avoid being seen. They waited for several minutes until the bulk of the crowd had dispersed, leaving the sheriff's department personnel alone.

"Mom, we should go," urged Tucker.

"In a minute. Let's see where they go first."

Lacey thought the confiscation teams would return to Key West and come back the next day. She was wrong.

Suddenly, they emerged from the side street and headed straight for the convenience store. They weren't traveling fast, making Lacey wonder if they intended to empty out the small establishment. When they slowed near the entrance, her palms started to sweat. She looked around for a place to hide so they could avoid any contact with the SWAT teams.

Then, unexpectedly, they turned into the lumber yard that adjoined the Penske Truck Rental across the street. There were more than a dozen moving trucks parked along the fenced utility yard.

Lacey shook her head and mumbled as she counted the trucks again.

"Reinforcements."

PART VI

Day twenty-nine, Friday, November 15

CHAPTER FORTY-TWO

Friday, November 15
Driftwood Key

Erin was the first to rise that day. She verily believed all women had a perception, a sixth sense, that was much more developed than a man's. Perhaps it had become a part of the female DNA over the millennia, inserted into the female genetic code as a protective measure. To Erin, it was almost supernatural. Over the course of her life, she'd discovered her brain could play tricks on her. Oftentimes, her heart made her blind. However, without a doubt, she could always trust her gut.

She tossed and turned all night, recalling the conversation she'd had with Hank on the beach more than a month ago. They'd just met and developed a mutual attraction for one another. At their age, mature singles were looking for a partner based upon more than looks. They wanted to laugh together. When seriousness was required, an intelligent conversation without rancor was a must. Moreover, they were looking for a best friend.

She and Hank had all of those things. However, it was the

serious discussion they'd had on the beach regarding nuclear war and the aftermath that stuck in her head. She'd never admitted this to Hank, but the day she was whisked away by the Secret Service, Erin wasn't surprised.

Her gut had told her that nuclear war would come to America. It was inevitable.

For a hundred years, as the U.S. became the dominant superpower around the world and the largest economic power, it had become a symbol of freedom and success that most nations should strive to emulate.

Yet, jealousy was a sickness, whether between individuals or nation-states. It's a form of hatred built upon insecurity and inferiority. As a result, the U.S. created a lot of enemies, even among her allies. Even within her own borders. Because, make no mistake, geopolitics are often born out of emotions. Those who resented America's success wanted desperately for the nation, and her people, to be knocked down a peg or two by whatever means available.

The evening the missiles had been launched from North Korea toward the U.S. mainland, Erin sensed they were coming. For a moment, she was thankful to be a member of the president's cabinet. An elite member of the government who'd be protected from the onslaught.

Then she thought about the people she loved. Friends. Family. Hank. Would they survive the nuclear detonations? What would happen to them when nuclear winter encircled the Earth?

To be sure, much of what she'd learned over the years about the prospects of nuclear winter was theoretical. At the time, a nuclear exchange had never taken place. During the conversations they shared, she said the aftermath of what happened during a nuclear war would bring a plague on the planet—nuclear winter. A climate catastrophe equivalent to a nuclear El Niño. An unrelenting winter that would poison the planet's atmosphere and threaten the world's food production.

Now her gut told her they were running out of time in dealing with this tyrannical mayor who ran Monroe County. Her attempts to thwart Lindsey's confiscation plan was as much out of self-preservation as it was to protect Hank and his family. The mayor's Robin Hood approach was untenable, and despite the fact it would fail, Hank and his family were destined to be prime targets during the implementation. By association, Erin would be imperiled as well.

Erin's thoughts had kept her up most of the night, and she constantly checked her watch, waiting for 5:00 a.m. when Sonny turned on the main house generator for an hour. She planned on transferring the photographs she'd taken to Hank's computer. Then she wanted to create flyers to be handed out to the residents of Marathon and posted on every street. They needed to rally the troops to take a stand against Lindsey. She knew, however, the Albright family couldn't do it alone.

At a few minutes before five, she got dressed for the day and made her way to the kitchen. She prepared the coffee, ready to press the on button the moment the generator started. Unknowingly, Sonny tortured her, as he was several minutes late. Normally punctual, he'd been up late patrolling the grounds with Jimmy before relinquishing the duties back to Peter.

Erin was wide awake and didn't need the caffeine coursing through her veins to hit the ground running. Within a second of the generator-supplied power turning on, she started the coffeemaker, flipped on the light over the kitchen sink, and rushed into Hank's office, phone in hand.

She was proficient on the computer and capable of using Microsoft Word to create most kinds of documents. Once she settled on the verbiage designed to evoke the emotions of shock and fear in anyone who read it, she printed six different flyers, each with a unique image of the Winn-Dixie carnage. By the time they were printed, she was ready to run them through the copier. At first, unsure of Hank's supply of paper and toner, she printed a limited quantity of three hundred She made a mental note to look up

Marathon's mayor, Juan Ramirez, to see if he had a means to print additional copies for distribution.

"You're up and at 'em," said Hank after he took a sip of his coffee. He glanced at his desk and noticed she didn't have any. "Can I get you coffee?"

Erin turned and reached for his mug. "Just a sip of yours," she replied. Then she smiled and gave him a kiss on the cheek. The two hadn't slept together. They'd been affectionate and related to one another as a couple. Somehow, taking their relationship to that next level hadn't come to fruition. They'd been a little busy, after all.

"What are you working on?" he asked as she handed the coffee back to him. Erin organized the six sets of flyers in neat stacks and used binder clips to keep them separated.

With her back to him, Erin caught her breath after a night of her brain working overtime and a frenzied morning preparing for the day. She slowly turned to Hank. "It's gonna come to a head today, Hank. I feel it in my gut."

Hank furrowed his brow. "I don't know, Erin. Mike and his buddies worked until well after midnight. They double stacked vehicles all the way down the bridge to Fred the Tree."

"Where?"

"Oh, sorry. It's a locals' thing. About halfway down Seven Mile Bridge, on the old road, there's an Australian pine tree growing out of a small patch of soil. It became a symbol of hope to locals following Hurricane Irma tearing through the Keys in 2017. Despite its shallow root system and a vicious storm trying to rip it apart, it survived. Fred the Tree, like the people of the Keys, was stronger than Irma's brutal winds."

The story caused some of the tension to ease for Erin. Maybe it was the anecdotal story about the Florida Keys or it was Hank's presence. She approached him and gave him a long hug. Then she whispered into his ear, "Today, you've got to be Fred the Tree. The people of the Keys need someone like you, Hank."

"Today?" he asked.

"I think so. It's time to get ready to take the lead."

"I don't think we're ready to face off with Lindsey."

"You have to be," she responded, patting him gently on the heart. "They need a leader, Hank. Not necessarily someone who does the greatest thing. They need someone who inspires them to do great things alongside you."

CHAPTER FORTY-THREE

Friday, November 15
Big Pine Key

The dim light of dawn woke Lacey up first. She and Tucker had decided to sleep on the boat and wait to see what the sheriff's confiscation teams' next move was. Overnight temperatures in the Keys dipped down into the low fifties, twenty degrees below normal. It was the first night that Lacey had slept outside since that fateful evening that Owen died. This was nothing compared to the bitter cold they'd endured. In fact, the temperatures in the Keys were similar to those in San Francisco at this time of year.

She stretched and then made her way down the dock to a concealed spot behind a stand of mangrove trees to relieve herself. As she peed, she listened for activity on Big Pine Key.

The Florida Keys were notoriously laid-back and not beset by the hustle and bustle of city life. Generally, the only noise an early riser might hear was the fishing boats going out for the day. On an island like Big Pine Key, there was no commuter traffic. Many people walked to their jobs or rode bicycles. Unless the weather was bad-tempered, most vehicles remained parked.

Lacey wandered through the home's entry gate onto the pothole-laden end of Avenue A. She stared down U.S. 1, looking for any signs of moving vehicles or police patrols. There were none.

"Hey, Mom," said a sleepy-eyed Tucker, who walked across the crushed-shell driveway in his bare feet. The teen had adjusted to the time zone change, but he'd never been a morning person. He joined her side, lifting his foot once, complaining about a broken shell he'd stepped on. "Anything?"

"No, not yet," she replied. "Do you feel like taking a walk down the highway to get a closer look?"

"Sure," Tucker replied and began walking away from her.

"Hey, mister. Go get your shoes."

Tucker rolled his eyes and shook his head. "This is how they do it in the islands, Mom."

"That was before the hospitals and clinics disappeared. There's broken glass everywhere."

"Oh, yeah," said the teen. "I'll be right back."

Tucker hustled back toward the boat, and Lacey yelled to him, "Weapons!"

"Check!"

A few minutes later, the two of them were walking along the shoulder of the road. Just a few blocks away, halfway between their boat and where the sheriff's deputies had slept during the night, two businesses had been looted. A small takeout restaurant, the Island Deli, had been ransacked, as was the Forks & Stix restaurant a couple of blocks down.

"I wonder how long it will take for every business to be broken into?" asked Tucker. "People will break into that shoe store, hoping there's a vending machine to clean out."

"Sadly, you're right," his mother replied. "There's not enough law enforcement personnel to investigate these crimes much less enforce laws."

"Especially when they're all doing one thing, which happens to be the same thing the looters are doing," added an astute Tucker.

Lacey thought for a moment and shrugged. In a way, her son

was right. Looters were breaking the law, but Lindsey and her cohorts thought they were within the law as they interpreted it. The result was the same.

Daylight allowed them to see a farther distance, and soon the bright yellow Penske rental trucks came into view. During the night, several had been removed from the chain-link fenced area and lined up along the shoulder of the highway. Lacey tapped Tucker on the shoulder and ran across the street to take cover behind an abandoned roadside taco stand.

They got settled in to watch for activity. It had been almost dark when they'd arrived back at their boat the night before, and Lacey, a relatively inexperienced boater, wasn't comfortable making her way back to Driftwood Key. Besides, she wanted to monitor the convoy of SWAT team vehicles to give her family a heads-up when they mobilized for the day.

The two of them waited for more than an hour, making small talk and observing their surroundings. A few local residents ventured out onto the highway to gawk at the SWAT teams' vehicles parked within the Penske compound. At one point, a pickup truck drove past them toward Seven Mile Bridge. About forty minutes later, it returned with a frustrated-looking driver behind the wheel. Lacey presumed Mike's roadblock worked.

"Mom, listen," said Tucker as he lifted himself off the folding chair behind the taco stand and slowly strolled into the parking lot. He held his rifle against his body and leg as he walked to keep from attracting anyone's attention.

Lacey did the same as she moved briskly to catch up. "Do you know what that sounds like?"

"I bet it's the two armored trucks that left yesterday with the other vans. They've come back."

"Which means they're about to get started on their day," added Lacey, who looked around nervously. "Come on, let's get a better look."

She tapped Tucker on the elbow and took off for the Tom Thumb across the street from Penske. Like before, she took cover behind the gas pumps as the low rumble of the approaching tactical vehicles grew louder.

"They're alone," observed Tucker as the trucks came into view. "I guess they plan on using these Penske trucks instead of the ones filled with stuff from yesterday."

"Most likely they were used as an armed escort. Let's see what they do."

They didn't have to wait long for their answer. Rather than turn into the utility yard, they pulled past the entrance along the sidewalk that ran parallel to the highway. Seconds later, several members of the MCSO SWAT team piled out of the vehicles and milled about while another man with stripes on his shirt walked toward the entrance to Penske.

"Dammit, Tucker. How're we gonna get back to the boat? We can't walk down the street with these things in our hands."

Tucker glanced around. There was a large, open area between their position and the taco stand where they had been hiding before. If they tried to run away, they could be seen within seconds once they broke cover. There was a crushed-shell driveway leading behind the Tom Thumb to where the dumpsters were located. Beyond that, he could see grass and then dense trees. It was their only chance.

"This way, Mom, before they wander farther away from their trucks."

Tucker hustled toward the building and quickly turned the corner in the direction of the dumpsters. Lacey followed him, and neither slowed down until they found an overgrown trail leading to the sparsely populated neighborhood behind the store.

Through the woods, there was a clearing and a large sand pit operated by an excavation company. Still afraid they might've been observed by the deputies, Tucker sought out another trail created by the locals through the dense vegetation. He was putting his hiking and camping skills to good use as he kept his bearings and identified safe paths through the trees.

Finally, they came out of the woods and ran onto a sandy road.

Although the road ended and took a sharp turn toward the beaches, a four-wheeler trail continued toward where their boat was docked.

"Thanks, son. I was freaking out a little bit."

Tucker nodded but immediately turned his attention to the trail. "Mom, we've gotta get to the radio and warn Grandpa and Uncle Mike."

CHAPTER FORTY-FOUR

Friday, November 15
Driftwood Key

"Okay, okay, Lacey, get back here ASAP. We'll take it from here." Mike shut down the transmission and turned to the group who'd gathered in the foyer of the inn. Anxious faces studied him as he issued his instructions. "It's go-time."

"So they're coming," said a concerned Hank. "I really hoped Lindsey would be satisfied with pillaging the Lower Keys."

"Yeah. Apparently, they've doubled the number of box trucks they're bringing and added a couple more patrol cars to their convoy. I'm thinking they wanna be prepared for a large show of force, kinda what we saw at Winn-Dixie."

Erin set her jaw. "Why would they expect different results from what they caused in Key West? We need to get going."

Hank nodded. "Agreed. It's all hands on deck today." He turned to Phoebe. "Can you and Jimmy handle patrols?"

"No problem, Mr. Hank," she replied before adding, "Jimmy is feeling much better, and he's not happy about being confined to Driftwood Key. Can you use him out there?"

Mike answered the question. "We can't risk it, Phoebe. Just because we're on a mission doesn't mean bad people aren't out there to take advantage of our absence. You guys have to protect Driftwood Key; otherwise, everything we're doing out there will be for nothin'."

She reluctantly agreed and turned to Sonny, who asked, "I'd like to help hand out flyers and talk to people. I think I can be convincing since I was sort of related to Lindsey."

"We really could use him, Hank," said Erin as she lifted up the stack of flyers. Hank assured her that he had plenty of toner and copy paper to last for years. While everyone geared up, they produced another three hundred flyers, and Sonny retrieved two Bostitch staple guns from the toolshed to secure them.

"Okay," said Hank, who assumed his role as the field general. "Mike, Jessica, round up your people and head for the bridge. Look for more ways to aggravate the confiscation teams as they approach."

"I have a few ideas. Hey, can we have Peter?" Mike asked.

"Sure. Grab him on your way out," replied Hank. "Erin, Sonny and I will be meeting up with Mayor Ramirez. He has some local business leaders lined up to help."

"Reverend Deb sent one of her parishioners to the gate last night," began Mike. "I was returning home when I saw the man walking alone toward our bridge. I scared the crap out of him when I came out of my truck with a shotgun pointed at him."

"Poor guy," said Hank. "What did he say?"

"Reverend Deb was busy yesterday. She managed to locate and speak with most of the clergy in town. They're one hundred percent on board with us."

Hank glanced at his watch. It was approaching eight o'clock, when he wanted to be at the mayor's office. "Guys, I love you all. Please be careful today. No matter what happens, our safety is most important. We can always get more stuff if it comes to that."

That morning, Sonny had run the generator for an extra hour to ensure the batteries on their two-way radios were fully charged.

Mike reviewed their choices of weapons and helped them load extra magazines in case they needed them. He really didn't want the family to get into a gunfight, but their experience in Key West told him to expect anything.

Hank and Erin hoped their diplomatic approach would avoid violence. The more the group discussed the personalities involved, they became convinced Lindsey had used this catastrophic event to seize power and control. Having Sheriff Jock do her bidding made her even more power hungry. Now it was up to the people of Marathon to take a stand.

While Mike, Jessica, and Peter prepared the bridge for the approach of the tactical vehicles, Hank, Erin and Sonny drove to the mayor's office. When they arrived, the parking lot was full of vehicles with an equal number of bicycles propped against the wall near the entrance to Marathon City Hall.

The Albright contingent was the last to arrive in the city council's meeting room, which was packed to a standing-room-only crowd. Multiple battery-operated lanterns were scattered throughout the space so everyone could see. Mayor Ramirez stood behind the lectern and was addressing the group when he noticed Hank enter the room.

"Hank! Everyone, most of you know Hank Albright, who owns the Driftwood Key Inn. His family is some of the original conchs."

Several familiar faces were in the crowd, and many stretched their arms out to shake Hank's hand as he approached the lectern. Erin and Sonny followed close behind. A couple of people even recognized Erin and called her by name.

Hank reached the mayor's side, and Erin handed him the pile of six hundred flyers. "Everyone, I'm going to be brief because we don't have much time. I know that Juan has called you here to help, and I imagine he's explained what's about to happen."

"Are you sure, Hank?" asked a woman near the front, whom he recognized as being a local attorney. "I know Lindsey can be overbearing, but this is a little hard to believe."

"Have you seen the video?" Hank asked, and then he turned to the crowd. "Has everyone seen the video?"

Many said no, and several replied that they'd only seen the photographs.

Juan stepped forward with a laptop. "Everyone, if you haven't seen the video, please step forward. I'm going to forewarn you. This is graphic."

The crowd shuffled around to allow those who wanted to watch get closer to the front. By the time Juan finished playing the video, the attendees regretted watching, and their anger had built to a fever pitch.

"What are we gonna do about this?"

"They should be arrested!"

"By who? Themselves?"

Hank retook the floor. "Okay, everyone. We share the same feelings. Trust me. This was just a part of the video we took. It was much worse, and let me add, it wasn't the first incident like this. Lindsey and Jock are running roughshod over the citizens and businesses of Key West. They aim to take their pillaging roadshow all the way to Key Largo if we don't take a stand."

"What can we do?" asked the female attorney near the front of the crowd.

Erin held some of the flyers over her head. "We know they're on their way. Our surveillance team watched them empty the Winn-Dixie on Big Pine Key. Their staging right now at the Penske Truck Rental, where they commandeered ten more box trucks." She was embellishing somewhat, but she felt it was necessary to keep this new batch of volunteers at a fever pitch.

"We're ready to help!"

"Yeah!"

Hank raised some flyers high in the air for everyone to see. "We need everyone to take some of these flyers. Go to your neighborhoods and spread the word. Knock on doors. Post these in prominent places. We'll do the same. We need all of Marathon to understand that their homes and belongings are at risk if we don't try to stop them."

"I'll take some."

"Me too."

"I have a generator and a copy machine. I'll make some more copies and have my entire family spreading the word."

Hank shouted over the enthusiastic crowd. "Wait. Wait. We need one more thing. If you haven't been down to the bridge, you may not be aware that we've blocked the road to prevent them from gaining access. That may not be enough. If you own businesses on the highway, you might want to make sure they're boarded up. Kinda like a storm is coming. Well, in a way, one is."

The group all made their way to the front and grabbed flyers. It was getting warm and stuffy in the city council's meeting room, so people were anxious to get going.

"Whadya think, Juan?" asked Hank after the two men stood to the side to allow Sonny, Erin and Juan's wife, Lisa, to pass out the flyers and offer suggestions.

"I went down to the bridge early this morning. It's a mess and definitely impassable."

"Good," added Hank. "I haven't had time to see for myself. I wanted to get the town behind it first."

The Marathon mayor agreed. "I think this has been a great start. Let's see how we're doing in a few hours when the convoy arrives. But I have to remind you that the county has plenty of road equipment capable of clearing this traffic jam your brother created. If they're determined, we won't be able to hold them off forever."

Hank grimaced and nodded his head as Juan voiced the same concerns he had. "I have an idea. Do you guys have enough gas to drive up to Islamorada and back?"

"I think so. Why?"

Hank whispered to Mayor Ramirez, who eagerly took in his instructions. He kept glancing at his watch as Hank spoke but seemed ready to take on the task.

"Now, I take it?" the mayor asked as Hank finished.

"Yes, and you'll need to hurry."

CHAPTER FORTY-FIVE

Friday, November 15
Seven Mile Bridge

Sergeant Jorge Rivera was exhausted. He'd spearheaded this operation on behalf of the mayor and his boss, Sheriff Jock Daly, from the beginning. He was known to be a micromanager. As a result, he insisted upon his tactical vehicle accompanying every major raid, and then, once the box trucks were loaded for delivery to the warehouses in Key West, he led the way back. He'd been operating on minimal sleep since the raids began, and his nerves had worn thin as the crowds surrounding the grocery stores became increasingly hostile.

It certainly didn't help his already surly attitude for the sheriff to dress him down the night before because of the continued loss of life during the raids. He tried to convince the sheriff that he didn't like his deputies being attacked and shot at either. However, since the beginning of the confiscation raids, word spread rapidly throughout the Lower Keys, and opposition was growing.

During their heated argument at the warehouse the evening before, Sergeant Rivera made the mistake of questioning the operation altogether. To make matters worse, he complained that Mayor Lindsey should have laid some groundwork prior to the raids so that the people knew their operation was designed to help them.

The sheriff hurled all kinds of vulgarities and threats at Sergeant Rivera. The tongue-lashing was the worst he'd ever witnessed, much less received. After he left the sheriff's office to get a few hours of sleep, he wondered who was under more pressure. The sheriff or him.

The convoy got a slow start leaving Big Pine Key that morning. One of the Penske trucks stalled barely a quarter mile over the water on the way to West Summerland Key. It took a dozen men and the front bumper of another truck to move the twenty-six-footer out of the way before they could proceed.

Then on the next island, Bahia Honda Key, the sand that had washed ashore from the hurricane slowed their convoy as it became difficult for the box trucks to discern where the road ended and the soft, sandy shoulder began. One of the trucks dropped its right-side wheels into the sand and became stuck. Sergeant Rivera could ill afford to lose another box truck, as there were no other rental locations until they reached Islamorada, and he had not yet sent an advance team in that direction to determine if the trucks could be seized.

After another lengthy delay to free the truck from the soft sand, the convoy of tactical vehicles, patrol cars, and box trucks was under way. They rumbled along past the Sunshine Key RV Resort, drawing dozens of people out of their motor homes and trailers to view the spectacle.

Interestingly, unlike what they'd experienced the last several days, this group stood on the sidewalk between the chain-link fence and the highway, cheering them on. It was as if they were being treated to a parade. Sergeant Rivera's spirits lifted when one of the armored tactical vehicles sounded their siren, causing the onlookers to jump up and down while exchanging high fives.

Feeling better, he radioed the sheriff's department dispatch to advise them that his convoy had entered Seven Mile Bridge at Little Duck Key. He expected to arrive in Marathon in ten minutes.

He was wrong.

Throughout yesterday and today as they'd traveled up U.S. 1, they rarely met any kind of operating vehicles. Stalled vehicles were everywhere, but most had been pulled to the side of the road. When he first began to encounter the abandoned cars and trucks on Seven Mile Bridge, he wasn't all that surprised.

Just like a traveler on a long stretch of interstate between exits, motorists often miscalculate the amount of fuel left in their vehicle and run out of gas. People don't intend to run out of gas. It just happens when they push their luck. Sergeant Rivera believed every driver pushed their luck in the apocalypse.

They slowed their pace so all of the convoy could stay together in case of a breakdown. Backing up and turning around wasn't an option on the two-lane bridge cluttered with broken-down vehicles.

Riding in the lead vehicle, he ordered his driver to slowly wind through the debris field of inoperable vehicles. His focus remained on each car in their path rather than what lay ahead. That was why it came as a shock to him when the convoy was forced to come to a complete stop halfway across the bridge.

"What the hell is this?" he asked of no one in particular. There were four deputies in the tactical vehicle with him, but none of them had an answer other than stating the obvious—a traffic jam.

Sergeant Rivera bounded out of the truck and held his right fist in the air, indicating all vehicles should stop. The three deputies in the back seat piled out, and the driver remained in his seat as he'd been instructed. Rivera turned to the second tactical vehicle and used hand signals to those members of the SWAT team to disembark. These two lead trucks had remained with him throughout the raids. They were his best people—team A.

He glanced in all directions, pausing briefly at the sight of Fred the Tree, which he'd never given a second thought to when he'd passed it before the collapse. He thought for a moment and issued his orders.

"You three, make your way up the highway and see how far this goes. Do you see these skid marks? Somebody went through a lot of effort to block this highway. I wanna know how far it stretches. Go!"

The men immediately took off in a steady jog, looking for gaps between the parked vehicles and maintaining their weapons at low ready in the event of an ambush. When they were out of sight, Sergeant Rivera retrieved field glasses out of his vehicle and climbed onto the hood.

After getting his balance, he focused on the men as they made their way up the road. Then he adjusted his vision and looked toward Marathon. He shook his head in disbelief. He pulled the binoculars away from his face and rubbed his eyes. He looked again and dropped several F-bombs.

"I don't need to wait for those guys to return. Get me the sheriff on the radio!"

"Yes, sir!" his driver shouted back.

It took several minutes for Sheriff Jock to respond to the radio call. By the time Sergeant Rivera had explained what he'd observed, the three members of team A had already returned. Their chests were heaving for air after jogging in the dense, sooty air. Sergeant Rivera asked the sheriff to stand by while he got the report from his men.

He retook his seat in the tactical vehicle and closed the door behind him. Then he instructed his driver to get out. After taking a deep breath to steady his nerves, he reached out to Sheriff Jock again.

"Sheriff, these cars are blocking the road all the way to Marathon. My men tell me there are hundreds of vehicles parked bumper to bumper, sideways across the road. It's impossible for us to pass."

"Who the hell did this?" the sheriff screamed through the radio.

"Sir, as my men reached the other end of the bridge, several people met them part of the way. The guy in front said his name was Hank Albright. I think he's the owner—"

"I know who he is!" the sheriff screamed, cutting off his sergeant.

Sergeant Rivera tried to ask the sheriff what he should do, but the communication had been terminated. He angrily threw the microphone against the dashboard and slammed the back of his head against the seat out of frustration. *This isn't worth the aggravation*, he thought to himself.

CHAPTER FORTY-SIX

Friday, November 15
Seven Mile Bridge

After the confrontation with the three members of the sheriff's SWAT team, Hank was filled with anxiety. He began to question whether they were doing the right thing by confronting the deputies. They were dressed in full body armor and helmets. They carried automatic weapons compared to the variety of guns available to the Albrights.

Hank was about to broach the subject of abandoning this whole crazy notion of staring down Lindsey's standing army of sheriff's deputies when he heard a voice in the distance. He turned to see who it was.

A half mile back, Lacey and Tucker were racing between the cars, waving their arms.

"Dad! Dad! We're here!"

"We're coming, Grandpa! Wait for us!"

Hank and Erin turned around. Mike and Jessica, who were walking alongside them, paused as well but kept their attention forward toward the looming standoff. Peter rushed back to greet his sister and nephew. They half-hugged and slapped each other on the back as the two of them continued toward Hank.

Peter waited behind, as off in the distance, Sonny, Phoebe, and Jimmy were also walking briskly toward them. Peter shouted to his father to let him know the Frees were on their way as well.

Moments later, half a mile away from where the SWAT teams waited, all of the residents of Driftwood Key were huddled together in the middle of the highway, surrounded by disabled vehicles.

After everyone caught their breath, Peter began laughing as he studied the jet-black tactical vehicles. He'd seen the military equivalent before. In a way, the scene didn't appear all that different than the war zones he'd reported from during his career.

"Guys? Are we nuts?"

His question lightened the mood somewhat. The group shared in his laughter, and several wrapped their arms around one another.

"That's how we roll," quipped Tucker, the youngest of the clan.

"You betcha!" said Phoebe, who hugged the teen.

"Let's go see what we're dealing with, shall we?" asked Erin. She took Hank by the arm, and the families made their way through the cars as if they were on a casual stroll to church on Sunday. It wasn't until they reached the void between the vehicle blockade and the menacing SWAT teams that reality set in.

As soon as they stepped into the open and away from the protection of the two sedans parked bumper-to-bumper, Sergeant Rivera approached them. He was flanked on both sides by two members of team A, who pointed their weapons at everyone from Driftwood Key. Had they pulled their triggers, the Albrights and Frees would be dead within seconds.

"Who is Albright?" snarled Sergeant Rivera as he stomped toward them, emboldened by his armed deputies.

"I am," Hank responded.

Sergeant Rivera scowled at Hank, and his deputies raised their rifle barrels menacingly.

Peter stepped forward. "I am."

Lacey smiled and held Tucker's hand. "We are, too."

"Same here," said Mike as he and Jessica joined Hank's side.

Erin and the Frees also stepped forward to join the Albrights.

Their actions enraged Sergeant Rivera. "You're a bunch of smart-asses. I've got the green light to arrest every last one of you."

"Do it, Sergeant!" challenged Mike, the former detective.

"I know who you are, Albright," Sergeant Rivera hissed. "They stripped you of your shield."

"Wrong, Rivera. I couldn't be a part of all of this." He waved his arms at Rivera, his men, and the line of vehicles behind him.

Sergeant Rivera angrily stepped forward a few paces, and Mike slid his hands on top of his holstered weapon. Suddenly, all of the deputies' guns were raised and pointed directly at Mike.

"Sergeant Rivera!" shouted his driver. "It's the sheriff for you!"

He shot Mike a nasty look and stomped back to his truck. The members of team A lowered their weapons slightly when Mike removed his hand from his. He stepped backward to join the others.

"Mike, not a good idea," cautioned Jessica, who rarely tried to tell her husband what to do. This time, he agreed with her and muttered that he was sorry.

"What's happening?" asked Phoebe.

"My guess is that Sergeant Rivera is no longer running this show," replied Erin. "It wouldn't surprise me if we're soon told—"

"Albright! The sheriff is going to deal with you himself. He told me to ask you this question."

"What's that, Sergeant?" asked Hank politely with a hint of sarcasm.

"Two things. One. Do you know what martial law means? Second. Do you know what lock 'em up and throw away the key means? Think on that until he arrives."

With that, Rivera ordered the rest of his SWAT team members from their tactical vehicles. He waved them forward until there were sixteen men standing shoulder to shoulder, weapons ready, facing down Hank and the others.

Not that Hank wanted to, but he felt compelled to give his

family an out. He spoke in a loud whisper so the SWAT team, who was less than fifty feet away, couldn't hear him.

"We can back off and go home. There's nothing wrong with living to fight another day."

"No way, Grandpa!" said Tucker a little too loudly, drawing a tug on the arm from his mother. He lowered his voice as he continued. "They'll just come to our home next. We have to take a stand. Out here. In the open."

Hank wrapped his arm around his grandson's shoulders and hugged him. Tucker, who had lost his father to the aftermath of nuclear war, was ready to take a stand even if meant dying in the process.

"Mr. Hank, what do you think?" asked Jimmy.

"Jimmy, you're not truly free until you no longer live under someone's thumb. Tyrants like Lindsey will never be satisfied until we comply with all of her crazy demands. I want to live but not as a prisoner of a despot like her."

"Then we stay," said Lacey.

"I agree," added Peter. "Terrorists are everywhere, and they take many forms. I've seen them in action overseas and in Washington."

Erin laughed. "I can vouch for that. Let me tell you about my boss." She and Hank exchanged high fives before wrapping their arms through one another's in a gesture of solidarity.

"Mike?" asked Hank.

"I'm still here, right?" he responded.

"Hey. Frees don't know any other way except to be free." Sonny's family grasped each other's hands and squeezed.

A long standoff began between the two sides. The SWAT team never blinked, nor did the Driftwood Key contingent. Then the vehicles ahead of them roared to life. All of them. At the same time. In the distance, they could hear a low rumble and the sound of tires squealing on the concrete pavement.

"Are they turning around?" asked Sonny.

"I don't know," replied Mike. "I can't see around them."

The SWAT team members held their positions and made no

efforts to return to their vehicles. For nearly an hour, the standoff had kept both groups paralyzed, staring at one another. One side capable of causing the death of the other in mere seconds. The vulnerable side stood proud, prepared to die for what they believed in.

CHAPTER FORTY-SEVEN

Friday, November 15
Seven Mile Bridge

The trucks and patrol cars jockeyed for position until they were parked along the concrete wall bordering the two-lane highway. The SWAT team never turned to observe their activity. The eyes of the men peered at their targets under the visors of their ballistic helmets. Like the parting of the sea in the biblical context, the vehicles made way for the new arrivals.

Approaching the front of the convoy were two front loaders utilized by the Monroe County Roads & Bridges department. The behemoths barely squeezed between the sheriff's convoy of trucks and patrol cars until they reached the front. Then the two Caterpillar 988Ks designed to clear sand and debris caused by storm surge pulled beside each other. The operators stared at Hank and his family for a moment before dropping their buckets to the concrete pavement with a loud thud that shook the concrete roadway.

"Dad," yelled Peter so he could be heard over the loud rumble of the 541-horsepower diesel engines, "those machines could pick up the cars and toss them over the rail. I don't know if we should—"

"Hang tough, Peter," Hank said reassuringly. "Stare back at them and don't show any fear. We have to stay strong."

Suddenly, the operators shut down their machines. The hissing and popping of the engines cooling off sounded like they were in the midst of a den of angry vipers.

The standoff continued for several minutes with neither side showing any signs of retreat. And then Mayor Lindsey Free emerged between the two enormous machines with Sheriff Jock Daly by her side.

Her face was red with rage, yet her voice was eerily calm. She wasted no time in addressing her nemesis.

"Hank, just who do you think you are?" she asked as she walked closer to him.

The SWAT team moved slightly to let Lindsey and Jock through. Sergeant Rivera moved along the side of the road so that he could provide visual instructions to his personnel if needed.

As Lindsey and Jock approached, Rivera motioned for the deputies to move closer as well. The gap was being closed between the two groups, which meant the Albright group was in even greater peril. There would be no time to run and take cover.

"I should ask you the same question, Lindsey," Hank shot back without a hint of trepidation in his voice. "I'm not going to make this personal. You have history with some members of my family. However, that's not what this is all about. This is about the Florida Keys and its people. It's about what the role of government is during a crisis. It's about maintaining the rights and freedoms we enjoy as Americans."

"Lofty words, but that's not reality, Hank. You have no idea what I have on my platter. You live in a fancy place on a beautiful little private island, insulated from the despair of your neighbors."

"That's not true!" Hank shouted back at her. "We've suffered, too. My daughter lost her husband. The father to my grandson. My son, Peter, came close to death countless times, especially when he was only a dozen miles from ground zero in Washington. My brother, Mike, a decorated and highly respected detective for you, Jock, was almost murdered at the hands of a homicidal maniac." Hank paused and moved next to Jimmy, who was standing alongside his parents.

He continued. "And how about your nephew, Jimmy. Remember him? Your irresponsible actions in blowing up the bridges almost killed him. But for the grace of God, he would've died because he was forced to volunteer for your crazy scheme."

"You volunteered him!" Lindsey's calm demeanor had been whisked away as Hank continued to stand up to her.

"Don't be coy with me, Lindsey. Your message to me on the front porch that day was loud and clear. Offer up a member of my family or you'd bring your wrath upon me."

"Whatever, Hank. Enough of this. It's time for you people to get out of the way. We've got work to do."

Hank looked down and then glanced at Fred the Tree. Like so many others in the Keys, Driftwood Key had survived the onslaught of Hurricane Irma that year. His family, the Frees, and all of the people of the Keys had stood strong as the storm pummeled their homes.

He stood a little taller and stuck out his jaw slightly. "No, Lindsey, you don't. You've already crossed the line from governing to tyranny. You don't have the authority—"

"What? Are you kidding me?" Lindsey was incredulous. "We're trying to find a way to help people survive the most devastating catastrophic event that's ever hit our country, much less the Florida Keys. The only way to keep order and prevent people from dying is for somebody like me to take control."

"It's not the only way," Hank argued as he took a couple of steps closer to Lindsey and the menacing gunmen. "You have to appeal to the residents and business owners of the Keys. You have to lay out a plan that incorporates our churches and communities to help one another. Bringing in the goon squad to steal from businesses in the name of the greater good only fosters resentment, and it gets people killed in the process."

"You're out of line, Albright!" yelled Sergeant Rivera, who took Hank's statement personally.

"When you're the mayor, you can do it your way!" shouted Lindsey. Her attitude was obvious. She was no longer interested in talk. She turned angrily toward Jock. "Are you gonna move these people out of our way, or do I have to do it?"

Hank tried to appeal to Jock's sense of decency. He was a law enforcement officer and had trained with the finest in the nation. Hank hoped Jock was growing weary of Lindsey's tyrannical demands.

"Jock, this isn't your idea, is it? Maybe you don't know that there's a better option, but I believe there can be if we bring people together instead of dividing them."

"I'm just doin' my job, Hank," he replied unenthusiastically.

Mike stepped forward to address his former boss. "We swore an oath, Jock. We promised the people of the Keys we'd never betray the public trust. We assured them we'd maintain the highest ethical standards, and this is important. We made a solemn vow to uphold the values of our community. How do these raids uphold the standards you and I both swore we'd adhere to?"

Jock grew quiet and avoided eye contact with Mike. Hank noticed some of the fight drain out of his body. Lindsey did as well.

CHAPTER FORTY-EIGHT

Friday, November 15
Seven Mile Bridge

In every potentially violent confrontation, there was a point of no return. It was that precise moment during which the two opposing combatants either decided the fight wasn't worth the trouble, or, in the case of a highly charged, emotional showdown, a mistake was made that resulted in blood pouring onto the streets.

Lindsey became more agitated and animated as she turned on her sheriff and lover. "Dammit, Jock! I'm ordering you to arrest these people. Take them down and move them out of the way."

Jock stared back at her, his body frozen from indecision. Or perhaps he refused to comply with her demands because he disagreed with her. Regardless of his thoughts in the moment, the impulsive mayor was prepared to act on her own.

She shoved Jock forcefully in the chest, causing him to lose his balance. He stepped back a couple of steps until he was near his line of armed SWAT team members. With fire in her eyes, Lindsey followed him, her finger pointing toward his chest as if she were prepared to shove him again. Instead, she caught everyone off guard.

Lindsey abruptly turned and reached for the barrel of one of the deputy's rifles. He deftly pulled it away, but she wasn't deterred. She grabbed for another. And another. All of the men were protecting their weapons as the wild-eyed Lindsey tried desperately to grab a rifle. Then all at once, the SWAT team and Sheriff Jock turned their attention back toward the Albrights and Frees.

Less than a quarter mile away, the sound of shuffling feet approached. Then muffled voices filled the deathly silence that had come over the Seven Mile Bridge. Everyone turned to focus their attention on the heads and shoulders that rose above the hoods and trunks of the cars blocking their advance. People turned sideways to slide by. Others used the bumpers to climb up and over the obstacles.

Hank Albright began to cry. Erin hugged him, and then the rest of his family gathered around. Tears flowed. Nervous laughter poured out of their mouths, stifled by some as they clamped their hands over grinning lips. Smiles and hugs were generously shared.

For as far as the eye could see, the people of the Middle and Upper Keys were coming. Hundreds of them. More likely, thousands. Some looked disheveled. Others appeared injured in some way. A few needed the assistance of a friend or family member to join the rest.

They were coming to stand up to Lindsey and the sheriff. They were holding their heads high with confidence and pride to support Hank and his family. Those who could manage a smile did. Those who still had tears to shed let them come out without any misgivings.

This was their fight, too.

In the middle of the pack, County Commissioner Bud Marino walked alongside the other two commissioners who would oppose Lindsey. They were accompanied by the attorney Mrs. Morton, who would provide them the legal means to oust the tyrannical mayor.

Near them were members of the clergy led by Reverend Deb. They were from all denominations, creeds and colors. They were calm, carrying the power of God in their hearts.

Mayor Juan Ramirez, his wife, Lisa, and the mayors of Islamorada and Key Largo were next. They smiled and nodded at Hank, giving him a thumbs-up and fist pumps.

The emotional scene swept over the residents of Driftwood Key. Weeks of trial and tribulation had come to a head. They'd set out to confront Lindsey, fully expecting that this might be a fight they couldn't win. They'd expected Jock's deputies to raise their weapons and even kill them on her orders.

However, today was not their day to die. It was their day to start a new life. As the new arrivals surrounded the Albrights and Frees, the power of their spirit and energy engulfed Hank. He accepted their gracious show of support.

He set his jaw, took a deep breath, and turned to Lindsey. He was about to speak when something remarkable happened.

Sheriff Jock Daly walked away from Lindsey and joined Hank by his side. He adjusted his uniform and confidently turned to face his soon to be former lover.

"Enough is enough, Lindsey. No more."

Next, Sergeant Rivera crossed the imaginary line in the sand that stretched from one side of U.S. 1 to the other, pointing directly at Fred the Tree, the symbol of the Florida Keys' resiliency. He was followed by the entirety of his elite SWAT team who'd carried out Lindsey's demands.

With a defeated look on her face, yet still unabashedly proud enough to hold her head high in utter defeat, Lindsey spun on a dime and marched away between the massive blades of the front loaders designed to clear a path for her. Now, the only path she could follow was back to Key West, where she would resign in disgrace.

As soon as she got in her car and drove off, the tensions eased, and everyone, all thousand-plus, cheered. They cried. They celebrated. And for an afternoon, they forgot they were in the midst of the apocalypse.

They were Conchs once again.

THANK YOU FOR READING NUCLEAR WINTER: DESOLATION!

If you enjoyed it, I'd be grateful if you'd take a moment to write a short review (just a few words are needed) and post it on Amazon. Amazon uses complicated algorithms to determine what books are recommended to readers. Sales are, of course, a factor, but so are the quantities of reviews my books get. By taking a few seconds to leave a review, you help me out and also help new readers learn about my work.

Sign up to my email list to learn about upcoming titles, deals, contests, appearances, and more!

Sign up at BobbyAkart.com

VISIT my feature page at Amazon.com/BobbyAkart for more information on my other action-packed thrillers, which includes over fifty Amazon #1 bestsellers in forty-plus fiction and nonfiction genres.

READ ON for my **AUTHOR'S NOTE** as I share some final thoughts on the **NUCLEAR WINTER** series and to see what's coming next—**BLACK GOLD**, book one in the **TEXAS FOREVER** series, available on Amazon.

AUTHOR'S NOTE

June 14, 2021

It has been six years to the day since I published my first novel, THE LOYAL NINE, book one of the Boston Brahmin series. I have written about a wide variety of potential catastrophic events, all of which have a basis in scientific fact or have occurred in our planet's history. With the Nuclear Winter series, like my other novels, my goal was to introduce readers to the potential threats we face following a nuclear exchange and what to expect as the events unfold. Through the experiences of my fictional characters, I hoped to let you imagine the scenario for yourselves and play it out in your mind so that you'll be prepared when catastrophe strikes. Each event is unique in its own way, and nuclear winter ranks alongside the eruption of the Yellowstone supervolcano in its potential to devastate the planet.

I started this series with a basic premise, a warning of sorts:

Nuclear war may kill millions.
Nuclear winter will kill billions.

Preparing society for something of this magnitude would be near impossible. It's the kind of worst-case scenario that politicians talk about in hushed tones while in private and the general public cannot fathom. As a result, the potential for nuclear winter is accepted as scientific fact. However, like so many other catastrophes I write about, the world crosses its fingers and prays it never happens.

Here are the salient points of my research that I hoped to have conveyed to readers in the Nuclear Winter series.

While it is true that millions at ground zero of the detonation would perish, in the aftermath, hunger and starvation would plague the survivors of a nuclear war. Millions of people would starve to death in the first few years following an all-out nuclear war.

World food reserves at any given time would be frighteningly small should production fail. They have amounted in recent years to about two months' supply at present consumption rates. In the United States, food stores would feed the population for less than a few months subject to distribution constraints.

The means to transport the food from sites of harvest or storage to the consumers would no longer exist. Transportation centers would be shut down. Roads, bridges, as well as rail and port facilities, would likely be rendered inoperable.

A breakdown in agribusiness would be an inevitable consequence of a nuclear war. Without the means to harvest, process, and distribute those crops that survived, there would be much spoilage.

So much of the social and economic structure of society as we know it would be destroyed. Relationships that we take for granted would disappear. Money would have little or no value. Food and other necessities would be obtained, when available, by barter.

More likely, as people became desperate with hunger, survival instincts would take over. Armed individuals or marauding bands would raid and pilfer whatever supplies and stores still existed. Those fortunate individuals who had the means would hoard their resources and soon become the victims of the crazed behavior of starving and desperate survivors who would ransack warehouses and attack individual homes.

Law enforcement would not exist, and many would be killed in the fighting between those trying forcefully to obtain possession of food and those trying to protect their own homes, families, and food supplies.

A reduction in average temperature by even 1°C at the Earth's surface because of the absorption of solar energy by soot and dust in the atmosphere would shorten the growing season in northern latitudes and markedly reduce or prevent maturation and ripening of grains that are the staple of human diets.

But the debates that have been heard are not of whether a nuclear winter would occur but how many tens of degrees the temperature would be reduced and for how long. During most of the growing season, a sharp decline in temperature for only a few days may be sufficient to destroy crops. The lack of rain that has been predicted after nuclear winter settles in would contribute to crop failures. Since most of the wheat and coarse grains are grown in the temperate regions of the Northern Hemisphere, which would be the zones most affected by a nuclear winter, it is evident that a nuclear war, especially during the spring or summer, would have a devastating effect on crop production and food supplies for years.

After the atmospheric soot and dust finally clear, the destruction of the stratospheric ozone would allow an increase in hard ultraviolet-B (UV-B) rays to reach the Earth's surface. In addition to the direct harmful effects to the skin and eyes of humans and animals, these hard ultraviolet rays would be damaging to plant life and would interfere with agricultural production. If the oxides of nitrogen increase in the troposphere, there may occur an actual increase of ozone at the lower levels of the atmosphere. Ozone is directly toxic to plants.

There would likely be a deterioration of the quality of the soil following a nuclear war. The death of plant and forest coverage because of fire, radiation, the lack of fertilizers, and the probable primitive slash-and-burn agricultural practices of survivors would leave the soil vulnerable to erosion by wind and rain.

Water supplies would be seriously reduced after a nuclear war, especially if there is a corresponding collapse of the electrical grid. Dams and large irrigation projects may cease to function. Reduced rainfall, which is predicted in some models of the climatic effects of a nuclear war, would interfere with agricultural productivity. If freezing temperatures actually were to occur during the warm season, surface waters would be frozen and unavailable.

Radioactive fallout would contaminate reservoirs and surface waters with long-lived radioactive isotopes, primarily strontium-90, which has a half-life of twenty-eight years, and cesium-137, which has a half-life of thirty-three years. These elements in the groundwater would soon be taken up by plants and would enter the food chain. Eventually they would become concentrated in humans; the strontium would accumulate in bones and the cesium in cytoplasm, where they would contribute to the long-term burden of radioactivity in survivors.

Not only would food be scarce, but it would likely be unsanitary as well. The destruction of sanitation, refrigeration, and food-processing methods, especially in the remaining urban areas or population centers, would result in the contamination of food by bacteria, particularly by enteric pathogens. Spoiled meat, carrion of domestic animals and even human corpses are likely to be eaten by starving persons, as has happened in major famines in the past. Pathogens to which civilized man has lost resistance would be acquired from foods and water contaminated by excreta and flies, other insects, and rodents, which would likely proliferate in the aftermath of nuclear war.

But the hunger and starvation would not be limited to the combatant countries alone, or even to just the Northern Hemisphere. It would truly be a global occurrence. Even without the spread of the possible climatic effects of a nuclear winter to the Southern Hemisphere, millions would die of starvation in noncombatant countries. Today a large portion of food exports goes to parts of the world where millions of people suffer from undernutrition and hunger.

It is evident that hunger and starvation would decimate the survivors of a major nuclear war. Millions of deaths would result not only among survivors in the warring nations but throughout the world. The developing countries, in fact, would possibly be the main victims of this famine, as their populations may not be reduced as immediately as would those in the combatant countries. Starvation would be essentially global.

My initial research into this topic began with a book written in the early eighties by Paul Ehrlich and Carl Sagan titled *The Cold and The Dark: The World after Nuclear War*. This book was a record of a conference held in 1983 during which the scientists introduced the world to the concept of nuclear winter. For the first time, world leaders took note of the climatic and atmospheric consequences of nuclear winter as well as the profound effect it would have on all living things on Earth.

Forty years later, their warnings have been acknowledged, but one has to ask, have we done all we can to avoid a nuclear holocaust?

BLACK GOLD, book one in the TEXAS FOREVER series, available on Amazon by clicking here.

COMING SEPTEMBER 2021

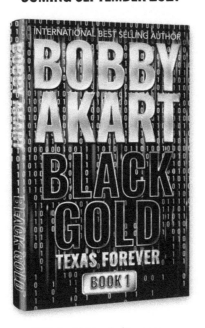

Oil is the lifeblood of America.
But some see it as poisonous to the planet.
How far will both sides go as a battle rages over Black Gold?

PRE-ORDER ON AMAZON TODAY

OTHER WORKS BY AMAZON CHARTS TOP 25 AUTHOR BOBBY AKART

Perfect Storm (a standalone disaster thriller)

The Texas Forever trilogy
Black Gold
Black Swan
Black Flags

Nuclear Winter
First Strike
Armageddon
Whiteout
Devil Storm
Desolation

New Madrid Earthquake (a standalone disaster thriller)

Odessa (a Gunner Fox trilogy)
Odessa Reborn
Odessa Rising
Odessa Strikes

The Virus Hunters
Virus Hunters I
Virus Hunters II
Virus Hunters III

The Geostorm Series
The Shift
The Pulse
The Collapse
The Flood
The Tempest
The Pioneers

The Asteroid Series (A Gunner Fox trilogy)
Discovery
Diversion
Destruction

The Doomsday Series
Apocalypse
Haven
Anarchy
Minutemen
Civil War

The Yellowstone Series
Hellfire
Inferno
Fallout
Survival

The Lone Star Series
Axis of Evil
Beyond Borders
Lines in the Sand
Texas Strong
Fifth Column

Suicide Six

The Pandemic Series

Beginnings

The Innocents

Level 6

Quietus

The Blackout Series

36 Hours

Zero Hour

Turning Point

Shiloh Ranch

Hornet's Nest

Devil's Homecoming

The Boston Brahmin Series

The Loyal Nine

Cyber Attack

Martial Law

False Flag

The Mechanics

Choose Freedom

Patriot's Farewell (standalone novel)

Seeds of Liberty (Companion Guide)

The Prepping for Tomorrow Series

Cyber Warfare

EMP: Electromagnetic Pulse

Economic Collapse

Lightning Source UK Ltd.
Milton Keynes UK
UKHW011849010721
386496UK00007B/421/J